THE
ATWELLE
CONFESSION

JOEL GORDONSON

THE

ATWELLE

CONFESSION

SELECTBOOKS, INC.
NEW YORK

This edition published by SelectBooks, Inc.
For information address SelectBooks, Inc., New York, New York.

First Edition

ISBN 978-1-59079-430-2

Library of Congress Cataloging-in-Publication Data

Names: Gordonson, Joel, author.
Title: The Atwelle confession / Joel Gordonson.
Description: First edition. | New York : SelectBooks, [2017]
Identifiers: LCCN 2017006502 | ISBN 9781590794302 (hardcover : acid-free paper)
Subjects: LCSH: Gargoyles—Fiction. | Murder—Investigation—Fiction. |
GSAFD: Mystery fiction.
Classification: LCC PS3607.O5955 A95 2017 | DDC 813/.6--dc23 LC record
available at https://lccn.loc.gov/2017006502

Manufactured in the United States of America
10 9 8 7 6 5 4 3 2 1

To the memory of my sister Marilyn,
who could find the good in almost everyone and everything,
and would hold her tongue when she didn't.

"Disputes and delinquency leave a trail; the quietly effective does not."

G.W. BERNARD

The Late Medieval English Church (2012)

PREFACE

WHILE THE STORYLINE AND CHARACTERS in this novel are fictional, the discovery of rare half demonic-half human wooden figures carved in the ceiling of the parish church of St. Clement is a true event. The carvings were "re-discovered" in 2012 by a good friend, a medieval historian from Cambridge, England, during her study of the unusual facets of the church in Outwell, Norfolk. BBC coverage of the discovery can be read at: www.bbc.com/news/uk-england-19077388.

Told to me over dinner, her intriguing tale of unexpectedly peering through binoculars at something mysteriously unidentifiable in the dark ceiling of the church prompted my imagination and resulted in my rough outline of this book that same evening.

Later, during my research and writing of the manuscript, she generously shared with me her comprehensive knowledge of the numerous remarkable facets and the history of St. Clement's, including an ancient will of the prominent Beaupre family from the village.

St. Clement's is a unique collection of features and artifacts, especially for a church in a small village off the beaten path. Many of the descriptions in this book are taken from the diverse and fascinating aspects of the church. In addition to the carvings, the church houses an ancient wooden chest built with special compartments to hold important documents, an alms box with uncommon carving, monuments to influential families from the village, and a wonderfully worn spiral stone staircase leading to a porch and a parvis overlooking the nave.

The church is being lovingly restored and preserved, despite daunting obstacles, through the efforts of a dedicated group of parishioners who deserve admiration, thanks, and our support.

For information about the history of St. Clements, visit: www.norfolkchurches.co.uk/outwell/outwell.htm.

For information and photos about the current restoration of St. Clement's, visit: www.youtube.com/watch?v=azi7tSbG38c.

ACKNOWLEDGMENTS

I AM GRATEFUL, AS ALWAYS, to have in my life the many people who are essential for transforming an idea into a manuscript and then a book. My sincere thanks go to my agent William Gladstone, to the wonderfully supportive people at SelectBooks, to Dr. Claire Daunton for her knowledge and expertise, and to "all the usual suspects" who were rounded up routinely for advice and support. And of course, to Jeanette, who cared through all of it.

THE
ATWELLE
CONFESSION

PROLOGUE

Atwelle, a town in Norfolk, in the year 1532 Anno Domini,
the 23rd year in the reign of Henry VIII, King of England

THE TWO MEN WERE PALE from the scene they had just witnessed, though as younger men in armor they had seen death many times in battles long ago. One struggled to hold back unmanly tears. The other wiped from his brow the sheen of clammy sweat set by the shock. Neither could raise his eyes to meet the glare of the priest who stood under the full moon shining on the uncompleted stone walls surrounding them.

"These are the most horrific and ghastly acts that humans can commit anywhere and under any circumstances. But such vile deeds done in the shadows of this unfinished church—this holy ground—can be matched in God's eyes by no other sin."

The men kneeled on the ground in silence, unable to raise protest or defense.

"There can be no doubt," the priest continued, "that such abomination and heinous crimes shall be punished by excommunication through the pope's edict and by execution on the King's command. These are certain."

At this announcement, the shaken men looked up at the priest. One spoke with a plea in his voice. "Father, there must be some way mercy can be shown."

"Yes, Father," agreed the other. "What can we do?"

"You will do what any Christian who is responsible for sin must do," the priest answered. "You will give confession and do penance for these evil works."

Both men nodded humbly. Yet the priest gave them another stern look.

"And it will be public confession and penance."

"That will not happen, Father," one of the men declared immediately as if the loathsome sight they had just experienced could be denied.

"It cannot be," confirmed the other. "It would be our doom, the end of our families."

"Hear me and make no mistake," the priest glowered at them. "You will confess all in front of God and the world, and pay a dear price for God's forgiveness if you are even to dare ask for His mercy."

As the two men started to object once again, the priest silenced them with a raised hand.

"Hear me out, for you have no choice in the matter. Your wealth and power will proffer no immunity. But your families and fortunes will not be destroyed if you listen well and follow my instructions.

"These words, written under your signature and seal, will state the manner by which you shall do your public confession and penance. . . ."

Atwelle, in the year 2017 Anno Domini, the 64th year in the reign of Elizabeth II, Queen of England, Head of the Commonwealth and Supreme Governor of the Church of England

The old vicar hastily signed the letter under the low light of the desk lamp in his church study. After sealing and addressing an envelope, he searched his desk for as many stamps as he could find. The village post office was long closed at that late hour. He had no idea of the postage required for the envelope's distant foreign destination.

His arthritic knees complained as he rose from his desk and hurried outside down the dark wet street. Without his hat or coat, he felt the drizzle flatten his thin gray hair and trickle uncomfortably under his clerical collar. An unpleasant taste from licking the envelope glue still sat on his tongue. Slightly out of breath, he looked cautiously over his shoulder a few moments later as he approached the mailbox that stood like a silent sentry below a dim light at the entrance to the post office.

After carefully sliding his letter safely into the mailbox, his fingertips lingered on the slot momentarily during a desperate prayer. He drew in a deep breath and after the briefest pause exhaled a whispered "Amen." Turning to leave, the old man was startled by a figure standing behind him.

"Good lord, you gave me a fright! Thank heavens it's you," he said.

The vicar saw the familiar hand reach toward him and extended his arm to shake it in response. His open hand remained untouched—and then clenched—as a long knife slid smoothly between his ribs and through his heart.

ONE

1532

To the Church Wardyns of St. Clement's in the Parish of Atwelle,

I bryng to you God's blessings with this account of the progresse of the building of the new Church of St. Clement upon the consecrated grounde of our olde church in accordance with your dutys for accounts of the church.

By the Grace of God and the gyfts of many, the walls are but finished. Through the gyfts from the wydow of John Hukesley from his estate, the beams of the roof are partially secured for carving when all mony required for the ceiling is gyven.

Chapels honouring the two great and venerable families of Atwelle are pledged.

Much is yet to be done without prospect of sufficient mony from accounts of the churches bee hives and annual gyfts of sheep from those who worshipp. For the roof, window glass, tower, bells, bell ropes, and pews, great sums remain without account.

As our parish may be benefytted by riches over poverte with the King's grant of a porte opening from this lande through our waterway out to the sea, we pray for magnanymyte not penurye that our welth myght be ediffyed to build once again this obedient church as our predecessors were wont to doo.

Let us pray for pease within our Realme, without stryffe or contencyon, debatte or grudge, and with no sense of warre between His Majesty and the Holy Catholic Church, that well we in our church myght not be lefte wher we begann.

Father Regis Hollowell

2017 Margeaux Wood's stunning green eyes glanced nervously up and down the walls of dark wooden bookshelves that surrounded her with leatherbound books from floor to ceiling. The office of the Master of Maryhouse Hall was as intimidating as the man who occupied it, the head of one of the oldest of the ancient colleges of Cambridge University.

"We are certainly pleased to have you as a colleague and research fellow at Maryhouse Hall, Margeaux," said Master Hodges as he leaned forward with his hands folded on the massive oak desk between them. "But there is some concern about your research and how it remains unfunded."

Tall and handsome, with distinguished gray sideburns, the master wore a well-tailored dark blue suit and silk college tie. He looked to Margeaux like the veritable patrician who had just completed a stint in the cabinet and the House of Lords before becoming master of a Cambridge college, because that's precisely what he was. She tried to summon some self-confidence.

"Master Hodges, I assure you my research is exceedingly unique from an academic and historical standpoint. Though a small church in Norfolk, St. Clement's in Atwelle presents a variety of important questions that cry out for answers."

The master's right eyebrow rose in a dismissive response far worse than if he had laughed out loud.

"Margeaux, your credentials and work at the Sorbonne are impressive. Your publications in French academic journals are indeed noteworthy. But in this case, your interest in a collection of odds and ends in a rather undistinguished church on the edge of a remote Norfolk village is hardly the standard of research to which we aspire at Maryhouse Hall."

His smooth baritone voice sounded as if he had pronounced an indisputable verdict of "guilty" from the judge's bench.

"But Master Hodges, my conversations with the former vicar of the church have suggested several possible intriguing historical explanations that could explain and tie together the wide array of disparate and unusual features of the church. And I believe from his comments that there could be even more mysteries in this church."

"Is the former vicar Father Charleton? The chap who disappeared a few weeks ago without explanation?" he asked.

"Yes, that's him," replied Margeaux.

He gave her a serious look.

"Very bad business, that. As it happens, Margeaux, I am familiar with the church and some of its unique features."

"Really? I thought your field was law," she replied.

"In legal matters, one's responsibilities can lead to the unlikeliest of places."

"What sort of legal matter?"

"I'm not at liberty to tell you. Solicitor/client privilege, I'm afraid," he demurred politely. "But in any event, I am not alone in questioning your research. It's surely borne out by the lack of any interest in funding your project."

"Well I admit I have had several grant applications denied, but there are more pending. And," she quickly added, "I also have some private funding in the works, Master Hodges."

His eyebrow raised doubtfully once again.

"There is something special about this church. I know it," she insisted. Both her French accent and the natural pretty pout of her lower lip became more pronounced with the conviction of her words. "I have no doubt that this undistinguished little church, as you call it, actually has important historical significance and that my efforts there can reap great rewards."

"Yes, of course," he replied curtly as he stood up and gestured at the door. "How nice to see you again, Margeaux. Do keep me informed about the funding of your research."

Behind her smile and courteous nod, Margeaux was fuming.

TWO

1532 Father Regis picked his path cautiously around the puddles in the mud of the main road through Atwelle. Watching each step he took in his plain leather shoes, the priest considered with equal care the three men he planned to engage. Two of them were the wealthiest and most powerful men in the town. The third was the village idiot.

The priest focused his thoughts first on Richard Lanham, toward whom he was treading carefully for his first encounter. Next he would talk with his friend Peter over dinner to review his progress and to plan his meeting on the morrow with Francis DuBois.

He stepped aside as a horse approached from behind, its hooves pulling up out of the mud with a sucking sound. When he heard the horse stop, the priest looked back over his shoulder. The long sword and a broad smile below a thick, drooping red mustache left no question about the identity of the horse's rider.

"It looks a bit damp down there, Father. Can I give you a ride somewhere so you do not muddy yourself too terribly?"

"Aye, Sergeant. You can," answered the priest as he took the man's gloved hand to pull himself up on the horse.

The sergeant noticed that the hair coming out from under Father Regis's black cap was beginning to match the gray of his cassock as much as the black of the open woolen gown resting on his shoulders. The large silver cross hanging from his neck clanged against the hilt of the sergeant's sword as the priest slid up onto the horse.

"Thank you, Sergeant. Atwelle is in good hands and its peace well maintained under your protection as sergeant at arms."

"As the parish is in your hands, Father, as it always has been," the large man replied. "Where will you be goin' today then?"

"To the Lanham manor house," he answered.

"To visit another king's man, like myself," the sergeant noted with an approving point at the Royal Badge of the Tudor rose and crowned "H" on his cap. "And what would your pope be thinkin' about that, if he knew?"

"Any disagreements between King Henry and the pope are no concern of a humble priest in this parish."

"I wouldn't be so sure, Father. The disagreements between the king and the pope are starting to affect a great many people, humble or not. And that cross hanging around your neck puts you humble parish priests who live under the king's protection right in the middle of those disagreements, I would think."

The priest's brow furrowed as he looked into the mane of red hair on the back of the sergeant's head. With each rocking step of the horse, droplets of dewy mist fell from the thick red locks to the sergeant's leather jerkin over the green doublet on his wide shoulders. Each man pondered his position in the political tensions of the times as the horse plodded on, taking little notice when its path led through the middle of a small herd of longhaired sheep being driven down the road toward the market.

"Has the weather slowed construction of the new church?" the sergeant asked.

"Some. All the stones to finish the walls have been delivered from the quarry. But the workmen are waiting until drier weather to hew the timber for the roof beams."

"And until you've got some money to pay for their work," the sergeant thought to himself.

"Here you go then, Father," he said as he pulled up before the large handsome manor house of Richard Lanham.

With a hand from the sergeant, Father Regis slid off the horse's back. "Thank you, Sergeant. I shall pray for you."

"Thank you, Father. But I don't know that prayin' will do any good for me—unlike some other things," he answered with an affectionate pat on the intimidating sword resting against his thigh. "Do you know what this is called, Father?"

"I do not, Sergeant."

"Its style is known as a 'hand and a half' by the length of its hilt. But for those who know swords, it is called—"

The sergeant looked around to be sure no one else would hear.

"The Bastard," he said with a proud smile.

"Indeed," answered Father Regis. "Then I shall pray for your bastard as well," he said with a wry smile as he turned to make his way through the gate and up the path under several great oak trees to the main door of the manor house.

While waiting for an answer to his knock, he admired the substantial wooden beams curving symmetrically across the facing of the front wall of the tall house. Wooden beams, he was reminded, were his reason for meeting with Lanham. The thought raised a growing feeling of anxiety that once again gripped at his insides. He tried to ignore the gnawing doubt about his ability to succeed at the task before him. Finally, one of Lanham's servants opened the door and greeted the priest warmly before leading him through the dark, wood-paneled entry to the lord of the manor who welcomed him in the study.

"Father Regis, good to see you." The tall, handsome man waved his guest to a chair opposite him.

"And you, Richard. You must tell me, how is your son doing?"

Although the look in Lanham's eyes changed, the smile under his well-trimmed gray beard did not move.

"Christopher is doing well, thank you."

"And has he made a decision?"

Lanham's smile disappeared.

"He has decided to take his vows. He hopes to enter the monastery this winter."

"How wonderful!" exclaimed the priest, although he could see Lanham did not agree.

"How can I help you, Father?" Lanham abruptly diverted the direction of their discussion.

"First, Richard, I wanted to thank you again for your extremely generous gift to build a side chapel in the new church in the memory of your late wife. It will be a beautiful place of prayer and a worthy memorial to her sainted soul."

Lanham looked down at the floor. He thought about how he had made that gesture of a contribution to the new church because it was expected of him, but regretted now that the chapel would remind him of her painfully until the day he died.

"You are most welcome, Father."

"I also wanted to report to you on how well the building of the new church is progressing." Father Regis provided numerous details on the partially finished walls, on the planning and purchases for the interior, and on the efforts of the expert workmen from the region. Lanham nodded his approval and continued waiting for the real purpose of the priest's visit.

"Richard, you appreciate as much as any of our worshipers the beauty and importance of the firmament of heaven over our heads as we live our lives below dedicated to God."

Lanham now knew why the priest was there.

"So I know that you—more than anyone in our church, Richard—appreciate the beauty and importance of the roof of our new church, which protects us as we worship and pray to Him."

Lanham was thinking the priest knew full well that the people who most appreciated the beauty of God's skies above were his parishioners who dug all day in the darkness of Lanham's new salt mines. Yet he wasn't talking to them about a new roof.

"The walls are almost finished and soon will be in need of the crown of beautiful wooden arches pointing to the heavenly firmament above, through which you will ascend one day to join your sainted wife.

"With the completion of the walls, we are also ready for the installation of the windows of stained glass. Through their beautiful colors, we will see the story of the founding of this church two hundred years ago and its renewal with the building of this new edifice in our time.

"Richard, God needs your support to purchase the timber for the beams and construction of the roof, and the stained glass that tells the story of this church and your place in it. May we count on you for your help?"

The priest knew his request was in trouble when he saw the muscles of Lanham's jaw tighten in response. He waited through Lanham's silence, preparing to persuade Lanham with more detail on the budget.

"Who else is contributing to the purchase of timber and glass?"

"You, of course, for your love of the church, are the first to whom I came," answered Father Regis.

Lanham's hand stroked his bearded chin as his mind turned over the request. The priest prayerfully folded his hands on his lap.

"Father," Lanham finally spoke, "you know that my gift of the chapel and other support to this point have been exceedingly generous."

"I do know that, Richard. I give thanks to God daily and ask for His blessing on you for your selfless gifts."

"And you may know that my recent investments in the new salt mines are substantial and uncertain at present."

"I have no doubt, Richard, that you will do well in such business as you have in all your other commercial endeavors."

"Then there is the port in Atwelle," Lanham went on. "There are petitions before the king for the grant of rights to create an inland port through the waterways to the sea. I, as you know, am not the only person seeking these rights and revenues. So there is much uncertainty about the success of that project on which the profits of my mines and enterprise rest mightily."

"There is little question that with the efforts of you and others in the town, the reality of the new port will surely come to pass," announced Father Regis as if such commercial matters were the subject of his daily meditations.

"Well, the efforts of 'others in the town,' as you refer to them, are more certainly in their own interests than they are in the new port," responded Lanham.

The priest continued looking at him hopefully.

"What about our king and the pope?" Lanham asked. With a steady gaze he waited for a response from the priest.

"How do you mean?" Father Regis replied to avoid a direct answer.

"You know that the king is close to a direct confrontation on the authority of the pope over the question of the annulment of His Majesty's marriage to Catherine of Aragon," stated Lanham.

"Yes, but the king has reached out to the Holy See many times to resolve the issue. An ecclesiastical court or Papal Bull will surely resolve the question amicably."

Lanham shook his head at the priest's naiveté.

"All of that did little good for Cardinal Woolsey, who went from being the king's chancellor to being charged last year with treason. If Henry VIII, King of England, decides he wants a divorce, he will get it, even in the face of the pope's opposition.

"If that happens, Father, the situation could lead to each of us having to choose sides. What if the king orders all priests to pray for his new marriage? What will you do then if the pope forbids it?

"And what of me, I ask you. What will I be choosing if I decide now to make a large contribution to your church? An eternity in hell through excommunication by the pope if I say no? Or losing my head by the sergeant's sword upon the king's command if I say yes?"

2017 As the old woman handed over a cup of odd-smelling tea, Margeaux could not help taking a sidelong glance at her unusually long and thick gray hair. Its natural waves hung loosely over her shoulders down past her waist.

"I may be named Daunting, but I'm old and cranky and poor as a church mouse here at St. Clement's," the old woman complained.

"I know what you mean, Miss Daunting," the young woman responded, gingerly juggling the teacup too hot to touch. "Not having enough money is the story of my life also."

"What's your name again, dearie?"

Margeaux smiled patiently. Miss Daunting had asked that question several times in the two months they had known each other.

"I'm Margeaux—Margeaux Wood, Miss Daunting."

The old woman gave her a suspicious look.

"Your accent—are you French?"

"My mother was French, but my father was English. I was raised in both countries."

Miss Daunting's wary expression did not go away.

"Now explain something to me. I was told you were a fellow, but you're clearly a woman."

"I am a 'fellow,' because that is my academic position," Margeaux replied and smiled again. "A fellow of my college, Maryhouse Hall, at Cambridge University. I'm a don."

The old woman cocked her head with a funny look at her. "Don? I thought you said your name was Margeaux?"

Margeaux's smile started fading at the edges.

"'Don' is another word for fellow, like a lecturer. Except I don't lecture actually, I'm a research fellow in medieval history."

"So you're not working with the new architect then?"

"No."

"I didn't think so," huffed the old woman. "Architects *are* fellows."

Margeaux's smile was gone at that point.

"And he is a real Don, by the way," the old woman snipped. "His name is Don."

With a satisfied look from having reestablished her natural order of things, Miss Daunting took a sip from her teacup.

Margeaux was already unhappy at how her project in Atwelle was going, and this conversation was not helping. Like the premature winter weather in the autumn outside, the small office in where they sat felt cold and damp like St. Clement's, the ancient church to which it was attached. She took a sip of tea. Margeaux didn't know whether it was exotic tea or maybe just old like Miss Daunting, but at least it was hot.

"Would you by any chance have some sugar for the tea, Miss Daunting? I'm sorry. I didn't catch the name of the new architect."

"You didn't catch it because I haven't yet told it to you," the old woman replied. "It's Don, like yours. Don Whitby. A fine-looking young man, if I do say so. And he's supposed to be the best in the business when it comes to restoration of old churches."

Margeaux concluded that Miss Daunting would make no attempt to find sugar in an office that was as disorganized as the old woman's mind, so she took a sip and tried to ignore its odd taste.

"When does Mr. Whitby start on the church's restoration project, Miss Daunting?"

"I have no idea. I'm just a volunteer. I do almost everything here except preach sermons and give communion," she answered with both pride and frustration in her voice. "But I'm definitely not in charge of the architect. I don't get paid a farthing, though I could certainly use it."

"How long have you been here?" Margeaux tried to sound polite and interested while trying to figure out what she was drinking.

"Well, if by 'here' you mean the village of Atwelle, my family has been here for centuries. If you mean here at the church, I started volunteering full time a while before Father Charleton disappeared." She let out a small sigh of resignation. "You see, the Church of England is not doing very well here in Atwelle, and the congregation is not very large anymore. With the fund-raising campaign to refurbish the church just starting, Father Charleton needed help. So I volunteered on a full-time basis. Much more work. No more money," she grumbled before sipping her tea.

"It's so strange, Father Charleton's disappearance," remarked Miss Daunting. "Such a pity."

"Yes," Margeaux agreed. "He had such a wealth of information about the church. I learned so much about St. Clement's from him in my brief time here."

Miss Daunting nodded with a frown.

"And then in the middle of all the activity to start the project to fund and begin the church's restoration, he up and disappears. Vanishes!" Miss Daunting snapped her fingers loudly and shook her head.

"But wasn't it fortunate that Father Lanham arrived as associate vicar just before Father Charleton disappeared," Margeaux observed. "He should do well to finish his training here, don't you think?"

"Yes, that was unexpected," Miss Daunting replied. "It's not many small churches like ours that have a curate these days. Plus it's so special that we have him here with the Lanham name when we're trying to raise money to restore the Lanham side chapel. And now Father Adams has returned to Atwelle to replace Father Charleton after thirty years as a missionary in Haiti. So I've got two ministers plus an old leaky church keeping me busy," she concluded.

After a final gulp of the peculiar tea, the old woman set down her cup and brushed some long strands of hair back over her shoulder to look directly at Margeaux.

"So how is your little project doing here at St. Clement's? What is it again?"

Margeaux took a deep breath and made an effort to sound enthusiastic as she patiently described her research to Miss Daunting one more time.

"It's a research project on the church's unique collection of facets. It's quite exciting actually."

Miss Daunting gave her a questioning look.

"Unique? The church has been here for centuries. What's unique about it? One of those big government research grants, I suppose," she concluded in a disapproving tone of voice.

"I'm afraid not," Margeaux had to admit. "That's part of my problem. The funding for my research is still uncertain at this point."

At this news, Miss Daunting tried to look sympathetic.

"Well, maybe things will work out for you, dearie."

Margeaux took a hasty final sip of the tea and set down the cup and saucer.

"Now that I'm here, would it be possible to meet Father Adams?"

"I'm afraid not now. He doesn't seem to be available much, unfortunately. He's not a young man anymore, you know."

"Could I see Father Lanham then?"

"He is unavailable also."

"Then why am I bloody well here?" Margeaux wondered with frustration, thinking about the hour-long drive from Cambridge. "Perhaps they might be available for my next visit?" she asked Miss Daunting.

"Perhaps," the old woman replied. Thick tresses of her long wavy gray hair fell around her shoulders as she leaned over to stand up.

Margeaux rose and thanked Miss Daunting before departing through the door to the nave of the church. Though the low light of the late afternoon sky made the church seem like a dark cavern, no lights were turned on. Only a single candle burned on a wall near the large stained glass window behind the altar. She walked past the altar and stood before the base of the window, looking up. Then her eyes circled around the interior of the church.

"Not much to look at," thought Margeaux. "But for what it is worth in the end, this may be the only church in England with so many unusual aspects that haven't been studied and chronicled. And there's probably a very good reason for that," she concluded with excitement. "There is something that will make it worthwhile for me to be here. I know it."

Margeaux felt a shiver run through her body. Her jacket was too light for the early winter weather and the cold church. Something made her look around. She felt like she was being watched, but in the dim light she saw no one.

Stepping over a brass figure of a knight with his long sword inlaid in the stone next to the altar, she began walking quickly toward the long aisle between the empty pews. When she thought she heard something, she stopped. The cavernous church was as silent as it was dark. She started walking again. Now she thought she heard footsteps. Again, she stopped, but still she heard nothing. The shiver ran through her once more.

Halfway down the length of the church, Margeaux looked around at the gray shadowed walls and then up at the dark wooden ceiling arching high above. The small candle by the altar seemed miles away. Taking only a few steps, she halted abruptly. This time she heard a footfall after she stopped.

Now she hurried down the aisle as quickly as she could without breaking into a run. Her fingers finally felt the cold iron of the latch as she reached the large ancient wooden door at the main entrance of the church. Leaning back to pull open the door, she stepped outside and then looked back into the dark empty church. There was no movement, only silence. She shuddered nervously again.

"Funny how the dark can turn a church from feeling like a sanctuary to feeling so threatening," Margeaux thought with a shake of her head as the familiar sight of her car calmed her a bit. Turning back to close the door behind her, she started to reach out for the latch.

The heavy door slammed suddenly in her face, looming over her as its echo raced away inside.

THREE

1532 After his midweek mass, Father Regis tried to hurry through his parishioners' confessions so he could meet with Peter as soon as possible. He very much needed to talk to Peter to work through his concerns before addressing Francis DuBois the next day. But there were many men waiting to make their confessions, and most of them involved the local prostitute, Molly. She was a continuing annoyance for the priest in the confessional, but not a problem for the men in his parish who simply sought absolution from Father Regis to resolve the matter in their consciences.

He let the last man off with a mild penance and went to find Peter at the side door of the church. The two men did not pass a greeting once the door was opened. Peter simply followed the priest in silence up the narrow spiral stone staircase to the modest cell in an enclosed porch over the side entrance of the partially completed, roofless, and windowless church. Glancing about the small room where the priest lived his spare existence, Father Regis motioned for Peter to sit on one of two plain stools in front of a tiny table.

Peter sat quietly while Father Regis leaned over the fireplace stirring a thin stew heating in a small cauldron. After he had dished up the stew into two bowls, the priest filled mugs with ale from a cask and joined his friend at the table. Peter gave a moan of eagerness to start eating, but Father Regis started to pray a blessing for the food first.

Even with his hands folded and head bowed, Peter kept a steady eye on the food. Immediately after the "amen," he reached for his mug and drank the ale in a single quaff. Then he vigorously broke off some bread from a loaf, dipped it into the stew, and ate it as if it were his first meal in days. Father Regis refilled the mug from the cask and sat down again, watching Peter eat.

"I need your advice," the priest said to Peter after a moment. Without looking up, Peter gave a low grunt in response while he continued chewing.

"I met today with Richard Lanham to ask for his financial support for the roof and stained glass in the new church. He did not give it."

Peter stopped chewing and looked at Father Regis.

"Church!" he repeated in a monosyllabic exclamation.

"He is worried about whether his salt mines will be profitable, particularly since their success is dependent on whether the sea access to Atwelle can be turned into a port and make it a market town for the region."

"Atwelle!" repeated Peter with exuberance.

"Whether that happens depends on the competition between Lanham and DuBois. Each of them wants to be the key power if the town becomes a flourishing commercial center and port. And neither wants the port to be successful if it increases the power and influence of the other. So they both desire the port to be a success, but yet do not want it to be the other's achievement. A rather odd situation, is it not?"

Peter, with a mouth full of stew, nodded vigorously.

"Lanham is also concerned about the worsening relationship between King Henry and the Holy Church in Rome. He thinks a large contribution to the building of the new church could put him on one side or the other if the pope and king become openly opposed to one another.

"But I know he's a king's man. After all, the king has provided the money for the development of his mines. But that also puts him in a difficult situation since his son has just decided to become a monk."

"Monk!" echoed Peter.

"I am also sure that he's worried about his support for the king, because DuBois favors the pope. So if the pope predominates in any conflict with the king, DuBois is in a position to assert control in the shire, including the inland port. Good play, that. It would mean Du-Bois becomes wealthier from expanding his trade of his own crops and wool and also from the shipments of Lanham's salt."

Father Regis gave Peter a look of grave concern. Peter mimicked the concerned expression in his own face until the priest looked away and he was free to reach for his ale.

"But I have to confess to you, Peter, that I too am worried about the worsening tension between the Church and the king. I fear the implications of an open conflict to me personally as well as my plans for the new church. What do you think I should do?"

"Church! King!" Peter repeated emphatically before he picked up the bowl of stew and licked it clean.

Father Regis thought for a moment and then looked at Peter as the answer came to him.

"Of course! Church *and* king. Right you are again, my friend. The new church will be protected if I can get both Lanham and DuBois to support the roof and window construction. In that case, the church construction will be finished regardless of the dispute over annulment of the king's marriage. I must secure the equal support of both of them.

"But how to get rivals to join together as major patrons of the church construction, especially when the king and Church are at odds?"

The priest frowned, doubting that he could ever sort out an answer to his dilemma. He looked up to see Peter studying him with a look of concern through unwashed locks of hair. Father Regis smiled at Peter, so Peter smiled too.

"All finished, Peter? Here you go then," he said handing a broom to Peter.

Father Regis watched Peter dutifully sweeping the floor of the priest's cell. "We are so different, and yet so much alike," he thought.

He remembered back to the time years ago when he had returned to Atwelle after studying canonical law at Maryhouse Hall in Cambridge. He had great promise, all his tutors had told him. They had recommended him to the Archbishop of Canterbury, who had then expressed an interest in furthering his career. There was even talk of a position in Rome. In the end, he shamefully admitted even now, he had doubted himself and his abilities, and ended up coming back to Atwelle as a parish priest.

With a fond look, he watched Peter, who was merely moving the dust ineffectively around the floor with the broom. Peter, whom he had first seen years ago as a dirty little boy with a damaged mind, had always managed somehow to live with confidence on the street. A child unclaimed, but cared for by all.

"We belong to no one, and yet to everyone, Peter," thought Father Regis. "We are children of Atwelle, you and I. Our family is this town."

As Peter swept furiously at a corner, Father Regis shook his head at the irony. Peter had little intellect and yet lived with the comfort of complete self-acceptance, while he, a priest highly educated and admired by all, was often tortured by continual self-doubt. Father Regis once again resolved that just as he had given his life in service to Atwelle, so he would give the town the new church it needed and deserved. "You will not doubt your abilities," he admonished himself with jaws clenched. "You have a purpose."

"Peter," the priest interrupted him. Peter stopped and looked up from his task.

"Thank you," said Father Regis with a look of genuine fondness.

"Peter!" he answered, echoing his name joyfully as he began sweeping the room once more.

2017 The large door to St. Clement's was already standing open when Margeaux returned to Atwelle a week later. She peeked in cautiously. In spite of the bright morning daylight outside, the interior of the church seemed unusually dark until Margeaux's eyes adjusted, and light streaming through the stained glass windows beckoned her entrance. Her long scan down the nave revealed that she was alone. She was not surprised. Monday is a church's day of rest.

Margeaux walked slowly down the center aisle of the nave. After each step, she stopped and examined the walls and the ceiling of the church. The gray of the walls was interrupted with occasional unpleasant water stains. Although not of great height, the walls appeared taller because of the high arc of the roof above, which was constructed of wood so dark that its blackness seemed unending like the night sky.

When she reached the front row of pews, Margeaux stopped to look at a large arrangement of flowers in a funeral wreath placed before the pew on the left side. She moved into a pew on the opposite side, where she sat very still for a few moments with her eyes closed. Anyone watching would have assumed that she was saying a traditional prayer communicating with God upon entering His house of worship. But this morning she was communing with His house rather than with Him.

Her whole being, not just her body, felt enveloped by the surrounding stillness of the ancient church. No movement. No noise. It was a contemplative quiet that made the world outside seem all the more frantic, loud, and out of control. The stone walls stood strong and silent, providing a sense of impenetrable protection from the mayhem created by mankind.

The air seemed not to move at all. Like most old churches, it was cooler than the hot days and warmer than the cold days outside. But never quite comfortable. Damp without being moist. It was as if the air Margeaux was breathing had lingered in the church from the day five centuries earlier when the space was consecrated.

The ambient light seemed to come neither from the inside nor the outside. Shadows simply happened from uncertain sources. But when the sun touched the windows, the color and patterns of the stained glass were transformed magically into a message for upturned eyes. When the sun disappeared, the stories told by the glass disappeared as if behind a closed book cover. Then the golden glow of the church's candles would hint at the stories in the windows that were still there to be read with the sun of another day.

Margeaux stroked the smooth wood of the pew. She felt its hardness where it bore the weight of her body. For no reason other than the physical experience, she pulled down the kneeler and came to her knees as if to pray. It too was hard and uncomfortable. The thought occurred to Margeaux that she had never once sat in a comfortable pew in any church. Was there an intended purpose for a pew to be so physically unpleasant? Was the discomfort meant to symbolize something? Perhaps a form of mortification of the flesh that all worshipers should experience?

From her prayerful pose, she looked at the altar. Historically, it was the place of blood sacrifice. Between two large ornate silver candlesticks, a large silver cross sat solidly at the center of the altar to symbolize the sacrifice of Jesus, God's only Son—the act of ultimate selflessness and love that was to define His church. From the altar came the sacrificial body and blood of Jesus, which were consumed by his believers in the holiest of rituals. How ironic, Margeaux thought, that the religion from which Western civilization arose was based on a rite of symbolic cannibalism commanded by Jesus himself at the Last Supper. "Take and eat. This is my true body given for you." Was this rite intended as the fullest expression of a person's becoming one with God, Margeaux wondered.

She rose from the kneeler and sat back on the pew. Her eyes once again circled the expanse of the church from floor to ceiling.

"This is where life for a villager in Atwelle began," she thought, "even before birth."

Couples were wed. Babies were baptized. Religious education was consummated with confirmation of one's faith. Communion taken.

Confessions given. Marriages blessed. Weekly worship and reminders of things one did not otherwise think about in life, but should.

"And then here it ends," she concluded. She looked over at the wilting flowers left over from the funeral. "With peace of mind in the protection of this sanctuary." Protection. Sometimes real, sometimes imagined, she thought. Protection conditioned on faith. But protection none the less. Protection that mankind instinctively needs, and so picks this place, consecrates it, and seeks safety there for peace of mind.

"Can my project in this place give me peace of mind?" Margeaux asked herself. It was an ancient but unremarkable church neglected for centuries by scholars and now by people who no longer worshiped. There were no obvious scholarly analytical challenges here from intricate glass windows of brilliant colors below grand arches of wondrous architecture that reflected the power and glory of the society in which it was built. "But there are lessons to be learned, mysteries to be solved, and rewards to be achieved," she told herself, deciding once again to be optimistic. She picked up the binocular case she had brought with her and pulled its shoulder strap over her head. The lid snapped open, sending a small sharp echo through the silent church. Pulling the binoculars out, she then focused with great interest on the main stained glass window behind the altar.

Margeaux's gaze lingered on the window as she thought of her love for stained glass windows in ancient churches. How powerfully their light and colors told inspirational stories to illiterate parishioners for centuries—stories from the Bible or from the history of the church. The windows delivered those messages of beauty, wisdom, and power straight from God instead of through the filter of foreign words from a priest.

But as she scanned the large stained glass window to the east, she found none of these messages. There was no apparent story. Most of the window, the bottom two tiers, were filled with a large circle of fading reddish color. When the light came through the tall panes of this colored glass, Margeaux felt as if she were immersed in a pool of blood.

"The message of this window hardly seems religious," thought Margeaux. "Why would there be so much red?"

Above the expanse of faded red, however, were smaller panes of glass fragments forming a pointed arch at the top of the window. Margeaux peered at these fragments through her binoculars, desperately hoping to find something of interest. But outside of what appeared to be some heraldic crests, most of the detail in the glass panes was obscured by the accumulated grime of past centuries.

"Odd place for bird watching."

Margeaux jumped up at the sound of a voice close by, and turned to find a man sitting in the pew behind her. She instinctively swung her binoculars at him in frightened self-defense. The man managed to lean back just far enough that the binoculars barely flew by his face. He held up his hands in surrender.

"Whoa there! I've got nothing against bird watching. Honest."

He looked to be in his mid-thirties and had a pleasant face with smudges of dirt near his auburn brown eyes. His sandy hair looked like it was combed neatly in the morning with orders to stay in place and then left to fend for itself the rest of the day. As he stood up, Margeaux could see his tall, lean frame was dressed in workman's clothes.

"I'm told you're Miss Wood." He held out his hand. "I'm Donald Whitby, the architect in charge of the project to refurbish the church. But you can call me Don. No one else does."

Margeaux liked his winning smile at his own bad joke, but looked at his hand uncertainly. It was quite dirty.

"Oh . . . sorry." He attempted unsuccessfully to wipe off his hand on his shirt and held it out again. "I've been hanging out with dead people," he said shaking her hand.

Margeaux cringed inwardly as she quickly withdrew her hand from the briefest of handshakes. He noticed her discomfort.

"I mean—what I should have said is that I've been down in the crypt under the altar.

"Most people look up when they're in a church. That's what churches are designed to have them do." He looked up at the stained-glass window that Margeaux had been examining and then across the dark wooden ceiling above. "But I look first at the foundations. It's right down to the cellar for me. I always say, if the foundation isn't doing what it's supposed to, there's not much hope for the bits on top."

His cheery smile and lighthearted observation hardly seemed like he was talking about an ancient church.

"How do you do, Mr. Whitby. I'm Margeaux Wood."

"Pleased to meet you, Margeaux," answered Don. He meant it. She was beautiful. "And do call me Don; otherwise I'll think you're talking to my father."

After she smiled at his comment, all he could think about was her dimples.

"What is the crypt like?" asked Margeaux. "It's the one place I think I haven't actually seen in St. Clement's."

Her question reminded him that they were still standing in a church.

"I'm pleased to report that the foundations of this fine church are as solid as an architect could want. No worries from there about the bits on top here."

"What I meant was, is there a great marble sarcophagus of some lost saint down there or skeleton bones scattered about? Please tell me they are there."

"Neither are there, I'm afraid." He noticed her look of disappointment. "But it's quite dusty down there, if that helps."

When he saw that his attempt at humor had missed the mark and that she looked genuinely discouraged at his answer, he decided to give her more detail.

"Actually, there are four stone coffins sitting above ground in the crypt. They're an odd collection really, like the rest of this church."

He liked the way her face perked up with interest.

"Would you like to hear more about them?"

Watching her eager nod, he noticed how naturally pretty she was without wearing any makeup.

"Well, the largest tomb is the resting place of a priest named Father Regis Hollowell. From my limited knowledge of the history of the church, I believe he was the priest here when the church was rebuilt in 1532. Not a saint though, at least not that anyone knows. Sorry."

He enjoyed the dimples from her smile once again.

"The next largest sarcophagus is a bit more humble and its inscription unfortunately has been obscured. But it's interesting that there is a brass sword inlaid on the top. The third coffin is unmarked and smaller than the other two, perhaps for a woman.

"And the last coffin is plain and unremarkable except for a couple things. First, it's a coffin used for a burial in a grave rather than a stone tomb for above ground. That may explain in part why it has no inscription of any sort. And from its size, it appears to contain a small child."

Don was glad to see that her attitude of discouragment had been replaced by a slight furrow between her eyebrows, as if she were puzzling over a crossword clue.

"Now, Miss Wood, I understand that you are here working on some research project while I'm to fix the leaks in the roof and, with an inadequate budget, keep this church going for another five centuries. Be honest with me, Miss Wood. You're not really bird watching, are you?"

"I'm here to study the whole church," she replied. "And with no budget at present."

"Oh dear," he murmured in a sympathetic voice. "And what exactly do you mean by 'the whole church'? Sounds like a tall order."

Margeaux paused in thought. Don could see the excitement in her eyes.

"There's nothing about this church that strikes one as exceptional in any way. And yet, when you start listing a number of things in and about this church, the collection of elements appears to be quite idiosyncratic. And there's no single or logical explanation for all these elements to come together in one place."

"Like what for instance?"

"Well, you can start with the stained glass," she pointed past the altar to the largest window. "Why is there such a vast expanse of fading red? And the same color is predominant in smaller stained glass throughout the church except for the two side chapels."

"Maybe they bought it at a sale price when they saw an advert," Don speculated with a grin. "'Available This Century Only!'"

Margeaux gave him a mild scolding look for apparently not taking her seriously.

"When you were entering the crypt behind the altar, did you notice the brass on the floor?" she asked.

"How could I not?" he answered. "That knight with the long sword had the most remarkable mustache I've ever seen.

"If it is a knight," she replied. "There is no coat of arms or history suggesting his name, family, or station.

"Then there are the two side chapels," she continued. "They were the gifts of the two most prominent families in the town when the church was built. They're much more ornate with hammer beams and detailed carvings and windows. My guess is that they cost more than the whole rest of the church's decor."

"The Golden Rule," concluded Don. "He with the gold rules."

"Then there's the enclosed room in a porch over the brick vaulting covering the side entrance to the church. It was a 'parvis,' a priest's room," Margeaux explained. "Now it's the office study for the vicar. I love the narrow spiral staircase going up to the small landing at its entry. The priest could see the whole church from there. But watch for the stone steps. They're quite worn and uneven.

"And in the study is a unique iron-bound chest built with compartments to hold important books and documents. The only other one like it is in a college in Cambridge."

"The lectern there is interesting," said Margeaux with a gesture at the head and beak of an eagle extending out beyond the platform from which centuries of Bible verses had been read. "It's made of a brass alloy that was used to mass produce these, it appears. There are some others exactly alike in parishes around Norfolk.

"It's said that each parishioner was required to pay to the pope a tax called Peter's pence by putting coins into the beak of the eagle, which came out through its tail."

Margeaux pointed at the other end of the church to the west.

"In the opposite corners are the baptismal font and the alms box for contributions to the poor and orphaned. Both of them have similar carvings of very sad faces, obviously done by the same carver. It's rather unusual that those two items would have a similar motif.

"There are also—"

"Yoo-hoo, Mr. Whitby!"

His name echoing from the back of the church interrupted them. Looking up, they saw Miss Daunting waving at Don.

"Father Lanham will see you now."

"Thank you, Miss Daunting," he called back. "I'll be right there."

"I finally get to meet this bloke," he said to Margeaux. "You want to come along?"

"Yes I would," she answered without hesitation as they stepped from the pew and headed down the aisle.

"By the way," she asked him, "were you by any chance here in the church after dark a week ago?"

"Here in the church? At night?" He wiped the dirt from his face with his handkerchief as he walked. "Not a chance! I never go into churches at night. They're spooky as hell!" he declared as he ducked through a low door following Miss Daunting to the church office.

Margeaux suddenly felt once again like she was being watched. Stopping at the door, she glanced back over her shoulder. This time she saw the face of a man peering at her from the shadows of the small porch over the side entrance to the church.

"I'll know that face next time I see it," she thought nervously.

FOUR

1532 Margaret DuBois hurriedly poked her head around the thick oaken door to her father's study.

"I am going upstairs now, Papa, and will be ready very soon. Please, do not make us late this time."

"Have you finished your harp lesson?" her father asked, looking up from his desk. After studying the rows of numbers in the account books before him for many hours, he relaxed at the sight of his beautiful eldest child.

Margaret's long wavy auburn hair reappeared next to the door. "Yes, Papa."

"And you gave your teacher the coins I left you?"

"Yes, Papa. He said I do not need any more lessons."

"He said no such thing," retorted her father. "Do you know how many of my sheep had to be sheared to pay for shipping that harp all the way from Brussels?"

"Papa, please, *please* do not be late because of your meeting with Father Regis!"

"All right, all right," he mumbled as he tried to turn back to the long list of debts demanding his attention. He was interrupted by his wife.

"Francis, Father Regis is here to see you," she said from the door, without bothering to enter.

DuBois sighed wearily and thought, "Another meeting to discuss money I don't have."

Father Regis came into the room with a smile that attempted—unsuccessfully—to suggest he was there solely for the well-being of DuBois.

"Francis, it is good to see you. How are you feeling, my son?"

"Why does he always call me 'son'?" DuBois wondered. "We are the same age, after all."

"Father Regis, it is always good to see you. I am well, thank you. Do sit down."

"And how are your good wife and the children?"

"My good wife, like all things in life, Father, is a blessing and burden. And as for the children, I've lost count of how many there are."

Father Regis smiled. He knew exactly how many there were since he had baptized them all. After the obligatory discussion of the wet weather, the condition of the crops, and the price of wool, the priest eased into his real agenda.

"Francis, I wanted to thank you again for your extremely generous gift to build a side chapel in the new church to the memory of your family ancestors. It will be a beautiful place of prayer and a worthy memorial to their sainted souls."

"You are welcome, of course, Father." DuBois knew precisely where in the ledger lying on the desk before him was the entry indicating the number of unmade payments on the loan of money he had borrowed for his gift of the chapel.

"I also wanted to report to you on how the building of the new church is progressing."

DuBois was impressed by how well rehearsed Father Regis's report was. He easily covered numerous details on the nearly finished walls, on the planning and purchases for the interior, and on the efforts of the many expert workmen from the region who were on the job. Uncomfortable and uncertain about his ability to persuade DuBois, Father Regis stayed with the script he had memorized for Richard Lanham.

"You appreciate, Francis, as much as any of our parishioners the beauty and importance of the firmament of heaven over our heads as we live our lives below dedicated to God. So I know that you—more than anyone in our new church—also appreciate the beauty and importance of the roof over our new church that protects us as we worship and pray to Him."

Although DuBois appeared to be listening, he caught only vague references to a "need for the crown of beautiful wooden arches pointing to the heavenly firmament" and colored stained glass to tell the "story of the founding of this church two hundred years ago and its renewal with the building of the new edifice." He looked up at Father Regis when he sensed the priest was finishing.

"Francis, God needs your support to purchase both the timber for the beams and construction of the roof, and the stained glass to tell the story of this church and your place in it. May we count on you for your help?"

The priest knew once again that his request was in trouble from the immediate question in response.

"Who else is contributing to the construction and glass?" DuBois asked.

"You, from your love of God and the church, are among the first to whom I have come," Father Regis answered promptly.

"No one else?"

"I fully expect that Richard Lanham, your old comrade-in-arms from the war, will be making a generous contribution along with his similar gift of a side chapel."

A momentary scowl crossed DuBois's face at the sound of Lanham's name.

"Of course I am inclined to support your request, Father, and shall certainly consider it. However, I fear I must wait until I know what prices are fetched by the harvest and my flocks of sheep. The markets have been fickle these last years, and one must be prudent in one's expenditures."

DuBois glanced down at the long list of debts in the account book awaiting his attention.

"Then there is the access to the sea. If the inland port is completed and operated successfully under the control of the right people, my crops, wool, and meat will have ready access to the demand of enough different markets that there will always be a good price.

"So I regret, Father, that it is not within my power at the moment to provide a response to your reasonable and appropriate request."

Father Regis looked crestfallen. Inside he berated himself harshly for the stupidity of relying on the very same request that had not worked for Lanham. The priest tried to salvage something from his effort.

"Can you suggest, my son, when you might be in a position to offer your help, so I can secure prayers for your success in the meantime?"

Before DuBois could answer, Margaret was back at the entrance to her father's study.

"Papa, we must go now!" she ordered.

The sunlight through the small window in the study reflected off her beautiful hair. Her hair had grown so thick and long that at the age of sixteen she often needed help from her mother or a servant to brush it. But today, sitting before the mirror, she had brushed it herself. She was not overly concerned about how she looked. It was more important to her that she not be late.

"Father Regis," said DuBois rising from his chair, "I am instructed to proceed to my next obligation."

Knowing their destination, the priest gave him a disapproving look.

"But I shall bear your request foremost in my mind, Father, as I tend to my lands and flock. You can be certain that I will advise you on matters as soon as I am able. Now I must go, Father. I look forward to seeing you at Mass on Sunday."

As Father Regis stood to leave, a smile came over DuBois' face.

"Father," he interrupted the priest's departure. "You should come with Margaret and me to our event. You might find it entertaining."

Father Regis frowned and DuBois' amused smile grew since he knew the priest would not find the event entertaining at all, but would have to come to avoid giving offense by declining the invitation.

"Well—" the priest hesitated.

"It is done then!" DuBois announced. "You go on and get in the carriage with Margaret. I will be along in just a moment."

As soon as Father Regis left the room with Margaret, DuBois reached for his cloak and turned to leave. His wife slipped into the study and closed the door.

"We have no money to pay for a roof and windows in the church," she scolded. Her voice was harsh and accusing. "You have already purchased more land holdings and built the largest manor house in the shire, and after the poor prices for wool and our crops the last two years, you do not have the money to pay for it all."

Margaret opened the door. "Papa, we must go now!"

"I will be there in just a moment, my pet. You go get into the carriage," he said as he gently but firmly steered her out of the doorway and closed the door. He turned back to his wife.

"Money is only part of our worry," he said. "What also concerns me is the same discomfort of all prominent Catholics at the prospect of what the king may do. He has failed in all requests to the pope to allow him, as the monarch, to conceive a male heir with a new wife. His Royal Highness could end up as displeased with all major supporters of the Holy Church as he is with the pope. An angry king with soldiers and ships nearby seems a threat far more ominous at the moment than an unhappy distant pope."

"Then why did you not refuse Father Regis's request?"

"The church still has great power over its parishes. So much so, the Holy See may impose through the parishes a tax called Peter's pence to raise money for Rome.

"And above all else, I must maintain the appearance of power and influence. That is the reason for our debt to acquire more lands and build the manor house. You know I have to give the impression of power and influence to be able to position myself for gaining control of the Atwelle port.

"It will be a masterstroke for us. First, we will have access to all English ports as well as those across the channel on the continent for trading the crops, wool, and sheep from our expanded estate. And if I can also control the revenues from use of the port, including the shipping of salt from Lanham's mines, we could become the richest and most powerful family in Norfolk."

"But how will you pay the debts in the meantime?"

"We will sell our crops, wool, and sheep as always. Prices will have to go up soon. I will also raise the rents on my tenants once again."

He lowered his eyes to the list of debts.

"And as we discussed," he looked up at his wife, "we will sell off our daughter if we have to.

"Do not worry," he assured his wife with a kiss on her forehead. "Instead of paying a dowry to the groom, I will secure a financial arrangement from the groom's family for my permission for him to marry this beautiful young woman from a prominent family of means. That will solve all our immediate problems."

"Papa!" He heard the frustrated cry from outside. "We will miss the blood!"

2017 Don struggled to look serious and not smile. Because if he did smile, he knew he would laugh out loud. No stopping it.

"Who cuts these people's hair?" he wanted to know. Don looked again at the old woman's long gray tresses and the young vicar's bowl haircut. Through sheer willpower, he forced the corners of his mouth to remain immobile.

The four of them met in the crowded church office. Don and Margeaux sat on one side of a small cluttered table while on the other side Miss Daunting sat next to Father Lanham, giving him an occasional admiring look. Margeaux's initial thought was that she was grateful Miss Daunting was not serving them tea.

Moving past Father Lanham's haircut, Don noticed that the tall, thin young minister rarely blinked and had tiny pupils, which gave the impression of a continual and intense stare.

"Needless to say, we're excited about the church's restoration project, Mr. Whitby," said Father Lanham.

Don kept waiting for him to blink.

"However, we do have continuing problems with funds," the curate admitted. "How much do you think we can accomplish with the current funding?"

"Come on! Blink, dammit," Don's thoughts urged him until he realized they were waiting for his response. He looked up in the air thoughtfully and furrowed his brow to look professional.

"Um—well, the good news is that the foundation and crypt are in sound shape. If they weren't, you'd have two choices. Leave the church alone and see how many more years or centuries it lasts; or tear it down, build a new church, and wait for it to become ancient again someday."

Father Lanham did not seem to appreciate any humor on the subject of his church. His stare carried on uninterrupted.

"And the rest of the building?"

"The news is not as good, I'm afraid. But I'm hoping the problems may be fixable," Don answered.

"Yes?"

"I haven't been up there to do a close inspection yet, but it looks like the most serious problems are with the old wooden ceiling."

The assistant vicar and Margeaux leaned forward with interest.

"When this church was built," explained Don, "wood was used for the ceiling even though stone vaulting had been around for a few hundred years. Wood doesn't last as long as stone, and five hundred-odd years is not a bad stretch for a wood ceiling. But now there is water leaking onto the walls, which ultimately has a negative effect on the stone and everything below.

"In addition, the structural integrity of wooden arches after five centuries is anyone's guess. Over the centuries attempts have been made to put preservatives on the wood. That's why the ceiling is so dark. I suspect the most recent was creosote applied sometime before the Victorian period. But unfortunately over a long period of time with wood that old, any preservative with a harsh chemical base will start eating at the wood. So, ironically, we may need to preserve the wood from the preservatives."

"What will that take?" asked Father Lanham with a worried look.

"Well, we won't know until we can do a closer examination of every square foot of the ceiling." Don tried to be encouraging. "But we'll start while we're up there by inspecting the top of the stones where they meet the wooden ceiling. That should indicate where large problems may lie, and we can do temporary repairs at least to stop leaks as we find them to avoid further damage."

"Mr. Whitby, I know you're experienced in restoration of old churches. Do you have any estimate on the time and costs for such repairs? Funds could be very tight."

"I'm afraid not, Father. Not until we know the nature and extent of the damage. But I think I've already managed to save us a fair amount of money," offered Don. "Ideally we'd like to use a cherry picker for the inspection and repairs."

"A what?" asked the young curate.

"A cherry picker. That's a sort of bucket on an extendable mechanical arm attached to a small tractor with rubber wheels. It's easily adjusted to different heights and can be moved about quicker and easier than scaffolding."

Father Lanham nodded his understanding, and Don continued.

"But it's more expensive and would take quite a bit of money to hire for the time we'd be needing it. So instead I got a bargain deal on some older scaffolding that a small construction company I know is no longer using.

"But there's not enough scaffolding to line the entire length of the church, so we'll have to do the inspection in sections. My plan is to split the scaffolding into two smaller platforms, one for inspection of each of the side walls. We'll start at the back and then reposition the sections at each of the main roof beams moving from the back of the church to the front behind the altar. We'll do the chapels on either side of the nave last since they seem to be in better shape.

"Moving the scaffolding along for inspection will take more time. But at the moment, this church has more time than money," concluded Don.

"I hope that by proceeding in those stages, the fundraising will progress over time so we will be able to pay for each stage," said Father Lanham. "That will be the business of Father Adams. He'll be concerned mostly with the fundraising."

"Will I meet Father Adams soon?" asked Don. As the lead on St. Clement's restoration, he thought it odd that he still had not met with the new head cleric who had succeeded Father Charleton.

"I'm sure you'll meet him in time," answered Father Lanham. "But for now he's quite busy with his new duties.

"You will report to me on any developments and plans for the restoration project," the young vicar with the odd haircut instructed in a firm tone with added emphasis from his unblinking eyes. He turned and shifted his uninterrupted gaze to Margeaux.

"Now Miss Wood, can you tell us about your project?"

Margeaux described the numerous items of interest in the church and explained that it was historically significant to find them all in a single church.

"Are you at all concerned, Mr. Whitby, about Miss Wood's project conflicting in any way with your work on the church's restoration?" Father Lanham asked. "We wouldn't want either of your projects to be impeded by the other."

"No, not at all," answered Don. "If anything, her work might help us discover problems and how we should deal with them to preserve the church's antiquities."

Father Lanham's face took on a small frown as if he were not completely convinced.

"Very well. Miss Wood, do keep me informed of the progress of your project." He looked back at Don. "And Mr. Whitby, let me know if any concerns are raised in connection with your tasks."

"Father Lanham," she asked, "I understand Father Adams just returned from thirty years in Haiti."

"That's correct."

"Have you met much with Father Adams yet?"

"Only briefly, I'm afraid. But I'm sure we'll be working closely together soon on the restoration project and the other work of the church. Since I'm new and he's returning after a thirty-year absence, we'll both have some work to do on getting acquainted here."

Father Lanham stood up to indicate the meeting was now over. He shook their hands and left rather abruptly. Margeaux and Don headed from the office back into the church.

"He never blinked!" said Don.

"What?" Margeaux gave him a funny look.

"Oh, uh . . . nothing," he answered. They stood for a moment surveying the interior. An odd sounding voice behind them interrupted their silence.

"Here! Mr. Whitby, nice to see you again."

Margeaux turned around and found herself looking directly at an unshaven face of a man dressed in rough, disheveled clothes. She could smell him and the liquor on his breath.

"Ah, Squeaky," Don addressed him. "Margeaux, I'd like you to meet Squeaky, a longstanding resident of Atwelle and a great servant of this church."

"Aw, Mr. Whitby, I just sweep the place up twice a week for a hot meal."

"And a good thing you do!" exclaimed Don. "Wouldn't be the same place without you, Squeaky."

"How d'ye do ma'am," Squeaky nodded politely to Margeaux. He turned back to Don.

"Mr. Whitby, could I have a word? Sort of private like."

"Of course, Squeaky," answered Don.

Margeaux watched the two men walk over to the corner where she heard Squeaky say something about "standing me a pint or two" before Don pulled out his wallet and handed the man some money.

A ray of sun broke through the clouds outside, brightening the main window behind the altar. Margeaux hastily took out her binoculars to see if she could detect anything of interest in the grimy panes under the pointed arch.

"Can you make out anything up there?" Don asked as Squeaky headed briskly out the church door.

The look she gave him as she lowered the binoculars was filled with disappointment.

"No. I'm afraid not. But the pointed pane on top looks like it might contain heraldic crests."

"May I?" Don held out his hand for the binoculars and took a look at the window.

"The cleaning lady didn't quite make it to the top the last five centuries, did she? But you could be right. If those are coats of arms, I'll bet they are from the two prominent families of the area when the church was built—the families that built the side chapels."

Margeaux took back the binoculars and was having another look.

"Here's what I'll do for you," offered Don, who was feeling a bit sorry for her. "Unfortunately, we do have to start with the scaffolding at the back of the church and move to the front in stages. But I'll try to hurry the inspection along and let you know when we get close enough to the windows that you can have a better look. And we will end up in the front corners next to the window where you might be able to make up for the cleaning lady's neglect and clean the panes at the top for a proper look."

When he didn't get a response, he looked over at Margeaux. He quite liked the way her hair curled behind her ear as she peered through the glasses.

"That's odd," she said. "Can you make out what those are?"

She handed Don the binoculars. He took a look at the dark ceiling where she was pointing.

"I can't quite tell," he said after some hesitation. "Possibly, if we're lucky, we might have just found ourselves an angel roof." His voice had a hint of cautious excitement.

"What's that?"

Don leaned forward, squinting harder into the binoculars to see more clearly what the shadows and dark wood were concealing.

"A number of churches in this region have what are called 'angel roofs.' The name comes from wooden figures of angels carved into the hammer beams where the beam connects with the stone wall to brace the ceiling. But I can't quite make out whether that's what we have here."

He handed the binoculars back to her with a smile.

"We'll have a look in a couple days when the scaffolding goes up. Would you like me to call you when we're ready to mount the summit?"

"Yes, please," she answered as she handed Don her card, which he took eagerly. "Phone me as soon as you can," she called out over her shoulder with a wave as she exited through the large door of the church.

"That I will do," Don affirmed under his breath as he tucked the card carefully into his wallet.

He took a few more minutes walking the length of the church to plan out the stages for placing and then moving the scaffolding on the side walls. As he turned to leave, he paused and looked up at the ceiling once again. His hand came to his chin as he puzzled over how an angel roof could have gone unnoticed in the church for five centuries. A thought came to him.

"This may not be a good idea, old man," he warned himself after considering it briefly. But his curiosity led him on.

He walked over to a low door that had been used in centuries past to exit into the graveyard outside. Pulling out a ring of keys to every entrance in the church, he found a heavy iron key that he had used recently to check out the ancient door and its frame. With a shove from his shoulder, he pushed on the door until it gave way once again after some resistance. Outside he found what he was looking for in the untrimmed grass next to the base of the church wall.

Don reached into the blowing grass and lifted up a very long weathered wooden ladder that clearly was past its prime. He guessed that the ladder had been the main method of accessing the walls and the ceiling of the church for a long time. Ignoring the spider webs, dead grass, and dirt that clung to it, Don balanced the ladder with some difficulty on his shoulder as he carefully threaded it through the low door. With a dull thud, he banged his head hard against the stone at the top of the door frame.

"Ouch—damn!"

His curse echoed through the church. He paused and glanced about to see whether he had offended God, the Church, or anyone else who might have heard him. Fortunately, no one acknowledged his comment, allowing him to focus on the throbbing bump on his head.

"Sorry, God," mumbled Don as he struggled to maneuver the back end of the ladder through the low door. Heading over to the side wall, he hefted the entire ladder up above the pews. A clump of dirt fell off and shattered messily on the front pew.

"Da—," he started to say once again until he caught himself. "I mean 'dash it all!'" he corrected himself, again not quite sure to whom he was speaking. "I've got to work on some projects other than churches," he concluded as he lifted the long ladder into position up the side of the wall.

Stepping back, he wiped his hands, rubbed the protrusion on his head, and swallowed hard.

"Right, this is the hard part," he said out loud to buoy his courage.

Yet he knew the hardest part was yet to come. He looked up at the ceiling again.

"I love looking up at heights. Why is it that looking down from heights scares the hell out of me?" he thought, hoping that if he analyzed his fear it would go away. "Maybe this is a bad idea," he started to argue with himself out loud once again. But his curiosity seized him once more when he looked up into the dark ceiling. "I'll just go up a few rungs to start," he compromised. "Maybe I can see something from there."

Don stepped up to the ladder, took a deep breath, grabbed the side rails firmly, and placed his foot on the second rung.

"And perhaps I'll feel like going even higher," he encouraged himself with a hollow hope.

A loud snap echoed through the church as the second rung cracked under the weight of his foot. Don stepped back and surveyed the ladder cautiously.

"All right, that's enough," he said to resign from the effort and abandon his exploration.

But when he looked up again, he was struck by both the disappointment in himself and the lure of the mystery above.

"Come on, Lord Chickenheart. Buck up!" he mocked himself to meet the challenge.

Don tentatively placed his foot on another low rung and took hold of a rung at eye level. As he stepped up, the rung held.

Suddenly he felt a strong hand on his shoulder that firmly prevented him from moving any further.

"May I help you?" a deep voice asked.

FIVE

1532 Margaret was so excited she could hardly sit still in the carriage next to her father and Father Regis.

"Stone Sexton!" she exclaimed. "Can you believe it, Father? Stone Sexton is in Atwelle.

"Do hurry, John," she called out to the livery servant driving the carriage. "We can't be late to see Stone Sexton. He's here all the way from London."

DuBois was pleased at his daughter's excitement, but also slightly concerned that she was so eager to see such a bloody spectacle. He remembered taking her to that first cockfight over his wife's objection. It was a bit unusual for a young lady to be among the men shouting and gambling over the birds that were fighting to the death.

"It will be good for her—something different for the girl," DuBois had told his wife. "And after all," he added, "it's good enough for the entertainment of the Royal Court." He fully expected to bring Margaret home early once she became squeamish at the sight of blood, but surprisingly, she was fascinated by the battle. In fact, she was so enthralled that she took no notice of the men around her. It was as if only she and the fighting cocks were there.

DuBois admitted to himself now that taking her to view the blood sport reflected his desire to share that kind of experience with a son. He had sons, but they were still much too young for such pursuits. So he felt proud when Margaret next asked him to take her to the bull baiting. Once again, he was surprised at her reaction. The sight of watching a dying bull unsuccessfully fighting off a pack of dogs while chained to a post did not repulse her. Instead, it captivated her completely.

With this new bond between them, DuBois took Margaret to London to see Stone Sexton, the bear that all of England was cheering. The two of them wound their way through the seedy streets and busy brothels of the Bankside in Southwark to the Paris Garden, which for five years had been the most famous bear-baiting arena in the country. For the one penny admission and an additional two pence to sit in the tiers of seats directly above the pit where the animals fought, they were among a thousand people who watched the fabled Stone Sexton, chained to a post but standing proud, as it deftly fended off waves of attacks by the snarling English bulldogs. The crowd rose at the end with deafening shouts for the bloodied bear who stood up and roared at the last dog that whimpered away among the dead bodies of all the other dogs. DuBois remembered Margaret standing up with the crowd, but simply staring silently with fascination and admiration at the bear.

"Will it be like London, Father?" Margaret's question brought DuBois' thoughts back to the present as the carriage lurched to a stop. She quickly climbed down from the carriage without waiting for him to help her.

"No, Margaret. This is Atwelle, not London. They have built only a wooden fence around the area for the contest. We will have to stand, I fear."

He stepped down from the carriage after Margaret. Father Regis looked around uncomfortably as he stepped down from the carriage, hoping that no one would notice him.

"Papa, do you think they will let Stone Sexton off his chain? I've heard that they have been releasing him to chase the dogs."

Father Regis winced at this prospect. She headed straight toward the gathering crowd.

"And Papa, do buy us some hazelnuts," she called over her shoulder as she hurried past the men exchanging wagers and the jugglers without paying them any notice.

For a few extra pence, they eventually found themselves installed right up against the fence of the small arena. Standing next to them was the sergeant with a great smile below his prominent moustache. DuBois studied the fence with a dubious look. It did not seem much of an impediment to the force of the formidable bear and dogs he had witnessed in London.

"Some hazelnuts, Sergeant?" DuBois turned to the large man and offered him the sack of the hazelnuts traditionally sold at these events.

Reaching into the sack, the sergeant grinned his thanks. Father Regis declined the similar offer when DuBois held out the sack to him. Dubois smiled at the priest's obvious discomfort and then turned back to Margaret to hand her the sack.

"Here you go, my dear."

"Thank you, Papa," she answered. Turning to the man standing next to her, she kindly offered him some nuts as well.

"Why thank you, young lady." The man smiled at her as he took a few nuts from the sack. The audience quickly returned their attention to the center of the enclosed circle where a man raised his arms for attention.

"Good gentlemen and faire ladies," the master of ceremonies called out. He was unshaven, and his long greasy hair reached the shoulders of his bright red jerkin, which was frayed on its edges. "Welcome to our contest in the fine town of Atwelle.

"Is there not a more splendid way to spend a Thursday afternoon in the realm of our King Henry than attending a bear-baiting battle pitting the courage of this country's finest mastiffs against the fabled beast that has not only the strength of Taurus, but also the cunning of Ursus and the fangs and claws of the devil himself? I ask you again, is there not?"

The crowd comprised of almost every man in Atwelle answered with applause of anticipation.

"Then with your permission, and with great pride and special delight, I give you the legendary—Stone Sexton!" The ringmaster gestured grandly to a gate in the fence.

Loud cheers broke out as the large bear was led into the arena with a chain around its neck and another chain around a back leg. Two men with heavy sticks watched him warily as they held the chains and paraded the bear around the arena for everyone to see. But the bear did not seem much of a threat to anyone. It walked wearily with a slight limp and glazed eyes. Scars covered its face and body.

DuBois saw that the many battles that had brought fame to the bear and fortune to its owners in London clearly had taken their toll on the animal. It was apparent to him that the bear's owners were now bringing the bear out to the towns where its reputation could still draw paying customers to watch the end of the animal's illustrious career.

After circling the arena, the bear was led over to a heavy thick pole that was planted like a tree trunk in the center of the small circle. There the men fastened the chains to the pole. The bear sat down stiffly on its haunches and waited with a blank look for what it knew would come.

"Look, Papa. They've attached a pretty pink rosette of ribbons above his nose."

DuBois nodded. "If a dog is able to rip the rosette off the bear's face and escape unharmed, it is a prized possession for the dog's owner."

"It may look pretty to you," commented the sergeant, "but it's not pretty to the bear. It's there to impede his vision so that he's not so skillful in killing the dogs."

Both Margaret and Father Regis frowned at this information.

"Good gentlemen and ladies faire," the master of ceremonies called out once more, "Now I give you the bravest, most loyal and true, our own—English bulldogs!"

Four men, each with a leashed dog, entered through the gate. The dogs were stocky and well-muscled, with large, flat heads and wide, strong jaws. At the sight of the bear, the dogs started snarling and lunged so hard they pulled the men off balance at the end of their taut leashes.

"Remarkable beasts," said the sergeant. "Once they lock those jaws on an animal, they never let go unless they're killed first. I've seen four like these take down a buck elk that had a large rack of antlers sharp as knives."

"Stone Sexton!" the ringmaster announced once again as he gave a nod to one of the men pulling back on the leash of a lunging dog.

When the man allowed his animal to approach the bear, the dog began a series of thrusting jumps that almost pulled the man off his feet. His boots slid against the bare ground when he leaned back against each advancing leap of the dog's hind legs. As it grew closer to the bear, the dog began barking and snarling viciously.

The bear took no notice of the dog until it gave the smaller animal a desultory look when the dog drew close enough to threaten it. The man looked back and forth from his dog to the bear and tensed for the moment when the dog's attack would bring out the large animal's claws and teeth. Everyone in the audience leaned forward for the bloody confrontation.

But when the dog finally came close to the bear's leg, the fabled Stone Sexton merely reached out with a lame swat at the hound while still sitting against the pole. The dog instinctively jumped back though the bear's paw came nowhere close to striking. It immediately dove at the bear again, but fell back once more when the bear waved its paw in the dog's direction.

The master of ceremonies quickly signaled to another man for a second dog to enter the fray. It too pulled hard at its leash to get at the bear and, alongside the other dog, snapped at the sitting bear's back paws on the ground. Though the bear seemed half asleep and remained leaning against the pole, it managed a well-timed wave of a single paw to fend off every one of the uncoordinated attacks of the frenetic dogs. The pink rosette slid from the top of the bear's nose to the underside of its jaw where it looked pathetically like a comical pink beard.

Some boos eventually came from the crowd. A sleepy sitting bear and a couple of dogs scurrying about at the end of their leashes were not the paying customers' idea of a blood sport. The ringmaster pointed at the two remaining men and their dogs to enter the contest. In an instant the bear was surrounded by four barking dogs.

The bear sensed the increased threat from uncontrolled bloodlust in the dogs and lumbered to its feet. The dogs, straining against their leashes, instinctively began to work together, lunging in two or three at a time so that the bear could not fend off all their attacks, while a remaining dog waited for an opening to attack.

Though not ferocious, the bear's movements were still effective from years of battle. It moved with remarkable coordination to swipe a paw at one dog while moving its bared teeth in the opposite direction to scare off another dog. At the same time, the bear would shift its hindquarters out of the reach of the third dog, with an uncanny sense of how far the dog could move on its leash. The repeated attacks by the dogs drew no blood.

All the while, the bear defended itself without making a sound and created a power that seemed to compel the audience's silence as well. While the dogs lunged with their masters shouting and sweating and playing their dogs in and out on the end of their leashes, the crowd stood without moving or speaking.

Finally, a few jeers came from the crowd. The absence of blood in the blood sport they had paid to see was now intolerable. They eventually booed and loudly demanded their money back, drowning out the barking of the dogs. The ringmaster tugged nervously at the dirty cuffs on his sleeves until a disgusted look came over his face.

"A blood sport with no blood," he muttered with disapproval. "Unchain the bear and unleash the dogs," he ordered his men as he turned and walked away. "The bear is history anyway."

The crowd cheered the men as they slid along the flimsy fence and cautiously slipped up behind the bear to loosen its chains from the pole. When the other men unleashed the dogs, the crowd roared their approval as their unsatisfied lust for a killing took over. The sergeant looked uncomfortably around the crowd. Margaret dropped the bag of hazelnuts and grabbed her father's sleeve in excitement.

The fury of the dogs was fired by their freedom. Yet they did not attack immediately. They slowly circled the bear in a low crouch, growling until they sensed their best opportunity to kill. The bear stood still. Wondering whether the bear realized the danger, the crowd tensed with the threat of death.

On a silent command given thousands of years ago from primal instinct, all four dogs attacked at once. Two of them were able to sink their teeth in the bear's hind legs. Another went directly for the bear's throat while the fourth circled behind for a delayed move to the back of the bear's neck.

The pain from his hind legs awoke the bear. With a frightening roar, he rose up on his hind legs to a towering height. A sudden powerful wave of his paw knocked away the dog leaping for his throat. The crowd cried out as the dog flew to the ground and lay still from the death blow. The other dog held off its attack when it saw the bear rise up. The two dogs with their jaws locked on the bear's hind legs shook their heads violently to tear at the flesh. Reaching down to one of the dogs on his leg, the bear clawed the hound with both paws and pulled it away, immobilizing it with deep wounds from his claws.

"It will take that dog a month of licking to heal!" the man standing next to Margaret exclaimed.

The sergeant turned to look at the man, but his eyes fell on Margaret. Unlike the others who were cheering and yelling, she made no noise. She leaned forward, her face slightly flushed with small beads of sweat on her upper lip, as she was riveted on the mayhem.

When the bear turned to the dog on his other leg, the dog who had laid back jumped for the bear's neck and locked its jaws onto the back of the bear's shoulder. The bear roared and tried to reach for its new attacker. While the bear reached back unsuccessfully, the dog on its leg let go to leap for the other side of the bear's neck.

With the jaws of both dogs locked on each side of the back of the bear's neck, the bear roared with pain as blood appeared in the fur of its shoulders. Stumbling about the ring, the bear tried repeatedly without success to reach back to dislodge the dogs. He shook his body and shoulders to throw the dogs off, but they hung on while being thrown about by the bear's jolting moves. Finally, the bear fell forward to the ground on all fours, breathing heavily while the dogs hung off his shoulders.

The people in the crowd were shouting when suddenly the bear stood up tall on its hind legs once again. The sergeant watched the tip of Margaret's tongue slip between her lips and move to moisten them before she swallowed. After a few staggering steps, the bear stumbled to a stop before the fence in front of the sergeant, DuBois, Margaret, and the horrified priest.

Stone Sexton stood there silent and still, the dogs hanging stubbornly on the bear's shoulders, until the crowd grew quiet with anticipation. It was then that the priest saw the anger come into its eyes. Its anger was not at the dogs or the pain. The priest sensed an anger burning in the bear's eyes at all the injuries and indignities it had been forced to endure to make men rich.

The bear reached up with its claws to cut away the wretched pink rosette and ribbons hanging from the side of its mouth. Once its glazed eyes saw the rosette fall on the ground, Stone Sexton slowly reached his right paw across his body over his left shoulder and his left paw over the right side of his neck. With a single powerful move, the claws of each paw were thrust into the body of a dog and pulled down along each of their bodies tearing both of them almost in half. The blood of the dogs spurted over Margaret and the man standing next to her before the animals slumped to the ground with the life seeping out of them.

Stone Sexton looked up into the sky, reeled unsteadily, and then fell forward, crashing across the fence on Margaret and the man beside her, who was completely covered by the bear's body. Margaret's arm was pinned under the bear along with the man. Before the stunned crowd could even react, the sergeant unsheathed his sword and pushed DuBois aside. He reached over and with a powerful thrust stabbed the bear. Margaret felt the hot stench of Stone Sexton's last breath on her face.

The sergeant and DuBois pulled the bear's body off the man and Margaret's arm. The man was dead, his skull and chest crushed from the weight of the bear. Father Regis kneeled down next to the man and began giving last rites.

DuBois was horrified to see the blood of both the man and the beast on his daughter's sleeve and hand. "Are you all right, Margaret? Tell me you're not hurt," DuBois pleaded with a fearful look.

Pale with shock, she nodded to him. DuBois picked her up in his arms to carry her back to their carriage.

"Make way!" ordered the sergeant to clear the crowd. When DuBois began to move through the surrounding people, Margaret looked back once more at the bear and the man. A path quickly opened up. Father Regis rose from the side of the dead man and hurried after them.

"I am taking you away from here," DuBois tried to comfort her as he carried her toward the carriage, "You are safe now, Margaret."

Both DuBois and the priest saw the blood covered fingers of her hand that bounced with each step. DuBois wanted to wipe the horrible red stain off her delicate hand right then and there, but hurried on for fear of greater injury. Reaching the carriage, DuBois laid Margaret on the seat and Father Regis gently brushed her long hair away from her face. Her face, which had been white from the shock, was now flushed.

"Are you hurt, my darling? Can you move your arms and legs?"

"I am all right Papa. I am not hurt."

With Father Regis looking over his shoulder, DuBois looked up and down her body to confirm her words.

"Thank God!" he said, taking her in his arms once again. "My poor sweet daughter."

He rocked her back and forth gently. "Are you certain you are all right?" he asked after a moment. Seeing her quiet nod, DuBois with grateful tears pulled out a handkerchief to wipe the blood off her hand. His eyebrows pressed together in puzzlement. Father Regis also looked surprised.

Her moist fingers were strangely clean of the blood.

2017 The midday sun streamed through the glass panes in the garret window of Margeaux's office study in Maryhouse Hall. She looked out at the eclectic assortment of spires and chimneys rising above the other Cambridge colleges along the River Cam as she listened to her student read the conclusion of an essay prepared for the tutorial.

"Thus, the popularity of blood sports, especially the displays of bull and bear baiting for the royal family throughout the Tudor period, along with the documented use of these blood sports to entertain visiting diplomats and even royalty from other countries, were actually a reflection, if not an intended portent, of the concerted use of violence as a fundamental instrument of governance in both domestic policy and foreign relations."

Even after the student finished reading, Margeaux continued gazing thoughtfully out of the window for a moment before turning back to her student. Margeaux did her best not to show any reaction to the young woman's unusual appearance.

Standing out below her short, spiked hair—dyed jet black—the student's ears were pierced with so many studs and earrings that there was as much metal showing as flesh. Studs stabbed the sides of both her eyelids, which were painted completely black with heavy mascara. A fake diamond pierced the side of each nostril, and a metal stud punctuated the center of her left cheek. A painful looking silver ring exited from the top of her lower lip over black lipstick and looped into the skin below.

Margeaux resisted the thought of where else on her student's body there might be similar hidden adornments. Sight, hearing, smell, taste, and touch were all symbolically under attack. That was enough to contemplate for now.

"Well, Miss Weatherby." Margeaux tried to sound positive. "How can I put this? Your extremely detailed and rather graphic descriptions of blood sports lay an extensive groundwork for your interesting thesis."

"Thank you Miss Wood," her young student responded. "But if I may be honest, I am a bit concerned about all the essays I've been assigned on the late medieval and early Tudor periods."

"How so, Miss Weatherby?"

"Well," the young student tugged at a nose ring for courage, "the historical analyses I'm given to do always seem centered on rather dark elements of the times. I mean, the essay subjects have been satanic rituals, exorcisms, and punishment of heretics. They're all such dark and gruesome subjects, Miss Wood."

Margeaux looked at her with a bit of surprise, thinking that her personal style suited that course of study quite well.

"Dark and gruesome subjects are a part of all people and a part of life, whether we approve of them or not," she answered. "And they take us to places not everyone likes to go and most people prefer not to see. These places are not lit for all to observe easily. They must be discovered by someone who can recognize them and is willing to share the darkness."

"Yes, quite," answered Miss Weatherby who didn't know what else to say. Unable to think of anything in response, she was relieved when Margeaux's phone started ringing.

"I'll see you next Tuesday. We'll discuss your next essay topic then," Margeaux concluded as she answered the call in the same breath.

"Hello."

"Margeaux, it's Don Whitby. I just got word that the first scaffold is up to the roof in the back of the church. The workman said I would be very interested in what he found. Can you come?"

"I'm leaving now," said Margeaux. "I can be there in an hour."

"Me too," he answered. "See you then."

Grabbing her purse, she bounded down the three narrow flights of worn wooden stairs out into the sunlight where she walked briskly across the lawn to the gate at the Porter's lodge.

"There's a letter for you, Miss Wood."

The head porter, still in the black coat and bowler hat he wore to make his afternoon rounds, handed her a brown envelope.

"Thank you, Gerald."

She saw the return address and hurriedly started ripping it open.

"Not good news, I'm afraid, Miss. Your research funding request has been rejected by the government."

Margeaux stopped tearing the envelope and looked at him.

"How do you know that, Gerald?"

"It's a thin envelope. I've seen quite a few of them in my time, Miss Wood. There's no additional paperwork that goes with a grant of funds."

Margeaux frowned as she took out the letter and read the confirmation of Gerald's deduction.

"Sorry, Miss Wood."

"It's quite all right, Gerald. I'm sure my research will get funded." After her lie, she hurried through the college gate to her car.

The drive to Atwelle was becoming pleasantly familiar. Once Margeaux reached the outskirts of Cambridge and started winding her way through the villages and past the farms along the two-lane road, she relaxed. Her eyes often strayed from the road to the orderly fields, which were once low fen marshes and bogs that had been drained to create the farmland. She knew the real origins of the fields were belied by the settling of the roads on the soft ground underneath, and she quite liked the gentle rocking in the quiet of her car as it rose and fell along the wavy roads toward her now-familiar destination.

As Margeaux pulled into a parking space near the church and got out of her car, the first thing she noticed was the unusual activity around the building. Trucks were lined up on the road next to the church. Workmen were busily moving the pipes and boards for the scaffolding.

Don drove up briskly in a low, sleekly shaped sports car with the top down. He waved at Margeaux as he pulled on the hand brake with a jerk.

"That's quite a car," she said, complimenting Don as he climbed out. "What model is it?"

"It's a 1956 MGA 1500," he answered proudly. "Said to be the first mass production car capable of doing one hundred miles per hour. I've been restoring her for a while."

"Really? How long?"

"Oh, let's see. About . . ." Don's right thumb drummed along his fingertips as he added up his digits. "About fifteen years."

Margeaux gave him a funny look.

"Let me introduce you to her," he said. "This is my Sally. I've worked on her quite a bit, but she's pretty much original. Never been mucked with. You know," he added, looking as if he'd just sucked on a lemon, "like adding modified parts.

"Well except for a modified oil cooler," he admitted. "She doesn't like hot weather. Cold and wet is her preference. But the heater's great—at least on your feet. The rest of your body, not so much."

"So everything is original just like it was built in 1956?"

"That's right. Except I rebuilt the engine, the transmission, the front and back suspension, the gearbox, the differential, and the electrical harnesses. And I replaced the spoked wheels and all the nuts and bolts."

"That's original?" Margeaux said with a raised eyebrow.

"You bet. Except the leather on the seats is new, of course. Nothing's too good for my Sally. Go ahead, climb in and try out the seats," he urged her.

Margeaux walked up to the door, but then gave Don a puzzled look.

"There's no handle to open it."

"Just reach on the inside of the door."

Her fingers felt a wire running along the width of the door at the top.

"There's just a wire."

"That's right. Pull down on it."

When Margeaux gave the wire a tug, the door clicked open.

"Original?" she asked.

"You bet," confirmed Don.

"How do you lock the doors?"

"You don't. I guess in 1956, one didn't worry about that."

Margeaux climbed into the low-slung car. Surprisingly, her legs were able to stretch out their entire length with room to spare. She smiled as she looked into the tiny rear-view mirror on the dash.

"I think my mobile phone screen is bigger than this."

Don shrugged.

"In this car, where you're going is more important than where you've been."

"Very philosophical," replied Margeaux. "I can't be more than a foot off the ground," she commented, looking down.

"A bit less actually. I know my car," he replied with pride.

Margeaux surveyed the gauges and knobs on the dash.

"What's this knob for?"

Don climbed into the driver's seat and gave a frustrated look at the knob to which she pointed. "Not really sure what the hell that's for," he admitted.

"But it's original," Margeaux said.

"Of course it is," he responded with conviction.

She noticed that as he sat there, his head stuck up over the top of the low windscreen.

"I'm only the third owner," he told her. "The first was a colonel in the army. Awarded some medal for something or other. The second was a librarian who was rumored to be part owner of a brothel. Then I learned the colonel was the other owner and they were lovers.

"But come look at the engine," he invited Margeaux as if that was far more interesting than the story of the owners. They walked around the front of the car, which seemed to extend forward forever. Margeaux looked at a narrow strip of chromed metal that wrapped around Sally below her headlights.

"Is that really the bumper?" Margeaux asked.

"It is."

"What could that stop?"

"Doesn't it look good on her though?" was all Don replied as he opened the bonnet to show Margeaux the engine.

Margeaux had to admit the engine was an impressive sight. Its shiny metal looked clean enough for a tea setting.

"With all that engine, where did my legs fit?"

"I don't know where mine go either," Don answered. "And they're even longer."

Don stood there some time, admiring the engine.

"What's in the boot?" asked Margeaux as she wandered to the back of the car.

"I'll show you," he answered, moving to join her.

When he flipped open the boot, another shiny chrome spiked wheel filled the place for a spare tire. Two neatly folded blankets filled the remaining space next to it.

"Where do you put the luggage?" she asked.

"Luggage?" he asked in return as if her question was a bit silly.

He stood there another minute admiring his car.

"That's my Sally," he said finally with a fond look.

"I'm not at all versed in these matters, but may I suggest one small addition?" Margeaux asked.

What's that?"

"Paint."

Don nodded his head thoughtfully, giving her suggestion serious consideration before turning to her.

"By the way, are you French? I noticed a bit of an accent."

"Yes, on my mother's side. I lived and studied in France most of my life. But my Father is English."

"I *parlez* a little French myself," said Don. "Just enough to get in and out of trouble when I spent a couple of summers in France in my teens."

Their conversation was interrupted by a workman who came out of the church and approached them.

"Don, you've arrived," he greeted the architect with a handshake. "Good to see you. How's Sally?"

"Doing fine, Nigel. Just fine.

"Margeaux, meet Nigel Green—a fine contractor and a fine man with a fine new baby boy." Don slapped the man on the back in congratulations.

"Nice to meet you, Mr. Green."

"And you, ma'am," he responded with a respectful nod and the proud smile of a new father. He turned back to Don.

"The scaffolding is old, but solid as a rock. You should have no problem. But do take care going up and down."

"Thanks, Nigel," said Don. "You're a sport."

"And you should find it very interesting at the top," the workman added with a wave as he walked briskly to his truck like a man in a hurry to return to the new responsibilities in his life.

Their eyes had to adjust as Margeaux and Don entered the dim interior of the church from the bright sunlight. Walking over to the back left corner of the nave, both of them strained to see the dark ceiling above the scaffolding.

"Let's go," said Don with pretended eagerness as he grabbed the metal ladder built into the levels of scaffolding pipe. A voice behind them stopped Don.

"Here! What's this all about?"

"Ah, Squeaky," Don stepped off the ladder and addressed him. "We're about to go up and have a look at the ceiling. Would you like to join us? You might discover something special up there."

Squeaky's hand came out of his tattered sleeve and scratched the whiskers on his chin as he looked warily up at the scaffolding. The excitement in Don's voice did not persuade him.

"I think not, Mr. Whitby. I'll leave it to you." As he turned to leave, Squeaky slipped a look at Don that confirmed he thought the architect was completely crazy.

This time Don stepped back and offered Margeaux the chance to go up first.

"After you," he insisted, using politeness to cover up his queasiness at the prospect of climbing the ladder.

With a nod of thanks, Margeaux grabbed the sides of the ladder and took steady rhythmic steps as best she could. Her skirt and shoes were not made for climbing. A moment later, Don followed slowly with his stare focused straight ahead, afraid to look up or down.

When he caught up with Margeaux at the top, he was surprised how dark it was despite the daylight coming through the windows and illuminating the floor far below. Margeaux grimaced at the dust, spider webs, and acrid odor of creosote as Don fiddled with a flashlight he had fished out of his coat pocket. He finally turned a beam of light on the wood above.

The two of them did not move for what seemed a long minute.

"Remarkable!" whispered Margeaux, her gaze transfixed.

"I've never seen such a thing," Don added, reaching up to touch it.

SIX

1532 The sergeant reined in his horse to a stop before the gate of the Lanham manor house. As his passenger slid from the seat behind him on the horse down to the ground, the sergeant noticed that the young man in the monk's cowl had already cut his hair into the traditional tonsure of a monk with the top of his scalp shaved in a bald circle.

"You know, I just dropped off Father Regis here recently. Seems like my civic duties now include the transport of clergy."

"I am not yet a monk, sergeant," the young man responded.

"Close enough, Christopher," the sergeant said as he smiled down at him. "When do you take your vows?"

"That has not been decided," the young man answered with an unhappy look. "But in the meantime, I offer you God's blessings along with my thanks."

"It will happen soon enough, I suppose," replied the sergeant. "Give my greetings to your father now."

With a wave and a gentle kick to his horse, he tugged on the reins to turn his horse back toward the town. Christopher Lanham hurried through the gate and into the manor house, where he headed directly to the dining hall. He was hungry. It seemed to him that he was always hungry these days from living in the monastery.

Richard Lanham rose from the table with his arms open.

"Christopher, my son! Welcome home. Come and eat. You must be famished from your journey."

As they embraced, Lanham looked with displeasure over his son's shoulder at the rough material of the cowl and the cut of the young man's hair. Lanham regained his smile as he stepped back and gave his son a friendly slap on the back before steering him to a seat at the table. Calling out for the servants to bring another plate and a mug of ale, Lanham resumed his seat at the head of the table.

"Tell me, son," he asked as he grabbed a chicken leg, "how are you faring with things?"

Christopher noted that his father did not specify what things or where. He responded in kind.

"They are well, father."

A servant placed a plate and mug of ale before the young man with an affectionate look.

"Good to see you, Geoffrey," said Christopher to the servant. "How are you and your good wife?"

"We are well, we are, Master Christopher. Thank you for asking," replied the servant, grinning with gratitude at the young man's question. "Is there anything else I can bring you, Master Christopher?"

"No thank you, Geoffrey. As always, you are very kind to me. Please give my blessings to your wife and tell her I look forward to seeing her."

"I will, sir. I will. Do come to visit us," the servant said with an appreciative nod and a slight bow as he backed out of the dining hall.

"A good man," said Lanham after the servant left the hall. "How long have he and his wife been here at the manor, I wonder?"

"My whole life, father," Christopher answered after his hands unfolded from a prayer of thanks before the meal. "At least nineteen years."

"Yes, indeed, your whole life." Lanham reflected on the statement. "What about your life now, Christopher? Do you still intend to take your vows and live in the monastery?"

His son stiffened, and the hand that was raising bread to his mouth stopped. "Father, I have completed my time as a novice. I have studied at one of the finest teaching monasteries on the continent. I am ready and the abbot is considering me for the service of the Lord. I plan to take my vows of obedience, poverty, and chastity for a simple life of service to my brothers and Christ as soon as I am deemed worthy."

Lanham frowned.

"Son, far be it from me to thwart God's plan or obstruct your desires. But can you forgive me if I express some fatherly concern about your choice?"

"Father, we have discussed this before. I have made my decision."

"Well if you are certain, what harm is there if I ask some practical questions?"

Christopher looked down and took a deep breath as if he were inhaling the patience he would need for the coming discussion. He pushed his plate away.

"Go ahead, father. Ask your questions of me."

"Do not take this wrongly, my son, but when it comes to a vow of obedience, I have to point out that since your mother died, you have done only what you wanted and no less. And no amount of caution or discipline has come close to dissuading you from doing your will and your will only."

"Father, my vow and my obedience will be to God. That will need no caution or discipline."

"Your obedience, Christopher, will be to your superiors in the friary. What makes you think you can subvert your strong opinions to follow their will? You have not tolerated that kind of authority in others.

"Even your own father," he added with a stern look.

"And the vow of poverty," Lanham continued. "You have had the best of everything since you were born. Again, what makes you think that by simply saying a few words in your vows that you will be happy living without all the creature comforts you have taken for granted your entire life?"

"As a novice, I have lived the life of a monk for over two years," Christopher retorted. Lanham pursed his lips.

"And most of that time was spent in a teaching monastery in Bavaria where the wine cellars and kitchens were better than King

Henry's. If that's what a vow of poverty entails, every peasant in the parish will be more than happy to take their vows as soon as they can sign up to join the monks.

"I am afraid, Christopher, that you have not the faintest idea of what poverty is and will be in the life you are vowing to live. And I daresay, without any doubt, you will not like it once you experience it."

Christopher took another deep breath and held his tongue.

"As for the vow of chastity, you are nineteen years old. How does that vow feel so far? Is it working well for you?"

Lanham paused for a moment to give Christopher a chance to think about the inevitable struggles of a healthy young man facing a chaste life.

"If that vow has been difficult for you the last three years, consider trying to keep to it for the rest of your life. Living in isolation with a handful of frustrated boys and shriveled old men will bring no great delight or comfort. But that, my son, will be your life."

Lanham waited for the young man to reply. After a long silence, Lanham carried on speaking.

"Now consider this, Christopher. A decision not to take these vows does not mean that you are embracing a life of sin or abandonment of God's will. What you would be doing is taking on the life and responsibilities that God intended for you. I know that because He would not have given you your life as a Lanham in this manor house if that were not so.

"You can live a life of obedience and simplicity in your devotion to God and His creatures while you carry on the family name and manage the holdings of the Lanham manor. It is the most honorable thing a man can do for his father. Without it, our name, our estates, and our family legacy will end. The benefits of living in isolation and reciting prayers all day cannot outweigh the good of preserving and fostering the gifts God has given you already."

Lanham paused a moment, but received no reaction from his son.

"Christopher, let me speak practically about a consideration that your life as a novice has not allowed you to appreciate. Your joining the order and living in the monastery is not necessarily a life of sanctuary. In fact, you may be walking into the middle of a great conflict that could put your life in peril.

"You may not know the extent to which King Henry is in a direct and serious conflict with the Holy See. The pope is refusing to annul the king's marriage to Catherine. And if the king is forbidden by the pope to remarry and take a wife who will bear him a male heir to the throne, His Majesty will effectively be at war with the Holy See.

"His Majesty does not treat with mercy those whom he thinks are his enemies. If Cardinal Woolsey can lose everything when the king questions his loyalty, the Church and all its servants could well lose everything as well."

Christopher looked skeptical.

"Do not think I am exaggerating on this point," Lanham emphasized. "If the pope levies taxes on the king's subjects while he denies the king the ability to preserve the realm under his son, there will be a war on the Church. And the life of your monastery and your own safety could be among the casualties.

"Imagine a legion of monks and nuns who have been chased from their abbeys and convents wandering hither and thither in misery seeking means to live. If you think such a thing cannot happen, you do not understand the depths of the king's antipathy to those who impede his will, including the Church."

Lanham looked at his son earnestly. "Christopher, here is the point about your decision that you should consider most seriously."

The son finally looked at his father to hear his last words on the subject.

"The only thing worse than making a vow you should not have made, is breaking it. If you do that, your respect for yourself is lost for the rest of your life."

Christopher looked back down at the food on the table. He no longer had any desire to eat.

"Thank you, father," was all the young man said before he stood and left the hall.

Lanham sat in deep thought, his cheek resting against his fist. He had no idea what his son was thinking. After a few minutes, he rose from the table, threw his cloak over his shoulders, and left the manor house. Once outside in the cool evening air, he walked resolutely toward the town.

With his long strides, it did not take long for Lanham to reach his destination. He stopped at an alley, where he looked about cautiously. Seeing no one, he stepped into the narrow lane, walked down a slight hill, and came to a low door in an ill-kept two-story house. As he raised his hand to knock, he heard voices inside approaching the door. Lanham quickly stepped into the darkness between two buildings next to the house.

The door opened to reveal the silhouette of a man against the candlelight in the room. Lanham watched the man reach out to put something in the hand of a woman and then kiss her before turning with a laugh to leave. The man walked right past Lanham, who pressed against a wall to remain hidden.

There was no mistaking him. It was Francis DuBois.

When Lanham was certain DuBois was out of sight, he walked back to the door and knocked. After a moment, the woman opened the door and eyed Lanham up and down.

"May I come in?" Lanham asked.

She took his arm and with a big smile pulled him in through the door.

"Of course, kind sir. You are very welcome here."

At opposite ends of the alley, two people watched Lanham enter the house. Peter sat on a stone stoop in the darkness of a doorway where he observed with mild interest all the comings and goings at the woman's house. Unseen at the other end of the passage, the sergeant followed Lanham's movements closely. After the door closed behind Lanham, the sergeant's hand tightened around the handle of his sword.

"Thank you for seeing me," Lanham said to the young woman as she took his cloak.

"Like I said, sir, you are very welcome. My name is Molly, but I'm sure you know that." She patted the ribbons in her blonde hair to make sure they were in place.

"I know your name," Lanham replied.

"I must say, sir, I never expected to see you here. But I am pleased to welcome you."

She sidled seductively up next to Lanham and pressed her breast against his arm.

"And is there something I can do to make sure that you are pleased to be here?"

Lanham's face took on a slight blush before it became serious once again.

"I am not here for myself," he said. "I am here about my son. I believe you know him well."

2017 "Ouch!" exclaimed Don as he quickly drew his hand back. He gave it a great shake to try to get rid of the pain. A throb immediately started around the sliver of wood under his fingernail.

Margeaux paid him no notice as she stepped behind him on the scaffolding to look up at the roof beam from a different angle.

"Here, let me have the flashlight," she suggested, taking it from Don to point the light upward from her new vantage point. Don, sucking on his injured finger, leaned over next to her to look where the light now fell. Another minute passed without words. Their fascination continued as their raised eyes kept moving over the mysterious being in front of them.

Eventually Don mumbled something unintelligible because of the finger in his mouth.

"What?" Margeaux looked over at him. When he didn't move, she pulled his hand away from his face. He hardly noticed, his gaze fixed on the roof beam.

"Well it certainly is not a roof angel," he repeated.

"Definitely not," she replied. Their eyes did not leave the object until they sensed at the same uncomfortable moment that the thing they were staring at was now staring back at them.

"He's an ugly brute," declared Don finally as the pain pounding in his finger continued to build.

Carved out of the beam arching up and over them was a grinning, beak nosed, devil-like figure about a meter in height. Its wide, penetrating eyes peered at Margeaux and Don out of the shadows of their sunken sockets. Below its intense staring eyes, a pointed triangular nose was carved into the top of an oversized protruding upper lip whose edges curled up into an evil smile. The smile revealed short crooked teeth crowded between two longer jagged fangs. Sticking out from the sides of its head were cauliflower ears whose ends abruptly curved upward to sharp points. Beneath the ears, two folded bat-like wings resembled a cape with a tall collar sitting on its shoulders.

"At least he's smiling," remarked Margeaux.

"Of course he is. He's got a lovely young lady to look at in front of him," Don replied.

The claw-like hands of the carving were resting on the shoulders of a smaller female wooden figure that stood before it on a semicircular platform affixed to the base of the beam. Carefully carved curls of hair surrounded her face and cascaded over the folds of her gown.

"Why would a gargoyle be here, inside the church?" Margeaux puzzled.

"Technically speaking, it's not a gargoyle," Don answered with the tone of an academic lecture. "In architecture, for centuries a gargoyle was a carved stone figure, usually a grotesque or frightening animal or demon-like form, which actually camouflaged a spout designed to convey rainwater from a roof and away from the side of a building to prevent erosion of the mortar between the stone blocks of the masonry walls.

"Again speaking technically, a sculptured figure of this nature is referred to as a 'grotesque' because it only has an artistic or ornamental function without being a waterspout. But now in layman's terminology, all such figures are often called gargoyles, whether ornamentation or waterspouts."

"But what is it doing *inside* the church?" Margeaux asked again.

"Good question. It doesn't make any sense that it's been placed here on the ceiling beams. Gargoyles were used to convey strong messages to worshipers who were for the most part illiterate. The first message was to scare people into coming to church by suggesting that a greeting from a nasty beast like this one was what awaited them if they didn't go to church. But the people who could see this fellow here were already inside this church.

"More importantly, gargoyles were placed outside the church to frighten away the devil and evil spirits. Their presence on the exterior assured everyone that evil was kept outside of the church's walls. If any carvings were inside a church, they were of Jesus, Mary, or the saints.

This one, however, puts the evil inside and directly above the worshipers' heads.

"It doesn't make sense," he mused as the two of them continued to examine the wooden carvings.

"Well," Margeaux offered after a few moments' thought, "cathedrals and churches of this era were called 'sermons in stone.' They spoke to the presence of evil, and represented how God was the only protection from a fallen world. Maybe that's why this carving ended up inside the church."

"But what about the fact that this figure is clearly some sort of demon, and yet it's next to a perfectly lovely human?" Don asked. "It's not just a devil or an animal alone."

"There seems to be a dual nature to the function of gargoyles," she suggested. "They look evil, but yet they keep out evil spirits or incite worshipers to do good. You could say they represent the struggle between good and evil. Maybe the human and demonic figures suggest a contradiction in the essential being of a gargoyle."

"Now you're sounding like an academic," accused Don in a friendly voice. "You've also forgotten another important possibility."

Margeaux turned away from the carving for a minute to look at him.

"Maybe the architect or the sculptor just thought this would be really cool," he grinned.

She responded with a dismissive look.

"I'm serious," he protested. "Don't underestimate the artist's joy of creation. They don't just think about what the church's message is. They make their own personal statements as well, consciously or unconsciously."

Margeaux begrudgingly acknowledged his thought with a nod before she noticed Don looking at the roof over the rest of the church.

"Do you see something else?" she asked. She strained in dim light to find what Don might be seeking.

"Well if we have this bad boy and young lady here, I'm wondering if there are more carvings on the other beams down the length of the church. There traditionally are twelve figures placed in the interior of church architecture, twelve being the number of disciples."

Don ended up focusing on the opposite corner at the back of the nave.

"We should have some idea soon. The scaffolding in the other corner over there starts going up tomorrow."

Don looked around once more. "What time is it anyway?"

It had grown dark while the two of them had been puzzling over their discovery.

"Let's go, Margeaux. Be careful now."

He held the flashlight on the ladder as he helped Margeaux start her long descent down. He hesitated before following her down.

"Don't like heights?" she asked.

"Not my favorite," he confirmed.

Margeaux finally reached the bottom and felt her foot on the solid stone floor. As she turned away from the ladder, a figure stepped up behind her.

"Don!" Margeaux reached up to grab Don's arm.

She recognized the man's face in the dim light, staring at her once again.

SEVEN

1532 Kneeling on the floor of her bedroom, Molly enjoyed one more time the satisfying weight of the leather purse filled with coins resting in the palm of her hand. She considered the task for which she had been paid handsomely in advance as she pulled back the floorboard to hide the purse. It was a simple task for such a great deal of money. Still, she questioned whether she wanted to do it.

She slid the floorboard back into place and covered it with the turned-back rug when she heard the knock on the door downstairs. It was expected. That would be her commission from Richard Lanham.

Molly smoothed the front of her dress and ran her hand over her hair in an attempt to feel that all was in perfect order. She quickly walked down the stairs to the door where she paused, took a deep breath, put on a pleased smile, and pulled it open.

There stood Christopher Lanham.

"Good day to you, Molly."

"Good day to you, Christopher," she greeted him. "Do come in."

She eyed his monk's cowl and tonsure haircut as he stepped by her while she closed the door.

"You have changed since the last time you were here, Christopher."

"You could say that." He looked around at the familiar setting. "It was kind of you to invite me," he said.

"It was kind of you to come."

"I have to say, Molly, that I am not entirely sure why you would have me here."

"I have to say, Christopher, that under the circumstances, I am not sure why you would come."

They stood there awkwardly for a moment.

"Where are my manners?" she finally exclaimed, taking his arm and leading him to a large high-backed chair with thick cushions. Then she pulled another chair around where she sat, facing him within touching distance. Christopher could smell her perfume. He inhaled deeply. The fragrance brought him a vivid memory.

"How long has it been?" she asked. "A year?"

"Two," he replied.

"And how did you ever—" she stopped with embarrassment at her clumsy question.

"How did I ever become a novitiate about to become a monk?" he finished her question.

She blushed.

"It's all right. I do not mind your asking, and I do not mind telling you."

She smiled as she thought how much he had matured since the times when he would come to her as a very young man to satisfy his energetic appetites.

"I can explain it entirely. My life with my father at Lanham Hall was not fulfilling. And the manner in which I spent my time was—" he gave her with a slightly embarrassed look. "Well let's just say some of it was ill spent."

He noticed a slight look of sadness pass over her face.

"Do not misunderstand me, Molly. I was not talking about you," he tried to apologize.

"Oh, yes you were." She smiled to ease his discomfort. "A young man's pursuing your, shall we say, unusual preferences, would be described by most people as ill-spent time."

Now it was his turn to blush. He looked down at the floor to hide it. When he raised his head, they smiled at each other.

"But it was great fun," he said with a laugh.

She laughed in return. "It was . . . different from most," she conceded.

"Well, even at my young age I had a sense that life should not go on like that. Then one evening when my horse came up lame near the friary in Walsingham, I went in and ended up spending the night. I spoke with several of the brothers the night through. By the time it was dawn, they had revealed to me an entirely different way of looking at life and my future."

He looked directly at her.

"It was then that I sensed that my calling might be to the service of God and the brotherhood of that order. I began my studies under the brothers at the monastery, then went to study among the monks in Bavaria. It was there that I learned how monks deal with what you called 'preferences' that are even more unusual than what you experienced with me."

Molly thought of the purse full of coins under the floorboard upstairs and felt uneasy. Christopher stood up and walked behind her chair. He leaned over and once again inhaled her perfume.

"There are still times, Molly, when I am unsure about this calling."

He placed his hands on her shoulders.

"It is a difficult life, and the requirements are sometimes hard to bear."

One of his hands moved around her neck and tightened. The other grabbed her hair. Suddenly he pulled her roughly to her feet.

"There are times when I don't think I can honor all the vows."

He put a hand over her mouth and with his other arm pulled her backside hard against his body.

"And there are times when I think I do not want to."

She felt his pelvis grinding against her and his teeth on her neck. With a duck and a twist, she freed herself from his grasp and stepped out of his reach. Facing him, she recognized the same look of strange lust in his face that she had seen before. He took a step toward her.

"Christopher!" Her voice stopped him cold. "You must take your vows."

He stood there tense with indecision about what to do. She could see the sweat on his brow.

"You want to do and you can do what you have to," she said in a firm voice. "You are strong enough for that life."

His look quickly turned to embarrassment.

"You have never refused me before," he said.

"I have never had a reason to before now," she answered.

"And if I gave you a reason not to refuse me?"

He drew a purse of coins out of his sleeve.

"Your father already has, and it did no good."

A dark look crossed Christopher's face. His hands clenched into fists. He gave her a long hard look before he spun around and lurched the door open to flee into the night. After a moment, Molly softly closed the door behind him and with a deep sigh, laid her cheek on its hard wood.

In the dark alley outside, the sergeant watched intently as Christopher hurried away. A moment later he followed the young man up the lane until he stopped suddenly and looked down to his left. Peter was sitting on a stoop in the shadow of a doorway.

The sergeant's hand crossed to the handle of his sword and started to slide the sword out of its scabbard. The large man watched Peter pull back in fear before throwing his arms pitifully over his head.

The sergeant stopped, slowly slid the sword back into the scabbard as Peter cowered below him, and started striding after the young Lanham.

2017 "Margeaux, I'd like you to meet Father Adams. The vicar saved me from certain death right here on an old ladder I was about to climb."

Don turned from the scaffolding and shook hands with the vicar. The cleric's grip was as strong as when it had prevented him from climbing the ladder two days earlier. Don grimaced slightly at the pressure on the sliver under his fingernail.

"Father, this is Margeaux Wood, the historian from Cambridge who is doing research on the church."

"Miss Wood." Father Adams held out a pale hand to shake hers. The strong bass of his voice surprised her for some reason. One would expect such a voice to come out of a much larger man.

The first thing she observed about him was his unusual cleric's collar. There was no traditional small white square or white band contrasting with his black clergy vest and suit coat. The band circling his neck was solid black, like his shirt and suit. His thick eyebrows were just as black, and seemed even darker beneath his closely cropped white hair.

Don could not contain his excitement. "Father Adams, we found the most remarkable thing on the church ceiling at the top of the scaffolding. There is a wooden gargoyle carved into the beam just above the wall stone."

"A gargoyle—inside the church?" The cleric squinted upward, trying unsuccessfully to see something in the dark ceiling.

"Yes," answered Don. "It's half demon and half human. And sitting in front of it is a smaller figure of a girl or woman. His claws are resting on her shoulders like she was his friend or daughter. It's quite extraordinary."

The vicar turned to Margeaux. "Have you ever seen anything like this before, Miss Wood?"

She felt slightly uncomfortable as the dark eyes under his bushy black eyebrows gave her a penetrating look. It was the same look she had seen when he had watched her earlier from the shadows of the church.

"No Father, I have not. But gargoyles in architecture are not something I've really focused on in my research."

He seemed content with her answer and looked up at the ceiling once again.

"Are there any church histories or other documents that might shed some light on how a gargoyle like this came to be here?" Don asked him.

The older man paused.

"I seem to remember a reference in some historical church documents to wooden carvings." He looked at Don and Margeaux apologetically. "But I've been away for many years, and my memory isn't what it used to be."

"The Caribbean, I understand?" Don asked with his usual pleasant conversational smile.

"Yes," was the vicar's curt reply.

"I believe someone told me you were in Haiti," said Margeaux.

"That's right," he answered before changing the subject. "Well, there's not much to be done about our gargoyle and his companion tonight, is there? We can't even see them in daylight."

Don pointed at the partially constructed scaffolding in the corner across the back of the church. "But I suspect we may find there are more like him on the other beams. And history teaches us that in your business, Vicar, good things come in twelves."

He gave the man an even bigger smile to reinforce his friendly attempt at humor.

"Except the commandments, of course. Fortunately there's only ten of them," Don added and smiled again in a losing cause.

"Yes, of course," answered Father Adams who showed no signs of being amused. "Let me know what you find, will you?

"Well, I must be going. A pleasure, Miss Wood, Mr. Whitby."

With a nod, he turned on his heel and started walking away into the darkened church. Don and Margeaux watched him disappear under the low doorway into the stone spiral stairway leading up to his study.

"Charming chap," noted Margeaux in a sarcastic tone after she heard the creaky wooden door close at the top of the stairway.

"Oh, he's not so bad once you get to know him," Don replied.

"Have you gotten to know him?"

"Not really." Don tried to avoid her mildly castigating look and changed the subject.

"So the platform in the other corner should be finished tomorrow." He put the enthusiasm back in his voice. "And the workmen should be done by early afternoon. Can you come back tomorrow and have another look?"

"But of course, *mon ami*," answered Margeaux. "But I really must be going now."

"Great! We should be able to see better in the daylight."

She had just decided she really liked his smile when she saw the eagerness in Don's face start to fade.

"Listen, I've got to fetch some things I left in the crypt. Can you make your way to your car all right?"

Margeaux could not help but see the slight shudder as he checked his flashlight.

"Yes, I'm fine. Do you really have to go down into the crypt? I know you said you don't like being in churches at night?"

He put the grin back on his face.

"Afraid I must, though afraid I am. Good night then. See you tomorrow."

As Don turned to head to the altar, he waved cheerily at the ceiling. "And a good night to you two up there."

Margeaux chuckled at him as she pulled on the heavy church door to close it. This time it did not seem so ominous, even in the dark, until once again, with her hand still on the cold iron of its latch, she was startled by a voice.

"Good evening, Miss Wood."

A man in a dark raincoat stood between her and her car. He dropped his cigarette to the ground and crushed it under his shoe.

"I'm Detective Richard Steele from the Norfolk Constabulary Investigations Division."

"Yes?" she asked, wondering what he wanted with her and why he would be there at night.

"We're investigating the disappearance of Father Charleton, the previous vicar here at St. Clement's."

"I'm sorry, Detective," she replied, "but I really did not know Father Charleton well. I only started my research project here at the church just before his disappearance."

"I understand, Miss Wood. But I'd like to ask you a few questions about Donald Whitby."

EIGHT

1532 Father Regis closed his eyes, and for a pleasant moment felt the autumn sun on his face as he waited by the market stall for the baker's wife. The warmth of the sun would soon be gone in the late afternoon, he thought. He could hear people around him hurrying to finish their purchases so they could get home and cook supper while there was still light.

"Father?"

He opened his eyes. The baker's plump wife was holding out a large loaf of bread that she had saved for him.

"Bless you, Lizzie," he thanked her as he tucked the loaf next to the vegetables in his cloth sack. He handed her a coin.

"That is yours, my dear."

"Why thank you very much, Father," she answered, pretending once again that the coin was enough to cover the cost of the bread.

"You're welcome," he replied. "Use it in good health for the Lord's work."

As Father Regis turned to head back towards the church, he heard a familiar grunting yell and turned around. There was Peter pushing people aside, and ignoring their irritation as he ran to catch up with the priest.

"Hello, Peter," Father Regis greeted him with a welcoming smile as he arrived out of breath.

Peter said nothing as he took the sack from the priest, put it over his own shoulder, and fell in behind Father Regis as proudly as a squire behind his knight. He followed the priest dutifully through the town towards the church. But as soon as he sensed the priest's attention was elsewhere, he peeked into the sack to see what he might be eating that evening.

"No meat," he thought with a frown.

When they reached the heavy wooden side door to the church under the shadow of the priest's room that extended above them like an enclosed porch over the entrance, Peter stepped in front of the priest and pulled it open.

"Thank you, Peter," Father Regis nodded politely.

Although they walked through the door into the church and were surrounded by tall, unfinished, windowless walls, they were essentially still out of doors. Father Regis paused and looked up at the sky in the late dusk light before stepping over to the small doorway of the narrow spiral stone staircase that climbed up to his cell. He ducked his head as he took a step up, with Peter following close behind. At the landing at the top of the curving stairs, he suddenly stopped.

A tall figure hooded in black stood there waiting for Father Regis, his hands folded calmly in front of him.

"Father Cuthbert, welcome." Father Regis tried to sound pleased to see him.

"Father Regis." The flat voice came from inside the hood of the black cowl. A bony hand came up to pull the hood back. Father Regis saw the familiar long crooked nose on the long thin face that never smiled. Wispy strands of hair floated around the crown of his bald head.

"Are you here with a message from the Bishop of Norwich?"

Father Cuthbert gave a questioning look over Father Regis's shoulder at Peter peeking at him from behind.

"Tis all right," Father Regis assured him. "This is Peter. He is a . . . simple person," Father Regis said. "He will not understand that of which we will speak. Come in."

Father Regis led the tall monk into the small room with a gesture. Peter squeezed in behind them.

"Have you eaten?"

"I am fine," answered Father Cuthbert. "To answer your question, I have come from the Bishop. That is what I do. God speaks to all of us in different ways. He speaks to me through the Bishop of Norwich."

"And what the Bishop of Norwich knows from God is only what you care to tell him," thought Father Regis as he took from Peter the cloth sack containing his purchases from the market.

With a gesture at one of the two stools, Father Regis invited Father Cuthbert to sit. But he remained standing after Father Regis seated himself. The sight of his black cowl made Father Regis uncomfortable. He was the only monk in the diocese of Norwich to wear the distinctive garb. While Father Cuthbert wore the black cowl on the authority of the bishop, Father Regis was thinking there was no doubt that the idea came from Father Cuthbert to give him the appearance of greater authority.

"To what do I owe the pleasure of your visit, Father?"

"My presence is not driven by any pleasure, Father Regis. I am here because matters are becoming serious between the Church in Rome and the king.

"Do you recall when the king levied a 10 percent tax on the income of every priest who received over eight pounds annually?"

Father Regis nodded with a frown.

"And then the king 'requested'—I use that term loosely—that the clergy lend him a quarter of their income and value of their goods."

Father Regis sat in silent acknowledgement.

"And do you remember two years later when the king tried to increase the tax on the income of priests to a third, but then abandoned the tax in the face of the church's opposition?"

Father Regis nodded again. Peter sat in the corner, ignoring them while scratching at his arm.

"Now there is talk that the king is going to ask Parliament to restrict how much land the church can receive under wills and bequests because the church has sworn a 'foreign' allegiance to the pope. There is even rumor of the king's seizing the property of any monasteries he believes owes allegiance outside the realm."

Father Cuthbert lowered his voice.

"The king is clearly constructing a campaign of fiscal intimidation to pressure the church to support annulment of his marriage to Catherine. It may go so far as to declare that anyone who claims that the pope has jurisdiction over matters of taxation or appointments to church leadership may be charged with treason. The monarch is beginning to act as though he is a servant of God ruling not just with divine approval, but at divine command."

Father Regis shifted uneasily on his stool.

"But we are not without the power to respond," Father Cuthbert went on. "We will arrange for a Bill of Liberties to be introduced into the Parliament that preserves the prerogatives of the church. And while the pope has always approved the king's recommendations for appointment of bishops and archbishops within the realm, the pope may choose not to move on those recommendations.

"Our lawyers have crafted means of getting around the restrictions on wills and bequests of land and wealth to the church by creating legal trusts in which the land and money are held by an overseer who ensures that the wealth is used for the benefit of the church. There may even be a Papal Bull forbidding clergy to give money to the king without papal approval and that only the pope can agree to financial demands on the church. The church would be claiming that it is exempt from taxes levied by the king.

"And further, for every penny that the king taxes the church and its clergy, there will be a levy of Peter's pence collected under papal authority from every person in the parish to offset the levies exacted by the king against us. That tax imposed by the pope and collected in the churches," Father Cuthbert concluded with a firm voice, "will mean there is a war of fiscal battles between the church and the king.

"And with the unspoken declaration of war, the first thing that will be eliminated by the royal defender of the faith will be the immunity of priests and monks against charges of certain crimes—the 'benefit of clergy' defense. Our clergy will have no defense against a charge of treason brought against them by reason of their allegiance to the church and the pope."

Father Regis felt sick to his stomach. Father Cuthbert seemed to tower over him, turning his world as black as the monk's cowl.

"So I am here, my brother, to remind you, as I am reminding all our brothers, that we repute and take our obedience of laws grounded only upon the scripture of God and the determination of the Holy Church. Though humble subjects of the king, we do not submit to the execution of charges and duty against us that are not prescribed by God, regardless of the crown's dissent."

Father Regis stood up. "I understand, Father Cuthbert."

A long dark sleeve extended out from the black cowl as Father Cuthbert placed his hand on Father Regis's shoulder. "I was certain you would. As you know, the bishop has seen fit to remove seven from the priesthood already this year. They will be excommunicated from the church and deprived of God's mercy." Father Cuthbert gave him a hard look. "I know you are not of that character."

He pulled the black hood back over his head and moved to the door. "And how are the funds and construction going for the new church building?"

"They are progressing," Father Regis answered in a weak voice. He hoped Father Cuthbert would not notice how pale he had become.

"Good. The bishop eagerly looks forward to the church's completion."

"May God be with you," was all Father Cuthbert said as he departed and began descending the spiral stairs.

Father Regis stood there staring at the floor while Peter watched closely to see if it finally might be time to eat. The priest looked up as two figures appeared at the open doorway to his room.

"Father Regis. A word with you, if I may."

The man who spoke looked familiar, but the distracted priest could not place him or recall his name. From the man's worn clothes, Father Regis knew he was a working tradesman. His shoulders were stooped as if he were still at work carrying some sort of heavy load. The priest also noticed the man's rough hands, which were clasped low in front of him as if he were a weary supplicant too tired to raise them in prayer. A woman stood beside him, carrying a small baby in her arms. Father Regis could sense her anxiety as she rocked the infant as though she feared it would start crying at any moment.

Peter gave them a disapproving look. They stood between him and his supper.

"Of course, my son," answered the priest. "What is it you wish to tell me?"

"Father, my name is Bittergreen, Robert Bittergreen. I am a wood-carver working on the church."

"Very good, Robert. Your work is important to the Lord and the worshipers of Atwelle. Your skills will stand in this church and be admired for hundreds of years."

"If my work is important, Father, why am I not being paid for it?"

The priest watched an anguished look cross the man's face.

"Father, I have a wife and a newborn son who need to eat. The church may be here for a thousand years, but I must feed my family tomorrow."

Father Regis said nothing.

"I do good work, Father. And I am told daily that I will be paid, but nothing is given to me. I show up faithfully to carve the wood we have, even while the others who are not paid are going back to their villages."

The baby started to whimper. Father Regis looked down at the floor.

"Father?" The man waited for an answer.

"What am I to do?" he asked as the baby started crying.

Father Regis turned and grabbed the loaf of bread out of the sack on the floor.

"Here. Take this for now. You will be paid," the priest tried to assure him.

The wood-carver gave Father Regis an unhappy look and took the bread. Then he grabbed his wife's arm and steered her and the crying baby to the stairs.

"Come to work on the church, Robert. The wood needs to be carved," the priest called to him as he disappeared down the spiral of stairs. "You will be paid soon!"

The words echoed around the walls of the church. Peter looked unhappy at the loss of the bread as Father Regis handed him a broom to sweep.

"You have seen my problem, Peter. If I don't acquire funds for the construction of the roof and windows soon, the building of the church is in serious jeopardy."

"Church!" repeated Peter in the same somber tone. As he swept the floor, he watched the priest put a few vegetables into a small cauldron full of water and start the fire underneath it.

Striking the flint over the tinder, Father Regis shook his head in discouragement.

"Neither Lanham nor DuBois will see their way clear to contributing to the church's construction until there is no risk to them from the dispute between His Holiness and His Majesty."

He blew softly on the glowing tinder until smoke began to rise.

"And even then, neither of them may be in a position to give money to St. Clement's until their battle for control of the inland port is resolved and one of them has secured great riches from his struggle."

Peter decided not to say anything because of the words he did not understand.

"Sadly, Peter, with the bill in Parliament and the competing taxes, the conflict between the Pope and the Crown has become worse. The realm will be filled with even greater controversy."

Peter swept the floor with harder strokes as he became more frustrated with the conversation. "Controversy" was another word he did not know. He was not even sure he could say it.

"Oh no," exclaimed Father Regis as he held an empty mug below the spigot in the ale cask. "There is no more ale. We'll have to do with water I'm afraid."

Now Peter was completely frustrated. No meat. No bread. No ale. And he still had no words to repeat for his part of the conversation.

"Father Regis!"

The two of them looked up as they heard the priest's name called out from below. They stepped out onto the landing and looked down the length of the church. Surrounded by the tall bare walls under the darkening sky, the imposing silhouette of the sergeant stood in the center of the church with his feet spread wide under his broad shoulders and his gloved hand resting on the handle of his sword.

"Father Regis!" the sergeant called out again, not seeing them in growing darkness.

"I'm here, sergeant," answered the priest. "Won't you join us for some supper?"

Peter gave Father Regis a critical look as the sergeant approached the spiral staircase with his long stride. Father Regis smiled as he heard the sergeant's long heavy tread turn into delicate steps on the tiny stone stairs. Peter hurried back into the room and sought safety by resuming his sweeping.

"Come in, sergeant. Come in!" Father Regis welcomed him at the top of the stairs.

The sergeant nodded his thanks as he ducked and squeezed his large frame through the door into the priest's compact quarters. He acknowledged the frightened man who was cleaning the floor with a harsh look. The sergeant took up so much of the small space in the room that Peter was forced to stand nervously next to the intimidating sword and was only able to sweep repeatedly the space right in front of their feet.

"We're having a light supper of vegetables in broth, sergeant. But you're welcome to join us."

The sergeant gave a dubious look at the small boiling cauldron in which a few odorless items were bobbing about.

"No, thank you. I have other plans for supper," he responded, trying not to belittle the priest's invitation. "But do not let me keep you from your meal."

"It can wait," answered Father Regis. He offered one of the two stools to the sergeant. The two of them sat while Peter continued sweeping the same space in the corner. "How can I help you?"

"Father, I wanted to talk with you without anyone taking notice." The sergeant gave a side look at Peter.

"I am sure you understand that you have little to worry about on that account. You may speak freely," Father Regis replied.

The sergeant glanced again at Peter and nodded at the priest. "There is talk about the levy by the Holy See of a Peter's pence. A pound for the pope from every hearth, I've heard."

The large man stroked his massive moustache waiting for a response until Father Regis finally spoke.

"Taxation by the Crown or the Holy See is not my business or within my knowledge."

"But Father, I am afraid it most certainly is. You will be asked to announce it, collect it, enforce it, and report for excommunication anyone who does not pay it."

"And what if I must?"

"Father, there is talk of a bill in Parliament laying punishment for exactions paid to Rome."

The sergeant paused to let the implications of his words sink in.

"You do not want to be on the side opposite the king, and I do not want to be on the side opposite you."

"What is the risk to those who pay the tax?" asked Father Regis.

"I have no idea what would happen to DuBois or Lanham, if that is what you are asking," the sergeant answered. "Our king is no longer tolerant of the pope and his stubbornness. His impatience is showing itself in harsh ways. He could seize the property of anyone who pays the tax, if he chooses not to do worse.

"All my moustache knows is that anything to do with this Peter's pence would not be a good thing for you, the families of Atwelle who pay it, or your church."

Father Regis remained silent. The sergeant let out a frustrated sigh.

"Look, Father. I am at the point where I am no longer even sure who I take orders from. DuBois wants me to do one thing and then Lanham wants me to do another because they both want to own every pence that moves through Atwelle and that precious inland port that they each want to control. And the king? Does he obey the church or go to war with the church? Where will his orders go in the end? I just want to do my job without having to take heads or losing my own."

Father Regis still said nothing.

Finally, the sergeant put his hand on his knees and rose carefully so that his sword did no damage.

"Well, there is that then," he said, trying to end diplomatically their inconclusive discussion. "Thank you for your hospitality."

As the sergeant started to move to the door, he turned to Peter.

"And you." He gave Peter a hard stare. Peter bent his head. "I'll not have you hanging about the lane to Molly's house any more. Do you understand?"

Peter gave a fearful nod. After a pause, the sergeant snorted at him and squeezed through the door to leave.

Once he heard the door close below them, Father Regis turned to Peter.

"Sit down, Peter," he ordered.

"Why would the sergeant be warning you to stay away from the lane to the house of—to the house of that woman? Have you been to see her?"

Peter was now upset as well as hungry.

"Peter no visit Molly." He instinctively knew he had to say something else to be believed, or he might not eat that night. "DuBois visits Molly!"

Father Regis looked at him in surprise.

"Lanham visits Molly!" Peter added.

Father Regis slowly stood up over Peter and asked, "How do you know this?"

"Peter sits by a door there. It dry. See them go into Molly's house."

"And the sergeant?"

"He saw them too. He saw me sit there. He touched his sword at me."

When Peter looked up, he expected Father Regis to be unhappy with him but was relieved to see the priest ladling vegetables into two bowls. Father Regis placed their bowls on the table and sat down, giving Peter a friendly smile.

"Peter, thank you once again for your help and counsel. When it comes to raising money for the roof and windows of a church, the Lord moves in mysterious ways. And you have given me the information to make it happen."

"Controversy," Peter repeated slowly with a proud smile at pronouncing the word he remembered hearing.

2017 Don telephoned Margeaux at the end of the next day. The scaffolding in the other back corner of the nave was now fully assembled, and Nigel Green had told him that another surprise awaited them at the top. Margeaux agreed to meet Don the following morning. As she drove up to the church and parked next to Sally, Don was standing before the large door at the entrance, waving at her with a smile.

"How's my favorite research historian today?" he asked in a cheery voice.

Don seemed to be his usual self. Although Margeaux gave him a pleasant smile in return, she wondered after answering Detective Steele's questions what Don's "usual self" really was. She had been thinking about that question all the way to Atwelle.

"Are you ready for another great discovery?"

She could tell he was anxious to get started.

"I'm certainly more prepared than for the last one." Margeaux pointed at her blue jeans and tennis shoes. "These should work much better for climbing up on a platform."

"Right you are," he responded. "I, on the other hand, dressed up for the occasion."

He pointed to his worn and dusty coveralls, though Margeaux could see the tie and the collar of a white shirt visible under the coveralls. Don pushed open the large wooden door and stepped aside to let Margeaux enter. She felt all the usual sensory adjustments of going into an old church. The air was cool on her skin. She squinted in the darker light. A slight mustiness filled her nose. The floor felt hard beneath the soles of her shoes.

Walking toward the scaffolding, they passed Squeaky who was idly sweeping at the floor with a large push broom.

"Mr. Whitby—Ma'am." He stopped to lean on the broom handle as he greeted them.

"Squeaky, we're going up the scaffolding again," Don announced. "It's another chance for you to ascend to the lofty heights of Christendom, perchance to observe with us another of its mysteries."

"Thankee, no," Squeaky responded as he quickly turned back to his job.

"Suit yourself," said Don with a shake of his head. "Sweep on, my friend. Sweep on!"

Don smiled at Margeaux when they heard Squeaky mutter the word "daft" as they walked away. When they reached the ladder built into the scaffold, Don held out a flashlight to Margeaux.

"Here you are. A present. Something anyone dealing with evil spirits should have—a source of illumination.

"Let there be light," he announced as he stepped back with a wave of his hand to give Margeaux the chance to lead the way.

Margeaux took the flashlight with a nod of thanks, grabbed the metal tubing of the ladder and started to climb.

"Don't look until I get there!" Don called to her when she stood up at the top. He paused frequently as he moved slowly upward.

"There," he said when he arrived at her side. "Ready?" They both pointed their flashlights at the roof beam in the ceiling before them and clicked them on.

The beams of light revealed a face just like the one they had discovered across the way. There was the same evil grin under the eyes peering out from deep sockets over a beaked nose. The creature's pointed ears and the cape over its shoulder framed its fangs that sat on either side of its crooked teeth.

"He's back!" said Don reaching out toward the carved figure.

"Don't touch it!" ordered Margeaux. "One bandaged finger is enough."

He pulled his hand back at her reminder of the throbbing in his hand. Margeaux explored the carving closely with the beam of her flashlight.

"It's quite remarkable how the detail is so similar to the first gargoyle. It's almost as though they came out of a mold instead of being carved by hand," she noted.

"But what this one is looking at is entirely another thing," said Don as he focused his light on the smaller carved figure resting on the platform at the base of the beam in front of and below the hovering demon. They both studied the figure on which the gargoyle's claw-like hands were resting.

"It's clearly some sort of priest or monk," said Margeaux. "His clothes could be a monk's cowl. They're not ornate like other Tudor dress. But the cut of the hair with the bangs and straight edges most certainly is the tonsure cut of the clergy at that time."

"Well, now we have a demon who likes both men and women. No gender discrimination here," Don replied.

They studied the carving for a few more minutes and then walked back to the ladder where Don shined his flashlight on the first rung. He took a deep breath before stepping carefully onto the top rung.

"You really don't like being up high, do you?" she noticed.

"Not so much," Don mumbled as he started the descent. Margeaux followed.

"Good morning, you two."

They heard the greeting as they reached the ground. Father Lanham and Miss Daunting stood waiting for them.

"We heard from Mr. Green about your discoveries up on the ceiling," the curate explained, "and were curious about what you found today?"

Don eagerly described the details of the carvings on the beams above as the young vicar and Miss Daunting listened intently.

"And Miss Wood here, our noted authority, is going to solve the mystery of the demon gargoyles of St. Clement's," he announced with great theatrics.

They smiled at her politely but looked unconvinced. "We should go tell Father Adams that we found a second gargoyle," said Don.

"He knows you are here and chose not to come," said Miss Daunting in a cold voice. "So I think there's no need to bother him with the news now."

Father Lanham tried to sound more pleasant. "Yes, well—nonetheless, congratulations on your interesting news."

The two of them smiled and turned to head toward the church office. As they walked, Don realized that the young man still may not have blinked during their entire conversation. Margeaux turned to him.

"Don, do you know a police detective named Richard Steele?"

Don gave Margeaux a surprised look. She could tell he had been caught off guard.

"Yeah, he was snooping around here recently asking questions about Father Charleton. Persistent bloke. Why do you ask? Did he talk to you?"

"Yes."

"What did you tell him?"

Margeaux didn't like that he asked this question.

"The truth."

"What's that?"

"That I did not know Father Charleton very long."

She looked directly at Don.

"Do you know anything about Father Charleton's disappearance?"

He looked off down the length of the church.

"Maybe."

A look of alarm came over Margeaux's face.

"I mean I don't know anything really," he continued. "But I found a black clerical collar in the crypt that only the vicars of this parish wear. The police think it might have belonged to Father Charleton."

His comment rekindled his own curiosity.

"I wondered why the vicars at St. Clement's wear a black clerical collar?" he asked. "A black clerical collar in a small parish in Norfolk. I'd never seen such a thing anywhere else. So I asked around a bit, and the parishioners told me the vicars here have always worn black collars. Might have done so for centuries, one of them said."

"There's a mystery behind that," Margeaux commented.

"That's more of a puzzle for a historian than an architect, don't you think?" he said as he turned to leave. "Now you have two puzzles in one church."

"Who knows?" he called over his shoulder. "There could be more."

NINE

1532 In the golden glow of the candlelight, Margaret's long hair was being brushed with lingering strokes by her handmaiden. Her mother came into her bedchamber and turned back the quilt on her bed. Margaret gave her a pout.

"Mother, why may I not go with Papa to any more animal contests?"

"My darling, you know why. We had such a fright with that bear, and besides, those events are no place for a lady from a prominent family."

"That is not true, Mother. You know as well as I that all the lords and ladies of the Royal Court view blood sports frequently. And the accident with Stone Sexton can be avoided easily. Papa would never let that happen again."

Her mother shook her head.

"Please, Mother. Please! Can I go with Papa again?" she begged as she crawled under her quilt.

"It is up to your father," was the frustrated answer. "You will have to talk with him."

"I will talk to Papa immediately," Margaret announced, putting her bare feet back on the cold floor.

Her mother stopped Margaret with a hand on her shoulder.

"My dear, you are in your nightclothes. You will wake the other children. And besides," her mother added with a disapproving look, "your father is off to watch those horrid cockfights at the tavern."

"Very well," she responded quickly, "first thing in the morning. I am off to sleep then," she said. "Give me a kiss, Mother."

As soon as she was alone, Margaret slid from under her covers and hastily dressed in the clothes she had just taken off. She drew her shawl around her shoulders as she tiptoed silently down the stairs and across the entryway where she slipped through the door, lowered the latch with a quiet click as it closed, and began the long walk under the light of the moon from the DuBois manor house to the town.

"A cockfight," she thought with excitement. While she walked, she remembered vividly the exhilaration of watching Stone Sexton, and the intense experience of actually touching the bear as it died.

When Margaret heard where her father had gone, she knew immediately what she would do. Once she reached the town she would make her way to a narrow alleyway that ran down a small rise. At the end of the alley was the back of The Greene Man tavern where the cockfights were held outside under torchlight. She could stand unobserved on the hill and watch the fights from a short distance.

Her long walk only made her more excited as she reached the town. She had no trouble reaching the alley without being seen, but now she hesitated. It was all in dark shadows until the bottom where the torches burned at the back of the tavern. At the sound of men cheering, she turned into the alley and made her way carefully down its dark descent.

Halfway down, Margaret started to move more quickly. She already felt a thrill from the excited shouts of the men watching the combat under the torches. Her eyes focused on the spot ahead where she knew she could see the spectacle.

"Not a good place for a young lady this time of night."

Though the voice was low, it made Margaret jump with fright. Her breath stopped as a hand reached out of the darkness and held her by the arm. Then she recognized the familiar large moustache in the glow of the torchlight, as the sergeant stepped toward her.

Before either of them could speak, a door opened across the alley. The sergeant pulled her with him into the shadows.

They focused on the man and woman silhouetted in the light of the open doorway. The woman leaned over and kissed her companion on the cheek. In turn, he gave her a playful slap on the rump and with a laugh handed her a small purse of jingling coins.

Margaret knew that laugh. Her eyes filled with tears as she watched her father walk jauntily down the alley toward the tavern, whistling his favorite tune.

When the door had closed and her father was out of sight, Margaret looked up at the sergeant. The tears were now running down her cheeks. She snatched her arm out of his grasp and fled up the alley.

As she reached the entrance to the alley, she was startled once again by someone turning into the lane. She recognized the simpleton Peter as she pushed by him and broke into a run in the direction of the Du-Bois manor house.

Peter watched her with mild curiosity for a moment, and then settled down into the shadows of his favorite doorway, where he started humming and rocking back and forth. He stopped abruptly when another figure turned the corner and walked purposefully down the alley.

The sergeant watched the tall man striding toward him in the darkness, until the man approached the door to Molly's house.

Molly had just reached the top of the stairs after counting the coins from DuBois. She was about to hide the small leather pouch under the floorboard when the front door was pushed wide open without a knock. Richard Lanham walked brusquely to the middle of the room

"You saw my son?"

"I did," Molly answered, looking down at him.

"But you have not seen him again." Lanham sounded cross.

"I have not."

"Is that because he did not want to see you? Were you not persuasive or persistent enough?" His voice was filled with irritation. "You were paid very well to make that happen."

"He very much wanted to see me again."

Now Lanham looked confused.

"He did not see me again because I refused him," she said.

An angry look came over his face.

"I paid you to do a job that you know how to do and do well," he said through tight lips.

Molly walked back down the stairs and stood in front of him.

"My job is not to maliciously ruin the future and soul of a promising young man by intentionally destroying his sincere commitment to a higher cause," she answered. "That may be his father's will, but it is not mine."

Lanham's jaw clenched and his face grew red. She reached into the folds of her dress and held out the small leather pouch.

"Here—take this money. It is you who wants to prostitute your son."

He stepped over to Molly, his flushed face in hers.

"You cheap, worthless whore!" he seethed. His hand raised to strike her.

At that moment, a large gloved hand grabbed his wrist from behind and held it firmly. Lanham's fist froze, suspended in the air.

"You will not be hitting a helpless woman," the sergeant said in a low growl, "no matter who she is."

The sergeant all but lifted Lanham off the ground as he led the man by his wrist over to the open door. With a threatening look, Lanham stomped out the door when the sergeant released his arm. The sergeant closed the door firmly and turned back to Molly. Her face was still pale from fright.

"Thank you, John. I am most grateful," she said to him, with relief in her voice. "But you know you should not be here."

The large man looked down at her.

"Molly, you know I love you."

His thick moustache moved slightly as his lip quivered underneath.

"You know I always have, and I always will."

2017 "So, Miss Weatherby, that's the essay subject I'd like you to research for your next tutorial," Margeaux concluded while trying not to look at the new piercing in her student's eyebrow.

Miss Weatherby lowered that eyebrow in thoughtful concentration.

"A black clerical collar . . . used for centuries by clergy in Norfolk. . . ."

Margeaux could tell she was intrigued. Miss Weatherby rose from her chair in Margeaux's college study and wandered over to the window to look out over the rooftops. Margeaux smiled. That view was where Margeaux also went instinctively to ponder any new question.

"Are you sure it's only used in Norfolk?"

"No," Margeaux answered.

"Does it predate the Reformation?"

"I've told you all I know," said Margeaux. "I confirmed its current use in Norfolk and I've learned that its origins go back centuries. The rest is for you to sort out."

"Black . . ." Miss Weatherby mumbled and mused another moment before looking over with an enthusiastic smile at Margeaux. "I'll do it, Miss Wood."

Margeaux returned the smile.

"I don't believe you have a choice, Miss Weatherby."

They both laughed.

"When we next meet, give me the preliminary results of your research up until that point, and we'll decide on a deadline for your essay then."

"Right!' exclaimed Miss Weatherby as she grabbed her bag of books and bounded toward the door.

"Oh, Miss Weatherby," Margeaux interrupted her departure.

"Yes, Miss Wood?"

"I don't mean to intrude on your personal affairs. But how is your brother doing, if you don't mind my asking."

"I don't mind," she answered, a slightly pained look in her face. "I heard that he was released from prison."

"Well that's good news. Have you heard from him?"

"No." Miss Weatherby shook her head. "It's such a shame really. He was such a good brother, as I told you. Brilliant, but troubled—a full year into seminary even and then to prison for dealing hard drugs. That's what drugs will do to you, I guess. They're bad business in the end."

Margeaux could not help but think that the figure with all the tattoos and piercings standing before her looked the least likely person to be lecturing against the evils of drug use.

"I'm sorry if I upset you," Margeaux apologized.

"No, that's all right. I appreciate your asking," she replied. The student's youthful exuberance returned to her voice. "I'm off to learn everything there is to know about black clerical collars!"

Margeaux listened to the student's feet hit every other stair for three flights down, and then watched her through the window as she walked toward the college library. Lingering at the window a few more minutes, Margeaux considered several questions of her own.

"Money and mystery," she summed up her thoughts out loud before grabbing her purse, locking the door to her study, and stepping carefully down the worn stairs. At the bottom, she headed for the college gate and her car.

"Miss Wood!"

Hearing her name, she turned to see the porter Gerald in his black suit and bowler waving at her. He followed the cobblestones that framed the lawn of the college court until he reached her.

"You have a couple of envelopes in your mailbox," he informed her.

"Are they thin?" she asked.

"I'm afraid so, Miss Wood."

Margeaux frowned.

"And it might be a bit worse," he added. "One of the items is an invitation to have tea with the master of the college."

"Why is that worse, Gerald?"

"Well, it's been my experience that research fellows who are having difficulty finding funding for their research are invited at some point to discuss with the master their position at the college."

He saw the look of concern cross Margeaux's face.

"But then again, maybe he wants to talk about something else," he offered to console her.

"And then again, maybe he doesn't," she responded in a grim voice. "Thank you, Gerald. I appreciate it."

Driving out of Cambridge, Margeaux resisted the temptation to release her frustration by speeding down the narrow streets. She eventually reached the outskirts of town and started to relax when she was surrounded once again by the flat fields of the fens on her way to Atwelle. After a while, Margeaux turned off her car radio so she could focus her thoughts on the strange situations that seemed to arise with every visit to St. Clement's.

What was happening at the church, she wondered. Who had tried to scare her at the church when the door slammed in her face? Why had Father Adams observed her at a distance instead of introducing himself? What did Don know that made the police interested in him enough to question her?

And what did the police think was going on, with all their questions? Should whatever happened to Father Charleton worry her now? Her project seemed to be moving along as she expected. Yet the situation was unsettling.

Then there were the gargoyles. A fascinating opportunity. Demonic figures placed inside the church. Hovering over figures that seem both protected and threatened.

"Well, we'll see the third gargoyle today," she concluded with anticipation as she pulled up to the church and climbed out of her car.

"Good morning, Miss Wood."

Margeaux looked up to see Nigel Green finishing a conversation with some of his workmen.

"Good morning. And please, call me Margeaux," she told him.

"Then call me Nigel," he answered as he shook her hand.

"And how is the new baby coming along?"

"Little Nicky is doing well, thank you. It's his father who could do with a little more sleep," Nigel said with a weary smile.

"The scaffold has been moved to the next roof beam, and you have another surprise in store today," he confirmed.

"Can't wait," she replied. "Is Don inside?"

"Yes, and you'd better go right in. I think he could use a bit of help at the moment."

Walking through the open church door, Margeaux saw Don talking with Miss Daunting and another woman. As she drew closer, Margeaux was surprised to see the woman arm-in-arm with Don, leaning against him. Her hair was big, teased and bleached blonde. Large eyelashes were glued to her eyelids that were heavy with mascara. Her red high-heeled shoes, tight red jeans, and bright pink top that revealed a great length of cleavage seemed grossly out of place in the church.

Miss Daunting noticed Margeaux approaching.

"Miss Wood, I'd like to introduce you to— "

"Hi! I'm Brandi, with one 'i.'" The woman held out her hand to Margeaux. Margeaux could not help but notice her long fake fingernails painted with polish that looked like it would glow in the dark.

"I'm Margeaux," she said, shaking Brandi's hand. "And I have two eyes."

Puzzling over the spelling of Margeaux's name, Brandi gave her a confused look. Don, who had managed to extract himself from Brandi, pretended to cough to keep from laughing. Miss Daunting resumed her introduction.

"Brandi is working with us doing odd jobs in the church and the fund-raising campaign."

"Been on holiday in Brighton," Brandi announced. "Working on my tan," she said as she reached again for Don's arm.

Don deftly avoided her grasp by pointing at the ceiling.

"There it is," he said to Margeaux. "All reassembled and ready for our ascent. Shall we head over?"

Margeaux nodded.

"Where's Squeaky by the way?" Don asked. "I have to offer my traditional invitation to join us. I love the way he refuses it."

"That horrid man? He drinks too much," declared Brandi.

"I haven't seen him about today," Miss Daunting answered.

"Too bad for him, then. We'll miss him," replied Don as he turned and started walking toward the maze of pipes and wood planks running up the church wall to the roof beam in the dark ceiling.

"Isn't he just luscious?" Brandi whispered with a wink to Margeaux as she walked by to follow Don.

"Friend of yours?" Margeaux asked Don a few seconds later as he started slowly up the ladder.

"You never know," he answered with a smile down at her before continuing his climb.

Margeaux was surprised at feeling a slight twinge of jealousy. They climbed steadily to the top. Don was careful once more not to look down. When they were both standing on the platform at the top, they clicked on their flashlights together.

There he was with the same evil grin as if he had been expecting them. This gargoyle was similar to the first two, but with slight variations from the hand carving. Also the point of one ear was missing—Margeaux couldn't decide whether that was by design or that it had come off over time—and the cape over his shoulders was a different design.

The biggest difference, as before, was the figure over which the gargoyle was leaning. The gargoyle's familiar gnarled claws were resting on the shoulders of a man dressed in plain clothes.

"A tradesman?" Don offered the question that was in both their minds.

"I'm not sure," Margeaux answered. "I'd say yes if he were holding some kind of tool. But that appears to be a cup or goblet."

They stepped nearer and examined the figure more closely with their flashlights.

"And his face has sort of a dull look about him," said Margeaux. "Look at his expressionless features and slack open mouth. I don't get the impression that the wood-carver was trying to suggest a man of any intellect."

The two of them puzzled in silence over the figure for a few more minutes until Margeaux started reaching into her coat pockets.

"I've come a bit more prepared this time," she said as she pulled out a tape measure, a pad of sketch paper, and a camera with a flash attached.

"That's a pretty fancy contraption. It looks expensive." Don eyed the camera.

"It is," she answered as she began measuring the gargoyle. "It's great for taking pictures in very low levels of light. I borrowed it from Gerald. He's a friend at college."

"Some sort of professional photographer?" asked Don.

She noticed he tried too hard to make his question sound casual.

"He's the head porter at college."

"The head porter is a professional photographer?" asked Don.

"No. But he's a man of many surprising talents." With respect to jealousy, Margeaux knew how to give as well as get.

After taking more measurements of both figures, Margeaux grabbed the camera and started shooting.

"Come on, let's have a little smile from you two," Don said to the carvings as if they were posing.

"That's spooky," said Margeaux after the camera flashed. "I could swear that gargoyle gave me a bigger smile. All right, now you go on over there and let me have a shot of the three of you with a big smile."

She looked over at him. The grin was gone from his face. He did not move or say anything. He just stared at the gargoyle and the figure of the man in front. After an uncomfortable moment, Margeaux picked up the sketch pad where she had written down the dimensions of the figures.

"Could you hold the flashlights so I can make some notes and sketches?" she asked.

Don was uncharacteristically quiet as Margeaux worked. Eventually he asked a question.

"Have you spoken to Detective Steele again?"

When she glanced over at him, his eyes were fixed on the gargoyle and the figure of the man.

"No."

When he said nothing more, she went on.

"He didn't ask anything particularly alarming or incriminating. I assume it was just routine to talk to me about Father Charleton's disappearance."

"But after all the time since Charleton disappeared, there must be some reason why the police are asking you questions now."

"Indeed," thought Margeaux. But she just shrugged in response.

After a while, Don started looking about at the ceiling and the church below.

"It's a funny thing about churches," he said. "A church is the house of God—consecrated ground, a holy place for His worship.

"Yet this sanctified place exists not because of God's holiness; it really exists because of the evil that people do. People are compelled to go to church because of sin. So this holy place is actually about evil people and their evil deeds. Ironic isn't it?"

She looked over at him. He was staring once again at the gargoyle.

"Well with all the evil people and evil deeds in the world, you could also conclude that the church is not irrelevant in today's society. There's nothing ironic about that," she responded.

Their heads jerked up at the sudden sound of a chorus of sirens pulling up outside the church. Margeaux and Don gathered their things quickly and hastily descended. By the time they reached the floor of the church, it was empty. Following the sound of commotion outside, they hurried through the open door where they were partially blinded by the flashing lights of two police cars and an ambulance.

Around the corner of the church, Margeaux and Don saw Miss Daunting and Father Lanham standing together with grim looks on their faces. Brandi was holding onto Father Lanham's arm, her other hand covering her eyes.

As they approached the group, Margeaux and Don saw two constables roping off an area around the tall grass against the wall of the church where Detective Steele was kneeling. When Detective Steele stood up, they could see a body lying next to the old wooden ladder leaning on its side against the wall in the grass.

"I found him lying out here," Father Lanham said to them. "It's Squeaky."

Margeaux saw Don's face go pale.

"Where's Father Adams?" she asked. No one answered or seemed to know.

Detective Steele looked toward where they were standing. Walking over, he blocked the group's view of the crime scene until he neared them and the two constables moved to the side. Margeaux looked past the detective. When she could make out the body in the tall grass, a sick look came over her. She saw Squeaky's arm slung over the side rail of the old wooden ladder. The arm was skeletal. No flesh, no muscle.

Margeaux stumbled over to the church where she placed her forearm and head against the cold hard stone of the wall to steady herself and erase the horrifying scene. She felt someone's hand on her shoulder.

"Are you okay?"

Margeaux heard Don's voice next to her. She reached over and pushed his hand away.

TEN

1532 DuBois sat hunched over the account book on his desk. His wife walked over and stroked his thick head of hair. In the sunlight streaming through the window, she noticed even more gray among his auburn waves.

"It cannot be as bad as all that," she tried to calm him.

"I am afraid it is, my dear," he declared. He frantically scanned the columns of numbers before him, unable to see any answers to his problems.

"But the workers in the fields have been bringing in so much grain and wool," she replied.

"And with the prices they are fetching, it is all worth a quarter of what we took in last year."

He slammed the ledger shut and leaned back, holding his head in his hands.

"And Lanham is up to his old tricks," he growled. "I learned today that he is corresponding with the king's chancellor with respect to establishing the port and controlling its revenues. Evidently he is trying to convince the king that if he is not given control over the port, he might not be able to give a return on the king's investments in Lanham's salt mine."

"Will that work?" she asked.

"It is a bold move if it does not ultimately anger the king as an extortionist threat."

"But if it does anger the king, it would put you in a good position to take control of income from the port, would it not?" his wife asked.

"That depends on the pope," muttered DuBois.

"The pope? How is that?"

"If His Holiness refuses to annul the king's marriage, or if a Peter's pence tax is imposed on all of us while the king is lacking funds for his treasury, we loyal Catholics will be in no position to expect anything favorable from the king. There is talk of the king strongly enforcing the Statute of Praemunire, which outlaws a religious tax to be collected and those monies sent out of the country. If there comes a Peter's pence upon us, it would be an offence under this statute that could result in the Crown taking our lands and chattels."

DuBois let out a scornful laugh.

"But if I don't come up with a solution to paying our debts coming due, we will have nothing to worry about. We will all be in debtor's prison without anything for the king to seize." DuBois slammed his fist on the writing table. "What can I do?" He stood up in frustration and stomped over to the window.

"Husband," his wife addressed him in a quiet voice as if to remind him of something.

He looked out into the sunlight before he turned to face her.

"I know," he said with a heavy sigh. DuBois walked over to the door of his study and glanced out in both directions.

"Where is Margaret?" he asked.

"I have not seen her," his wife answered.

DuBois closed the door firmly and returned to the window.

"All right. We will marry off our daughter for a handsome payment to us for the privilege."

His wife nodded with firm agreement. DuBois stared out as if hoping to find a solution to his dilemma in the landscape outside the window. "We need someone with significant wealth who is sympathetic to our position and has need of a young beautiful wife," he mused. "And we must find such a person quickly."

They both puzzled over the situation in silence. After a few moments, DuBois's face lit up with surprise followed by a satisfied smile. "It will take some doing," he said hesitantly. "But I think I have the unlikely answer."

His wife walked over to him and with a proud look, gave him a triumphant kiss.

"I knew I could count on you."

∽

While DuBois was making a plan to save his family, Margaret was on her way to do what she thought was necessary to do the same. She walked up to the door of Molly's house in the alley, swallowed hard to summon her courage, and knocked loudly.

A look of surprise came over Molly's face as she opened the door. From the girl's distinctive features and auburn hair, Molly knew immediately who stood before her.

"May I help you?" Molly asked with a cautious look up and down the alley.

"Stop seeing my father," Margaret ordered.

Molly studied her up and down, from her crescent-shaped cap to the puffed sleeves attached to the bodice on top of her gathered petticoat and skirt.

"Won't you come in?" Molly invited as she stepped back to open the door wide.

Margaret hesitated, but, not wanting to look weak, nodded and stepped in. Molly closed the door and turned to her.

"If you do not want me to see your father, maybe it is him you should be talking to, not me."

Margaret was at a loss for words. She never expected such a response; nor had she planned what to say beyond her command at the door. Her face turned red with embarrassment.

"You are a shameless harlot who is seeking to destroy my family," she finally blurted out.

Molly took a deep breath.

"Do you know why your father comes to see me?"

Margaret gave no answer.

"It is not because he does not love your mother—or you," said Molly.

The tears in Margaret's eyes now ran down her cheeks.

"Won't you please sit down?" Molly gestured to the chair in which DuBois liked to sit.

Margaret moved to the chair where she dabbed at her face with a kerchief. Molly gave her a moment while she looked at the floor to avoid sobbing.

"People visit me for a great number of different reasons," Molly said finally in a soft voice as she seated herself where she could look directly at Margaret.

"What is your name?" asked Molly.

Margaret sniffed and did not answer.

"No matter," responded Molly.

"You know," she went on, "everyone has personal desires and needs and tastes. So why do they come to me?"

Margaret looked up at Molly.

"Some people seek someone with whom to share these desires, needs, and tastes when they cannot find a person to share them with in their lives. That is what I do. I share people's special desires and inclinations. And I keep their secrets. Oftentimes, my dear, that keeps these people from destroying their lives—or even destroying themselves."

Margaret's moist eyes never left Molly as she listened attentively.

"So that is what this 'shameless harlot' may have done for your father and your family. Is there anything else you'd like to call me?"

After a moment of silence, Molly spoke again. "Well if you are not going to call me anything else, may I ask again what I may call you?"

"Margaret."

Molly paused for a moment.

"Margaret, do you have someone with whom to share your secrets? Especially your special desires or needs?"

"No, not really." Margaret's concern had turned away from her father.

"I did not think so," said Molly. She leaned forward and took Margaret's hands in hers.

"Do you want to share them with me?"

"I do not know," answered Margaret.

"Well now you know who I am and what I do. Come back again if you like."

Margaret gave Molly an embarrassed smile of apology.

"I will."

2017 The deep voice of Father Adams filled St. Clement's from the pulpit.

"I had the good fortune of knowing Cecil Tremont when he was a young man during my first tenure here at the church, and then came to know him again at another time in his life during my recent return."

Don turned to Margeaux sitting next to him. They had not seen each other since the day Squeaky's body was found.

"Cecil?" he mouthed silently to her with a look of surprise.

"Of course," Father Adams continued, "we all knew him as Squeaky."

Margeaux shrugged back at Don as if to say "I guess so."

She discreetly counted only twelve people in the church for Squeaky's funeral three days after his body was found. Most were from the church, including Miss Daunting, Father Lanham, and Brandi with an "i." Margeaux guessed that the few additional people mustered together in a single pew on that weekday afternoon were Squeaky's friends from the pub. She noted the irony that everyone there represented the two contrasting focal points of Squeaky's life, the church and the pub. And each place always brought him back to the other.

As Don listened to Father Adams moralize on how life's temptations can drag one down if one is not attentive to the threat of evil ways, he realized that the vicar was wearing not only a black clerical collar, but all the vicar's vestments were black, instead of the usual white surplice over a black cassock. He tried unsuccessfully to recall ever seeing black vestments before, even at a funeral, and puzzled over them for a while. The tone of the vicar's voice sounded the end of the eulogy.

"One can never know the source of every evil. Yet, it is like a lion seeking to devour whom it may. But sleep well, Squeaky, for the lion will seek you no more. Amen."

The organ started up a hymn, which the twelve people sprinkled throughout the pews stood to sing in the echo of Father Adams' booming voice. Then with the vicar's benediction, the service ended in an abrupt anticlimax. Margeaux watched Squeaky's mates file out of the pew to head for the pub.

"That's it," Don said to her. "Squeaky's life on earth is officially done."

Margeaux was not sure whether he was trying to be flippant as usual. Then she noticed Father Adams walk over to the side of the church where Detective Steele was obviously waiting to speak with the vicar.

"Don, have you heard anything more about Squeaky's death?" she asked.

"No," he responded. "The news reports didn't say much. Just the basic stats of his life. I'm guessing the police are keeping the details secret for use in interrogating suspects."

"Do they have any suspects?"

"Don't know," he answered. "They've talked to a lot of people."

"Did you see Squeaky's body after they found him in the churchyard?" she asked.

"No. I really couldn't see much of anything. But I think we'll discover some pretty suspicious characters at the top of these two scaffolds." Don clearly wanted to change the subject. "Are you ready to go up and question them?"

"I am," she said, grateful for the distraction. "But I have to hurry a bit. I have an important appointment back at college."

"Have you got your flashlight?" asked Don.

With a nod, she patted the pocket of her jacket.

"Then up you go," he said as they reached the ladder on the first repositioned scaffold. "Let's meet our fourth gargoyle."

At the top, they turned on their flashlights simultaneously. Margeaux said nothing.

"Well, what do you think?" he asked.

She looked over at him and remained silent.

"We've got our old friend," he said as he pointed his flashlight on the familiar pointed ears, sunken eyes, and grinning fangs. "And this other fellow looks sort of familiar."

Don moved the beam of his flashlight to the gargoyle's claws resting on the shoulders of the figure in front. Margeaux turned back to the figure.

"Looks like the same figure as across the way. Same simple clothes, a similar vacant look," noted Don. "But he's having a little trouble with his goblet. It's tipped downward at the end of his hand."

Don walked up for a closer examination.

"Well it's no wonder," said Don. "His arm is nothing but a bunch of bones like a skeleton. That's odd. What do you make of it?"

He turned back to Margeaux and saw the pallor in her face.

"Are you all right?"

"Let's go look at the roof beam across the way," she said.

"Don't you want to take some pictures or notes? This is rather interesting."

"Later," answered Margeaux. Her foot was already on the ladder to climb down. "Let's look at the next gargoyle," she insisted.

Don could barely keep up with her as she walked briskly down a row of pews across the aisle and past the remaining pews up to the other recently relocated scaffold. She started climbing without pausing. When he followed her to the top, Margeaux's flashlight was already shining on the wood carving in front of her.

"Wow!" said Don looking over Margeaux's shoulder. "She's almost as pretty as you."

Margeaux scanned the details of the gargoyle and the delicately carved female figure over which it hovered.

"What's that on the sides of her head?" he asked. "It looks like a wing coming out of each side."

"It's a roughly carved rendition of a headpiece popular for fashionable women in the Tudor period," she answered. "It was called a 'gable hood' because its pointed shape resembled the gable of a house. Those wings, as you called them, are decorated side panels called lappets. Gable hoods eventually became extremely ornate with a box-shaped back and two tube-shaped hanging veils that could be pinned up in a variety of fashions."

Margeaux, having sketched the previous gargoyle on that side of the church, noticed something further that Don did not. This gargoyle's fangs were framed by upturned lips in a slight smile, and its claws turned inward around the female figure's neck instead of simply resting on her shoulders.

Well, she's still not as pretty as you," said Don. "And you don't have a demon hovering around you, do you?" he jested lightly.

She gave him a questioning look without smiling.

"I have to go."

Don looked surprised.

"Are you sure you have to leave?" he asked. "This is good stuff."

"*Oui*. I have a meeting with the master of the college."

Margeaux quickly climbed down the ladder, left without saying goodbye, and drove faster than she should have on her way back to Cambridge. As soon as she arrived at the college, she looked at her watch. She had ten minutes before her appointment with the master, so she headed right to her study.

After unlocking the door, she moved directly to the window where she tried to calm her jumbled emotions and sort out all she had just experienced.

"No," she changed her mind. "First I have to think about my meeting with the master."

Taking a few deep breaths, she scanned the rooftops and looked down at the college court below. Her breathing suddenly stopped.

There was no mistaking the white hair and black collar of Father Adams walking on the cobblestones beneath her window.

ELEVEN

1532 All Father Regis could focus on were the rough calloused hands respectfully clasping the caps of the three men standing before him. Polite but defiant, the men had said their piece. Father Regis lowered his eyes to avoid their expectant looks.

"You and your men have done good work on the new church building. And more, you have been exceedingly patient. I only ask for a bit more of your indulgence. I can say no more good, except that you and your men will be paid."

"But Father," one of the men continued. Father Regis calmly endured their complaints one more time as if they could make a difference. But when he looked into their faces, he feared what he would hear next.

"Father, if our men are not paid their wages, they will no longer work on the church."

Father Regis took on as confident an air as he could muster.

"You will receive your wages, both for past work and to finish the church, in advance of its completion," he declared. "But you must continue your work until All Hallows' Day. If you do, the men shall see all their wages even before the winter."

The priest's voice was firm.

"You will receive your entire wages at once at that time. Just work through All Hallows' Eve. Tell your men."

The three men looked surprised and pleased. With a chorus of thanks, they turned to leave.

"Was that a lie?" the priest worried. "I do not know how it will happen, but I must have faith."

Struggling with his guilt, Father Regis noticed one of the men had remained standing before him.

"Is there something else, Marlowe?" the priest asked.

"Father, it's about Bittergreen, the wood-carver."

"I know him." Father Regis winced.

"Well, sir, he has a newborn child, and says he has no choice but to move on."

With obvious discomfort, Marlowe nervously twisted the cap in his hands.

"There are not many men his like—a good man, Father. And there are no men in these parts with his skill. Without him, I do not see how the construction can go forward. I will have no one, let alone a man of his skill, to fashion the roof beams or carve the screens and other fine woodwork."

"Are not all the men valuable, Marlowe?" Father Regis asked. "And do not some of them have children also?"

"Yes sir. But Bittergreen, sir—"

Marlowe stood there saying no more, waiting uncomfortably until Father Regis reached into a small pouch tied to the belt around his waist and handed two coins to the man.

"Say nothing of this to anyone, Marlowe. These are for Bittergreen."

"Thank you, Father," Marlowe said with a bow as he backed away.

Father Regis sat in silence for some time, paralyzed by the predicament he had created. He felt the need to talk with Peter for guidance, but there was no time. Lanham was expecting him. The priest felt guilty that he had started his plan to force the money for the church out of Lanham with Peter's knowledge of Lanham's visit to the prostitute in the town.

"Now I must see it through," he concluded.

At almost every step on his walk from the church to Lanham Manor, Father Regis changed his mind about what he should do and what he would say. He wavered between guilt and a strong conviction that he had no choice if he was to meet the trust of the workmen and complete his life's work at the church. He was so addled by the time he walked under the great oaks to the door of the manor house that he could not even bring himself to pray for guidance from God before he knocked.

It seemed to Lanham's servant as he led Father Regis through the dark wood paneling in the manor house to Lanham's study that the priest was oblivious to all around him. The servant was surprised when the priest refused to be seated while he waited for Lanham.

"Father Regis, do sit down," Lanham urged when he entered the study a few moments later.

"Richard, I feel that I must speak to you about the woman in the town named Molly," Father Regis announced in an agitated voice without any pleasantries.

Lanham's face hardened. "I have nothing whatsoever to say with respect to that woman," he dismissed the comment with a threatening look.

Only then did Father Regis realize how foolish and badly played was his gambit. In the end, his plan to extort money from Lanham was based solely on a statement from Peter, which Lanham now curtly dismissed. All he had at that point, he realized, was the word of the village idiot against one of the most influential men in Atwelle. Now he desperately feared that he had managed only to damage his prospects badly.

"Father Regis, I know you need funds for the roof and windows of the church."

The priest waited with his head lowered, expecting Lanham's wrath.

"And I believe we can possibly reach an agreement in order to make those funds available."

Completely surprised, Father Regis glanced up at Lanham with immense relief. "How can I help you?" he quickly asked.

"My son is not to become a monk. Is that clear?"

Father Regis looked puzzled.

"I am afraid not. I do not know what I am being asked to do."

"It may not be entirely simple, but the result is straightforward," replied Lanham. "You are to see that my son marries, and soon. I cannot do it. It is you who must."

Father Regis, his mouth hanging open, stared at Lanham in disbelief.

2017 "Please slow down," Margeaux ordered, "and take a deep breath."

Miss Weatherby gave Margeaux a look that said "Why ever would I do that." She shrugged her shoulders, took a perfunctory breath, and launched into a detailed report just as rapidly as before.

"Just start with a summary, if you will," Margeaux interrupted her student again before looking out the window of her study to listen carefully.

"There is very little information to be found on the use of black vestments in the Church of England. They are not mentioned or sanctioned in the general instructions on such things. So I started again with your reference to known use of black vestments in Norfolk. I went to Church of England data bases for the dioceses of Norwich and Ely in Norfolk and did a search for 'black vestments' among the various data bases."

"And what did you find?"

"I found a lot of parishes in Norfolk and a helluva lot of priests and vicars in those parishes going back centuries."

"Centuries?" asked Margeaux.

"Centuries," Miss Weatherby confirmed with obvious pride. "And a good number of them, too." Miss Weatherby paused for dramatic effect. "And I finally found it—a single reference to a black vestment next to the name of a priest. Almost five hundred years ago."

"What did you do then?"

"I went to bed. I hadn't slept in two days."

"Yes, of course. And after that?"

"I carried on looking at the long list of clergy for the last five hundred years in the church where I found the reference."

"Where was the church?"

"It's the parish church of Atwelle, a village on the edge of Norfolk. I had to look at a map to locate—"

"Yes, yes. I know the place. What did you find then?"

"As I said, there were no more references to 'black vestments.' But after that first reference, every priest and vicar thereafter was listed as 'OBV entrusted with the cure and protection of souls.' That designation goes on for centuries, repeated for every one of the listed clergy in that parish. I'm guessing the 'BV' stands for black vestment. I don't know what the 'O' stands for," Miss Weatherby concluded.

"Did you notice any of the names of the clergy on the list?" asked Margeaux.

"I jotted down some of the recent names," said Miss Weatherby as she sorted through pages of notes.

"The last one on the list is named Charleton. And the one before him is—" She turned over the piece of notepaper. "Adams."

Margeaux's stomach tightened at the sound of the name. "You're sure the name was Adams?"

"Yes, of course."

"Did you search any further? Are there any other parishes or dioceses with priests designated as OBV?"

"I've looked at Norfolk, Suffolk, Cambridgeshire, and Lincolnshire so far," Miss Weatherby answered with a weary voice. "I found no other priests' names with the OBV, though."

"You're sure? That's an enormous number of parishes."

"Can you see my bloodshot eyes, Miss Wood?" Miss Weatherby asked.

"I don't think you need to carry on looking at every parish in England, Miss Weatherby," Margeaux replied. The student looked relieved. "Now I'm afraid we'll have to end early. I must go or I'll be late for an appointment."

Miss Weatherby picked up her knapsack and stood up.

"Just write up a brief summary," Margeaux told her as she headed toward the door. "No need for a full essay quite yet."

After opening the door, Miss Weatherby paused in thought.

"Miss Wood, the 'O' in 'OBV'—"

"Yes?"

"Could it be like the 'O' in 'OBE'?"

"Order of the British Empire," nodded Margeaux. "Very clever, Miss Weatherby. That might be it: Order of the Black Vestments."

"I'll search for it," declared Miss Weatherby as she stepped through the door.

"Oh, and Miss Weatherby," Margeaux called her back into the room. "Please go to sleep at bedtime, won't you?"

Miss Weatherby pondered the instruction for a moment.

"Bedtime? What time is that?"

Margeaux smiled as she heard the footsteps once again hitting every other step down the narrow staircase. She was glad for the opportunity to smile about something before returning to St. Clement's to look at the sixth gargoyle and the next figure of another young woman.

An hour later, Margeaux pulled her car up to the church and parked next to Sally. Don was standing before the large door to the church where he was speaking with Nigel Green. Margeaux took a nervous breath and walked up to greet them.

Nigel gave her a friendly smile, while Don nodded an uncertain hello.

"Miss Wood—I mean, Margeaux—the scaffolding is done and there's another mystery for you," Nigel said with a smile.

Thank you, Nigel," she said curtly as she walked past them into the church and directly toward the repositioned scaffold.

"Did I say something wrong?" Nigel turned to Don.

"Don't worry about it. I'll see what's going on."

Nigel shrugged his shoulders and headed to his truck while Don hurried after Margeaux. He found her waiting at the scaffold's ladder.

"Aren't you going up?" he asked,

But then Don saw why she was waiting. Looking up, he saw a man descending the ladder. It was Father Lanham, who soon stepped down and brushed off his hands.

"Quite interesting," he said to them. "You should have a look."

Margeaux immediately started climbing. Don looked at the young vicar and thought how the unblinking eyes over the smile on his lips didn't fit together. Cautiously following Margeaux up to the top, Don found her standing back from the next gargoyle, keeping very still with her flashlight on the carving.

He walked up to the carving and shook his head at the appearance of the sixth gargoyle. "This guy is turning into one nasty piece of work. Look what became of that poor young lady in front of him. What do you suppose that means?"

Don leaned into the gargoyle and studied its claws closely. They circled the neck of the delicate female figure. But inside the gargoyle's grasp there was nothing.

The head of the young woman was missing.

"Shame," he said as he blew the dust off the spot where the figure's head should rest. "She had that pretty gable hat thing too."

Don turned around to see Margeaux's reaction. She had disappeared. He heard the sound of her feet descending rapidly on the metal ladder.

"Margeaux—wait!" he called out as he followed her down more slowly. She was walking briskly away. At the bottom, he ran to catch up with her.

"What's wrong, Margeaux?"

She turned away from him. He grabbed her by the shoulders and spun her back to face him.

"I don't know what's happened to you or whether I've done something to upset you. But I don't like seeing you agitated and not knowing what to do about it."

"There's nothing wrong," she said, turning away.

"That's not true, and you know it."

He tightened his grip on her shoulders to make her look back at him.

"You and I made an unusual discovery here that's intriguing and intellectually interesting. I thought we were enjoying discovering these mysteries together. I thought I could help you explain them and make something of your project beyond some grimy windows overlooking odds and ends.

"*C'est tres bien, n'est pas?*" He was even willing to try his French to sort things out. "Then all of a sudden you won't even talk to me. So don't tell me nothing's wrong."

Don slid his hands down her arms and took her hands in his.

"Now tell me what I can do to make things better."

"There's nothing you can do," she answered, trying to take her hands out of his grasp. He would not let go.

"Is it Squeaky's death?"

"That's part of it."

"What's the other part?"

"Will you please let go of my hands?"

He dropped her hands and tried to hold her attention with a look of concern.

"Don't you think there's something unusual going on, between what's happened and the gargoyles?" she asked.

"The gargoyles?" He looked at her first with surprise and then up at the dark ceiling. "How do you mean?"

"Well, after they found Squeaky, we saw the fourth gargoyle that suggested the death of the man in the carving with the gargoyle on the opposite side."

Don gave her a skeptical look.

"Look, Margeaux. Squeaky's death was tragic, but don't you think it's a little farfetched to tie it to the gargoyles? What possible connection could they have? The gargoyles are almost five hundred years old, and Squeaky was found before you and I saw the fourth gargoyle that suggested to you the death of the man in the third carving. You've got to be logical about this."

He saw Margeaux thinking about his argument.

"Now tell me," he gently ordered. "There must be something I can do to make you feel better?"

Margeaux looked up into the dark ceiling at the roof beams where the scaffolding would go next.

"There is. Could you have Nigel move the scaffolding to the next roof beam right away?"

"Of course," replied Don. "I'll finish the inspection of the beam with the first carving of the young lady and her gargoyle tomorrow morning and have Nigel start dismantling and moving the structure tomorrow afternoon. Will that help?"

"To be honest, I don't know," Margeaux answered.

TWELVE

1532 "You are spending too lavishly on this dinner," DuBois' wife had scolded him. "He's only a priest."

"Yes, but he is the one person in a position, unlikely as it is, to do what is necessary to save our fortune and secure our power. It is money necessarily well spent," he had replied.

Now, as they watched Father Regis happily holding out his wine goblet for the servant to refill, they were thinking that they both had been right.

A fire roared high in the large hearth of the dining hall in the DuBois manor house. Its golden light reflected off the family silver that adorned the long dining table loaded with sumptuous food.

"What a fine collection of beautiful silver, Francis," Father Regis observed with admiration.

"Acquired over the centuries," responded DuBois, "since one of my ancestors first crossed the English Sea as an officer of William the Conqueror."

The servant filled the priest's wine goblet to the rim from an ornate claret jug.

"More venison, Father?" DuBois urged.

Father Regis nodded his thanks as he finished drinking and set down his already half-empty goblet. DuBois gestured to his servant to serve the guest more meat.

"And possibly some of the lampreys in that delicious sauce?" Father Regis asked as the sweat beaded up on his flushed brow.

"Of course, of course," DuBois answered as he himself handed the silver bowl of eels to the servant to serve. His wife rose and took the claret jug to top up the priest's wine goblet immediately. When she finished, DuBois gave her a nod.

"Father Regis," she smiled at him sweetly, "may we offer you some humble entertainment while we dine?"

"And how is that?" he gave her a pleased look in return.

With a gesture from DuBois' wife, the servant opened the door at the end of the dining hall.

"You of course know our daughter, Margaret?"

"Know her? Do not jest, madam. I baptized her!" he replied. He stood up as Margaret entered the room holding her harp.

"My dear, how nice to see you," he smiled at her.

Margaret came up to him and curtsied.

"Father Regis, welcome to our home."

"Thank you, my dear. I did not know you played the harp."

Her auburn hair glowed as she sat before the fire on a stool placed under her by the servant. Father Regis looked over at DuBois.

"She not only looks like an angel, but she can sound like one too?"

They all laughed as Margaret blushed.

"Margaret, play us a ballad whilst we dine," her father ordered with an affectionate look.

Father Regis took another bite of venison and washed it down hastily with an indelicate quaff of wine before turning his full attention to Margaret. DuBois and his wife exchanged a knowing glance before she filled the priest's goblet once again.

Margaret strummed the harp in her lap for a few opening chords and started singing an enchanting tune in a delicate voice.

All in a pleasant morning
       in the Merrie Month of May;

Among the fragrant meadowes
        a younge man took his way:
And gazing rounde about him
        for pleasures he could see
At length he spied a proper Maid
        under an oaken tree.

So cheerful was her countenance
        and lovely to behold
She seemed as if that Venus faire
        was of the selfsame Mold
And many a smirk and smile she gave
        all in the Meadows greene;
I could compare her unto none
        but unto Love's faire Queene.

At length she turned her smiling
        into a sighing songe
Bewailing her bad fortune
        that she was a maide so longe;
There's many that are younger
        than I, that have been wed;
Yet still I fear that I shall dye,
        and keep my Maiden-head.

My father's rich and welthie
        and hath no daughter but me;
Yet want I still a husband
        to keepe me companie.
My yeares are younge and tender;
        and I am fair withall;
Yet is there nere a youngman
        will comfort me at all?

The blossoms of my beautie,
    I think, may well invite
Some batchelor of fortune goode
    to take me for his right:
For why I dare presume it,
    there's few doth me excelle,
As it is manifest and plain
    to all that know me welle.

At this point, the chords from Margaret's harp turned sad and her voice lost its cheery tone.

The God of love that sits above,
    Who knows me,
    Who knows me,
How sorrowful I do serve:

Grant my request that at the least
    He shows me,
    He shows me,
Some pity when I deserve.

That every brawl may turn to blisse,
To joy with all that joyfull is.

Do this my dear and binde me
For ever and ever your owne,
And as you here do finde me,
So let your love be showne:

For till I knowe this unytie,
I languish in extremytie.

As if with a hand made heavy by sadness, Margaret strummed on her harp the last mournful chord of her song.

Father Regis sat motionless with his mouthful of venison half chewed and tears filling his eyes. DuBois and his wife could barely conceal their pleasure as they watched him and then looked at each other.

"That was lovely, my sweet girl," said DuBois as he rose and kissed his daughter fondly on the top of her head. "Now say goodnight to Father Regis and it is off to bed with you."

"Goodnight, Father," said Margaret with a curtsy.

Father Regis could only nod as the tears were running down his cheeks. As she turned to leave, he reached over and took another long drink from his wine goblet.

"I must say, Francis, she is a remarkable young woman," he said when finally able to speak.

"Yes, Father. We have been blessed. She will make a wonderful wife to someone, hopefully in the near future, as she would be such a beautiful bride."

"But I fear for her prospects, nevertheless," added DuBois with a worried look.

"How can you doubt that she will marry well?" Father Regis replied.

"Because she, like her family, is a devout Catholic. And I fear what may become of us if the king takes retribution on Catholics after the Holy See stands in the way of his divorce."

Father Regis frowned as he reached again for his wine.

"Just as I fear for the rebuilding of our church," DuBois went on. "With such a threat, who can feel unfettered to give handsomely to the work on a church whose obedience continues to lie with the Holy Church in Rome."

DuBois paused to let his statement of Father Regis's principal problem weigh on the priest's mind.

"I myself would give you all the money you need for the church, but I alone cannot reach the sums you need."

DuBois paused.

"Nor can Richard Lanham," he added before taking a thoughtful sip of wine.

"The king's grant of rights to create and control the inland port in Atwelle languishes as His Majesty takes no action on any issue while he is distracted by his conflict with the pope and his desire for an heir. In the meantime, Lanham is not making sufficient revenue from his salt mines because without the port he cannot transport his salt to foreign markets.

"And Lanham has his own problem with having an heir. He cannot convince the king's chancellor to grant him rights for the port if he has no suitable heir of his own to carry on with the right to revenues from the port."

"But Lanham has his son Christopher," replied Father Regis.

"Let me ask you, Father Regis," said DuBois. "How do you think the king, who is fighting the pope for the right to bear a son, would take the advice of a chancellor who recommends giving royal rights to revenue that will end up in the hands of a monk?"

Father Regis said nothing.

"These are our circumstances, Father. Neither Lanham nor I as rivals can move the king. I cannot obtain the grant of rights to the port because of my family's long and loyal affiliation with the church, and I am running out of money. Lanham cannot obtain the grant of rights to the port because his son is about to take his vows as a monk, and Lanham is about to run short of money when he must make payments to the king on His Majesty's investment in the salt mines."

DuBois waited a moment before delivering his next point.

"And as a result, there is nowhere for you to go for sufficient sums to complete the construction of your church."

The priest sat there looking dejected.

"There's only one solution to all these problems," DuBois stated.

Father Regis still could only stare at the eels congealing in the sauce cooling on his plate.

"Though he will not speak to me, Lanham and I must combine our causes if we are to secure the king's grant of rights to the port and if you are to secure the funds you need for the church. And we must combine our causes by joining our families in a way that I obtain the funds I need to avoid losing everything I now own and in a manner that Lanham obtains a son who is an heir acceptable to the chancellor.

"Father Regis, look at me," directed DuBois. He took a deep breath. His wife eyed the priest intently.

"I want you to approach Richard Lanham to propose that my daughter become betrothed to his son with an ample payment to me for the privilege. Obtain his agreement to meet with me. And you must convince Christopher Lanham that he should not become a monk and should marry my daughter. If you are successful, there is a chance that there will be money to complete your church."

Father Regis laughed out loud.

"This is not a laughing matter, Father. I am deadly serious about making this happen."

"So am I, my son," replied Father Regis raising up his wine goblet as if to toast his good fortune. "I assure you—so am I."

2017 At a slow, measured, rhythmic pace, Father Adams and Father Lanham walked with Don down the aisle of the church, moving gradually toward the altar. Don observed how they both kept their hands folded before them as if they were prepared to start praying at any moment. He also noticed that each also kept his voice low as if practicing for prayer. Father Adams paused and looked up at the scaffolding that rose like a great blemish on the smooth wall of the church.

"So your discovery of the gargoyles on the roof beams continues today, Mr. Whitby?"

"Yes," Don replied. "Margeaux and I are going up the scaffold that has been moved down to the next roof beam. We expect to see a seventh wood carving there."

"Tell me more about what you've found."

Don described the order and detail of their discoveries and concluded that they were quite unique.

"Most unusual," Father Adams commented after listening closely. "Do you have a theory about these carvings? What they mean and why they were put here?"

"Not really." He decided not to mention Margeaux's suspicions about the gargoyles suggesting Squeaky's murder.

"And Miss Wood's project—studying the church?"

"She really hasn't been able to do much with the stained glass. I expect she'll see more soon when the scaffolding moves closer to the altar. She seems focused on the gargoyles at the moment."

After a few more of their rhythmic steps, Don turned to Father Adams. "Father, I don't mean to appear to be overreaching my responsibilities, but can you tell me how the fund-raising for the restoration project is going? Some of the companies and men working on the church have approached me. We will have some more pretty hefty bills coming soon, and I don't wish to be in the uncomfortable position of asking people to continue working when payment for past work continues to be in arrears."

Father Adams cleared his throat.

"I'll be honest with you, Mr. Whitby. At the moment, the amount of funding is not where we had anticipated it would be. However, I can report that I am close to arranging a substantial source of funding that alone will cover all the remaining costs of the project."

The vicar turned to Don with a smile.

"And, I'm happy to say, there should be a sizable sum left over at the end of it."

"That is gratifying to hear, Father," said Don. "You'll have to forgive me if I ask about this subject again. I've heard that before when working on churches."

"Yes, of course," replied Father Adams with a sigh. "I understand."

Don paused when they reached the point where the length of the nave intersected with the transept to create the form of a cross in the church's architecture. He pointed to the side chapel on the left.

"Father Lanham, if you don't mind my asking an obvious question, does the Lanham Chapel have any connection to your name?"

The young man smiled patiently as if it was not the first time the question had been asked.

"Yes, it does."

Don and Father Lanham wandered over to the side chapel while Father Adams continued walking down the length of the church, looking up frequently at the roof beams in the dark ceiling.

"Did you grow up in Atwelle?" Don asked him as they paused to inspect the Lanham chapel.

"No, I did not. The family name goes back centuries here, but we have not been in Atwelle or Norfolk for quite some time."

"How did you come to be the curate here?"

"My religious obligations were not planned," he answered. "In fact, they were rather unforeseen."

"What led you to become a man of the cloth?"

"It was the unexpected influence of a person in my life."

"Who was that?" Don was intrigued.

"I'd rather not say. It's a private matter. But she has defined my life to come."

Don saw Margeaux marching toward them and then glanced down the church at Father Adams. He lowered his voice, "Father Lanham, I'm interested in a curious thing about the attire of the clergy here. I've noticed that Father Adams wears a black clerical collar and black vestments. Can you tell me their significance?"

Margeaux walked up to them before Father Lanham could respond to Don's question. "Father Lanham—Don," she greeted them. "Can we head up the ladder now, Don?"

"Good morning," Don responded more formally than his usual manner. He turned back to the curate. "Excuse me, Father, but Miss Wood is keen to get on with business. Would you like to join us?"

"Thank you, no," Father Lanham responded as he moved off. "I should be joining Father Adams."

Don walked quickly to keep up with Margeaux. "As promised, we were able to move the platform as soon as possible to take a look at our next discovery. After you," he offered with a sweeping gesture.

Margeaux started to climb with her small rucksack filled with the flashlight, camera, binoculars, and notebook slung over her shoulder. Don followed dutifully.

At the top of the scaffold, they were greeted once again by the demon carved into the roof beam. There was the same evil grin with the exposed fangs and crooked teeth, the sunken eyes, the pointed ears, and the clawed hands reaching out to the smaller figure before him.

"I certainly recognize our old friend," said Don as he and Margeaux peered closely at the carving. "But the wood preservative and moisture have caused more deterioration to these carvings than the others. What do you think the smaller figure is?"

Despite its badly disfigured head, Margeaux thought she knew what the figure was. She instinctively reached out and stroked its unclothed body with her fingertips.

"I believe it's an infant," she said with a slight quaver in her voice. Her fingers moved from the carving's small plump belly up to its disfigured head where her touch lingered for a moment. "How soon can you move the scaffolding to the next carving across the way?" she asked as she pulled her camera out of the rucksack and started snapping photos.

"I don't know for sure," Don answered. "We're not really done with inspection and repairs on the ceiling where it is now."

He picked up Margeaux's binoculars and began examining the ceiling. Margeaux lowered the camera and looked directly at Don.

"Please hurry and move the scaffolding as soon as possible," she urged. Her request sounded almost like a plea. She looked once again at the carving of the baby and across the church to the opposite roof beam.

"I'll do what I can," he mumbled.

Margeaux gazed across the church to the roof beam at the other side. If there were similar carvings on that beam like the others, they were hidden in the darkness of the ceiling.

"Promise me you'll move the structure over there right away," she ordered.

"All right. All right. I said I'll do what I can," he responded as he placed his foot on the ladder for the first of his cautious steps down.

Margeaux placed her things back in the rucksack and walked over to the ladder. She paused and pointed her flashlight one more time at the small figure in the gargoyle's grasp. After a worried look, she quickly followed.

THIRTEEN

1532 Peter grinned with pleasure as Father Regis unexpectedly offered to refill his mug of ale from the cask in the priest's small cell.

"It is all quite remarkable, Peter. Unbelievable, actually," Father Regis exclaimed with uncharacteristic exuberance. He hummed the ballad he had heard from Margaret DuBois as he also drew himself a rare second mug of ale. Peter drank his ale in one long gulp and belched with another grin as he listened to Father Regis. He had never heard the priest hum before or seen him so happy. With monotone grunts, he tried to imitate the tune coming from Father Regis. The odd sounding combination of their voices filled Father Regis's room, where they had shared a humble dinner earlier than usual that day.

"You have no idea of my predicament. The workmen were demanding their wages with the threat of stopping their work on the church. And I promised their entire wages for the coming year by All Hallows' Day though I have not even a farthing to pay them."

The priest laughed out loud. "Then the good Lord provides for me like an unforgotten sparrow and a lily of the field who does not toil or reap."

Father Regis clapped his hands in sheer joy.

"First, Richard Lanham to my utter surprise instructs me to see that his son Christopher marries and marries soon. Then, to my amazement, Francis DuBois tells me that I am to propose to Richard that his daughter marry Lanham's son.

"And if I do, I shall be rewarded with the money to finish the church. I have that from both Lanham and DuBois."

Father Regis could not suppress another gleeful giggle. He had been talking so quickly that Peter did not even have the chance to repeat any words to please him. Sensing an opportunity, Peter held out his mug hopefully. The priest took the mug, distractedly refilled it, and handed it back without thinking.

"But how to convince Christopher not to take his vows, you might be asking." He looked at Peter with a conspiratorial expression. Peter wiped the ale from his chin.

"I know exactly how, Peter. Because I myself once faced the decision of whether to take my vows. I know the best tool to change Christopher's mind."

Father Regis turned to Peter as if he expected his grinning friend to venture a guess on what that tool was. Peter's smile grew tentative as he looked around uncertainly, thinking that Father Regis expected him to say something.

"'It is Margaret, Peter. The girl herself. What better persuasion to give up the vow of chastity than placing before him for the taking all the apparent and enticing advantages of foregoing that vow? And all with the encouragement of his priest and her family."

Father Regis gave Peter a look of pleased satisfaction before turning serious. "You will have to leave soon. No need to sweep today, my friend. Christopher Lanham will be arriving shortly, and then DuBois is dropping off his daughter so I can discuss with both of them my thoughts for the side chapels for their families."

The priest gave Peter a confident look. "Clever, eh?"

Peter watched Father Regis pacing about the small room and kept smiling though he had no idea about what the priest was talking. Father Regis eventually settled back onto his cot and fell into deep thought. Peter's eyes glanced around nervously as he did not know what to do in the unexpected silence.

"But I can only do so much," Father Regis muttered. "How can I . . ." his thought trailed off unfinished.

"Father Regis."

At the sound of a young man's voice, the priest leaped up from his cot and took Peter's arm.

"Go now, Peter. Go!" Father Regis all but pushed him out the door and down the narrow spiral stairs.

"Hello, Christopher," Father Regis greeted him with a brotherly embrace.

Christopher and Peter glanced at one another as Peter scurried through the door in the unfinished walls before Christopher stepped back and spoke to Father Regis.

"Father, it is good to see you. Bless me in this holy place."

The young man kneeled before him.

"Yes, yes," he said with a distracted look as he placed one hand on Christopher's bowed head and made the sign of the cross with the other.

"Thank you for inviting me here to discuss the designs for the family chapel," Christopher said as he rose from his feet.

"Of course," answered Father Regis. "We happily are approaching the time when such matters must be considered."

He smiled at the young man.

"I've also asked that someone from the DuBois family be here as well. I thought it made sense for both families to be present to discuss the plans for their chapels so that they can complement one another and the church without duplication."

"Yes, of course, Father. As you deem fit," said Christopher.

"Father Regis," another voice called out.

"I believe that is Francis DuBois," said Father Regis with a nervous smile as he turned to go to the door in the wall.

"Welcome, Francis," the priest greeted him. "And who do we have here?" Father Regis asked when he saw Margaret standing next to her father. Against her dress of deep green velvet, Margaret's cascading auburn hair was breathtaking.

"My apologies, Father. I cannot stay because of unexpected business," announced DuBois. "So I have asked Margaret to speak with you about the family's chapel. I expect she will be using it much longer than I," he said with a laugh.

"Oh, Christopher—I did not see you there. Greetings to you," said DuBois as he walked over to shake the young man's hand. DuBois looked up and down at Christopher's cowl. "You have become a man since I last saw you. How is your father?"

"Yes, it has been a while," answered Christopher. "My father is well, thank you."

"Christopher, this is my daughter Margaret." DuBois led her over by the hand to him where she gave a curtsy.

"Good day, Father Lanham," she said.

"Good day, Margaret," he said. "But I am afraid that despite my appearance, I am not yet a monk. Please, call me Christopher, just as you did when we played as children."

Margaret nodded shyly. DuBois and Father Regis exchanged a furtive look of approval.

"I am off to my business then," said DuBois. "Margaret, the carriage driver will come back and wait for you after I am delivered to my destination. Christopher—Father," he gave the two men a short bow as he turned and left.

The three of them strolled along the unfinished walls as Father Regis described the construction and the plans for completion of the church.

"It is quiet now that the workmen have gone home for the day," Father Regis observed as they walked through the blocks of stone and timbers of wood. He picked up a shovel that lay in their path and set it to the side. "It can be quite a commotion when they are at work."

He stopped and pointed to his left and right.

"Ahead of us will be the altar, and to the right will be the DuBois family chapel dedicated to your ancestors, Margaret. The Lanham chapel, dedicated to the memory of your sainted mother, Christopher, will be to the left."

The three of them talked for some time about the plans for the chapels. Father Regis was pleased at how the two young people seemed quite interested, and commented not only on their own family chapel, but on the other's chapel as well. Father Regis seized the mood of the moment.

"My children, we have more to discuss I am sure, but I must excuse myself for awhile to attend to a pressing matter. May I leave it to you two to carry on alone until I can return?"

"Of course, Father, if it is all right with Margaret," said Christopher with a deferential bow to the young lady.

"That would be fine, Father. We will have everything worked out by the time you return," she said with a smile.

"That would be lovely," said Father Regis from the bottom of his heart as he turned to go with a wave.

The two of them wandered on.

"Margaret, it is nice to see you again."

"And you too, Christopher," Margaret said, more relaxed now that it was just the two of them.

"It seems long ago that we played together as children," he commented.

"In some ways it does," she agreed. "But I suppose that in other ways we remain the same as we were then."

When they reached the spot where the altar was to be built, they found a dark hole in the ground.

"What is down there?" asked Margaret.

"That is the crypt from the original church," answered Christopher.

She peered into the darkness.

"Are there dead bodies down there?"

"I imagine so. The original church was built centuries ago. Crypts were built for burials."

"Remember when we played among the graves in the churchyard?" she asked while circling around the hole to look in from a different angle.

"I remember getting into trouble for it," he answered.

"We imagined there were witches and devils doing horrible things," she giggled.

"Yes," he replied. "And I learned later that in fact they exist and actually do those horrible things."

Margaret looked up at him abruptly.

"How do you mean?"

"When I studied at the monastery in Bavaria, I learned that the monks there dealt with all sorts of witchcraft, sorcery, and rites of Satan committed by villagers in the region. There were even books in the library on how to recognize such evil and exorcise it from places and people."

"Was any of it like we used to play among the graves in the churchyard?"

"Now that I think about it, it was." He smiled at the memory.

"Tell me about it," she insisted.

"Are you sure?"

"Yes."

Christopher looked around to confirm they were alone. He described the details of several satanic rites and sorcerer's rituals that he had studied at the monastery. When he finished, he noticed that her face was quite flushed.

"Margaret, I am sorry if I upset you," he apologized. "I should not have told you about—"

She walked over and fell to her knees before him, the velvet of her dress in the dirt at the entrance to the crypt. "Father, I want you to hear my confession."

"Margaret, I told you, I am not yet a monk. I cannot take your confession."

"Father," she repeated in a firm voice. "I want *you* to hear my confession."

2017 Margeaux was curled up in her favorite overstuffed chair in the corner of her college office. She smiled as she read out loud the cover page to Miss Weatherby's essay.

"'Satanic Rites in Bavaria in the Fifteenth Century'—more in the series by Miss Joan Weatherby," Margeaux announced to the empty room. She turned the essay over and set it down when she heard the knock on her door.

"Come in."

Margeaux immediately recognized her visitor by the black bowler hat that entered first.

"Good afternoon, Gerald. May I help you?"

"Good afternoon, Miss Wood. Sorry to interrupt."

"Yes, Gerald?"

"Well, Miss, there's a man here to see you."

He looked slightly uncomfortable.

"You're not jealous, are you Gerald?"

"Not at all, ma'am," the porter replied. "He says he's a policeman."

Margeaux frowned. "Short dark hair and a dark blue raincoat?"

"That would be him, Miss Wood. Would you like me to show him up?"

"I suppose so," replied Margeaux without enthusiasm.

Gerald paused at the door.

"Miss Wood?"

"Yes, Gerald?"

"Is everything all right?"

"Yes, of course."

Gerald did not look convinced.

"If you need anything, at any time, you'll let me know, won't you?"

"Yes, thank you, Gerald."

The porter turned to leave.

"Oh, Gerald," she called to him, interrupting his departure.

"Yes, Miss Wood?"

"Have you noticed a visitor coming into the college—a white haired clergyman wearing a black clerical collar?"

"Why yes," he answered. "Quite often lately."

"And you let him through the gate?"

"Of course," Gerald replied. "He comes often to visit the master of the college."

"The master?" she asked with surprise.

"Yes, ma'am. Should I get the policeman now?"

"Oh, yes. Thank you."

A few minutes later she heard the footsteps of the two men trodding up the narrow staircase. Gerald ushered in Margeaux's visitor and left the door slightly ajar as he exited the room.

"Good afternoon, Detective Steele," she greeted him as she rose to shake his hand. She noticed he wore the same dark blue rain coat and smelled of nicotine. She also thought he looked as if he was missing a few hours of sleep.

"Good afternoon, Miss Wood. I'm sorry to trouble you, but would you mind answering a few questions?"

"Of course not, Detective. But I've told you everything I know about Father Charleton and Don Whitby and Squeaky. I really don't think I have any more information that would be helpful."

"Miss Wood, how well do you know Brandi Knowleton?"

"Is that Brandi with one 'i'?" she asked.

Detective Steele gave her a look after the odd comment.

"She is the young woman who assisted at the church," Margeaux answered. "I met her only once, at the church when she had just returned from her holiday."

"Do you know if she had any enemies or was particularly afraid of anybody?"

"No, not really. We never really talked beyond our introduction. That was the night they found Squeaky in the churchyard."

As he wrote her answer down in a notepad, Margeaux asked, "Detective Steele, why are you asking me questions about Brandi?"

"We're questioning anyone who came into contact with her recently," he responded.

"But why ask questions at all? Is she suspected of some sort of wrongdoing?"

"Miss Wood, Brandi Knowleton is dead."

Margueax's face went pale. "How did she die?"

"I'd rather not say, Miss Wood."

Margeaux looked down at the floor for a moment and then back up at the detective.

"Was she decapitated?"

Detective Steele immediately stood. His notepad fell to the floor as he reached hastily into his pocket.

"Miss Wood, I must tell you that you do not have to say anything." He went on reciting in a rote cadence. "But it may harm your defense if you do not mention when questioned something which you later rely on in court. Anything you do say may be given in evidence."

"Detective, you don't have to give me a statement of my legal rights—"

He pulled a set of handcuffs out of his coat. "Miss Wood, please stand up very slowly, turn around, and place your hands behind your back. Do not make any sudden moves or try to flee."

"Detective, let me just explain."

"Do as I say—Now!" he commanded in a loud voice.

As she stood to turn, the door burst open. Gerald, complete with bowler hat, stepped between Detective Steele and Margeaux.

"I don't think you'll be doing that to Miss Wood while she's on these premises," the porter growled defiantly at the detective.

Detective Steele brought his mobile phone up to his mouth.

"Dispatch, this is Steele."

"Detective, Gerald, just hold on a minute!" Margeaux interrupted. "There's no need for any of this. Detective, may I just explain something to you?"

Steele looked at Gerald and brought the mobile phone to his mouth again.

"Gerald," Margeaux addressed him as calmly as she could. "Thank you, but there's no need for you to intercede here. I should talk to Detective Steele alone. Would you mind leaving the room please?"

Gerald hesitated.

"Everything's quite all right, Gerald. Please . . ." she pointed at the door.

"I'll be right outside the door, Miss Wood," he assured her.

"There's no need for that. Thank you."

She waited for him to close the door.

"Detective, may we please sit down so I can explain something?"

"I don't believe so, Miss Wood. There's no one outside the Norfolk police who knows Miss Knowleton was beheaded, except you apparently. You're in deep trouble, Miss Wood."

"I did not know that the poor woman was decapitated, Detective. I was surmising, and I believe you should know how it is that I could suggest that this happened to Brandi."

She sat back down in her chair.

"Please, Detective, sit down. And I think you'll need that notepad."

Steele sat down cautiously and without taking his eyes off her, picked the notepad up from the floor.

"I don't know anything about Brandi's death, Detective. But here's what I do know."

Margeaux proceeded to tell him about the discovery of the gargoyles. She described how they had found the gargoyle and the carving of the man with the skeletal arm soon after the death of Squeaky, whose arm she had seen was also skeletal.

Ignoring Steele's suspicious looks, Margeaux then told him about the discovery of the gargoyle with its claws around the neck of a young woman, followed by the gargoyle paired with the carving of the young woman with no head.

"It was troubling to see that, Detective," she went on, "but it had no meaning until you told me that Brandi was dead. I just guessed at how it happened. I'm sorry my guess turned out to be right," she concluded with a disbelieving shake of her head.

Detective Steele still looked at her skeptically. "What possible connection could there be between recently discovered gargoyles carved centuries ago and murders in Atwelle?"

"I don't know, Detective. But don't you think it's too remarkable to be coincidence?" she asked.

"Who knows about these gargoyles?"

"Well, Don Whitby and I discovered them."

She looked to see if the detective had a reaction, but saw none.

"Anyone else?"

"The church staff—Father Adams and Father Lanham. Miss Daunting."

"Anyone else?" he asked again.

"Well, Squeaky and Brandi knew that we had found the gargoyles, but I am not sure how much they knew about the details of the carvings. And I suppose anyone else those people might have told or anyone who might have climbed up for a look on their own. But I don't know who that might be."

"Have you told anyone else, Miss Wood?"

"No."

He looked at his notes and flipped over the pages.

"Not much of a lead, really. I can't move forward with this information."

He stood up.

"And I don't suppose I can interview the gargoyles, can I?"

The detective saw Margeaux was not amused.

"Miss Wood, I'm not going to take any action against you at this time. But let's just keep this discussion between you and me for the time being. Will you do that?"

"Yes," she agreed. "But what about the other gargoyles?"

"Which ones are those?" He flipped open his notepad once again.

"We think there might be others on the roof beams farther down the nave."

Detective Steele closed the notepad and slipped it into his coat pocket. "Why don't you just let me know if you find anything important when you get there, all right?"

Margeaux was trying to think of a response to make him take her seriously when the detective's phone rang loudly.

"Hello." He stood completely still as he listened intently for a moment. "I'm leaving Cambridge now. I'll be there in an hour."

Detective Steele quickly moved to the door. "I have to go. Thank you for your interesting observations, Miss Wood, and let me know if you see or hear anything suspicious."

Margeaux listened to Steele's heavy steps thumping quickly down the stairs. She threw herself into a chair and leaned forward with her hands covering her face. When her phone rang unexpectedly, she answered it quickly.

"Margeaux, this is Don."

From the sound of his voice, she knew he was upset.

"Brandi's dead!" he said. "They think she was murdered." Don paused. She could tell he was gathering himself. "And I just talked to Nigel Green. He's frantic. His baby boy has disappeared. The police think he may have been abducted."

There was no hesitation before her response.

"We have to look at the next gargoyle—now!"

"That's why I called," he replied. "Hurry!"

FOURTEEN

1532 A quick kiss on the cheek was the usual greeting for the sergeant.

"It hurts," he thought, "for what it is not."

Molly closed the door behind him and invited him to sit. He maneuvered the sword in its scabbard belted around his waist so he could lower himself into the chair. Unsure of his words, he tugged on one end of his great red mustache until Molly finally broke the silence.

"You are looking well, John."

The sergeant cringed at the formality of the conversation.

"Molly, may I speak plainly?"

"Of course, John. You are always free to speak your mind to me. I hope you know that."

"I would rather speak my heart, Molly."

Molly closed her eyes and sighed.

"John, you know that can lead to nowhere good. The desires of our hearts were forbidden long ago."

"That is my point, Molly. What happened to us—what was done to us—was long ago."

"And never to be undone," she said.

"And why not?"

"Because, John, nothing has changed. You came from a family of privilege. I came from a humble family, and my father often crossed the law. Now you are a man of consequence, respected and relied upon by all who live in Atwelle.

And I am," she paused, "let us just say that I am like my father."

"Yet we deeply loved each other when we were young," he said with a plea in his eyes, "and as to that, nothing has changed either."

"John, your feelings and your logic cannot prevail. You know that what you want simply cannot be."

"Molly, do you no longer love me?"

The sergeant could see that his question caused her pain.

"I will not answer, John, for even if I do love you—as deeply as I certainly did and as long as I am able—it could change nothing."

"My feelings, my words, they mean nothing to you?"

Standing, she walked over to the sergeant, placed a lingering kiss on his cheek, and stepped back to look into his eyes.

"No, John. They mean everything to me."

She watched the big man's eyes fill with tears. He stood and quickly wiped them away with a gloved hand.

"John, you must go now," she ordered in a soft voice.

He didn't move. She touched his cheek with her fingertips before going to the door, which she opened. She bent her head to indicate there was nothing more to be said.

The sergeant walked to the door and stopped beside her, staring straight ahead without moving. Her eyes stayed fixed on the floor. The two of them remained still, as if standing close without a touch or a look was all the pleasure they could share. A long moment later, he walked out into the dark alleyway without a word.

Molly moved to the stairs, but instead of going up she stood there a few moments dabbing her face with a kerchief. There came another knock on the door. She squeezed her eyes shut, wishing she were not there to answer it.

The door opened abruptly. DuBois stood scowling.

"You are to stop seeing my daughter," he declared in an angry voice.

She shook her head at the irony that his daughter had said the same to her about him. Molly decided to answer him as she had answered his daughter.

"If you do not wish me to see your daughter, maybe it is her to whom you should be speaking and not me."

She watched his face grow red and jumped as he slammed the door shut.

"You have met with her repeatedly," he accused. "Why have you done so?"

"It is she who has come to me," answered Molly. "The reasons were hers."

"I forbid you to see her again!" he shouted at her.

Molly turned her back to him. "I am afraid it is your daughter you will have to forbid, for they are her visits. And why do you assume that she visits for a reason that calls for them to be forbidden?"

"If she is coming to see you, it can be for no good."

She wheeled around with a hurt look.

"Is that why you come to see me—for no good?"

DuBois looked flustered at the question until the anger in his face softened.

"Look, Molly," he tried to reason with her. "I simply cannot have my daughter in your company."

Now it was Molly's face that turned angry. Her fists went to her hips in a defiant stance.

"And why is that, good sir? How can I be good enough for the company of the father but not good enough for the company of the daughter?"

He was at a loss for words and conceded the loss of momentum.

"Molly." His voice now tried to sound friendly. "You know what I am trying to say. I do not mean to insult you."

"Well you are doing a fair job of it."

She gave him the hurt look once again, this time with a pout.

"I guess what I am asking for is your help," he said. "Whatever it is you talk about with her, I ask you to let her be taught such things by another."

"If your daughter visits me to be taught something, it is likely something someone should have taught her before. Perhaps she is asking for my help, just as you are now."

DuBois realized he was continuing to lose ground in the battle he had started.

"I am sorry to have spoken so harshly. You can understand a father will sometimes go too far to protect his daughter."

Molly thought of her drunken father throwing a mug of ale at her when she was a young girl. When she said nothing, DuBois dug a small purse of coins out of his doublet.

"Look, I am sorry if I offended you." He handed her the purse as a conditional surrender. "Take this, and please have nothing to do with my daughter again. Would you please do that, my dear?"

Molly accepted the purse, then took his arm and steered him over to the door.

"You have nothing to worry about, my dear DuBois. Her visits to me are very different from yours."

"I am sure," he said with a smile of relief. "But how is it that they are different?"

Molly gave him a smile in return that vanished as quickly as it appeared.

"She does not have to pay for me to see her."

The door slammed in his face.

DuBois stood there in stunned silence. Wondering if he had been successful in his task and whether he could ever see Molly again, he headed down to the tavern at the bottom of the lane, hoping that a mug of strong ale would help him make sense of his encounter.

Hearing the door slam, Peter leaned out of his favorite seat in the dark doorway up the alley. He watched with curiosity as DuBois stood before Molly's house for a moment before walking down to the tavern. Then a smile came to his face as he realized that he could please Father Regis by recounting what he had just seen.

Peter turned quickly at the sound of a footstep in the lane right behind him. Too late, he threw his hands up in a futile attempt to protect himself. A long-handled spade swung full force into his face, followed immediately by another blow.

2017 Margeaux pulled her car up as close to the church as she could park. The building was completely dark. The wind howled out of low black clouds that made the whole town seem like it sat in a shadow of the season's early nightfall.

She sat there nervously for a few minutes looking for any movement or lights that she hoped would indicate Don was already there. The only movement came from the trees bending violently in the turbulent wind. Finally, the headlights of a car swept across her as Don wheeled in and skidded to a stop next to her.

As they got out of their cars, they looked at each other without speaking before moving to the main entrance to the church. There the cold gusting wind buffeted them while Don fumbled to find the key that unlocked the door. He cursed when none of the keys worked to open it.

"Do you have your flashlight?" he finally asked her in exasperation. He blew on his hands to warm them as Margeaux fished the flashlight out of her rucksack.

As she pointed the light toward the key ring, he struggled uncertainly from key to key until he held up an oversized iron key.

"Follow me," he shouted at Margeaux over the wind rushing through the large oak trees. "This will get us in."

With her skirt whipping about her knees, she trailed Don around the corner of the church past the tombstones leaning in the untrimmed grass. When they reached a low door at the side of the church, Don jammed the large key into an ancient rusty lock, twisted it hard, and jammed his shoulder into the heavy wood to push the door open.

Once inside the church, the two of them searched along the wall to find a light switch. Margeaux's flashlight finally focused on a single switch. But when she flipped it, the only light that came on was a single light bulb off to the side in the DuBois chapel.

She and Don hurried back to the wall across from the scaffold on the opposite side of the church from where they had viewed the gargoyle holding the baby. Margeaux pointed her flashlight at the roof beam above. They strained their eyes to see up into the black ceiling.

"This is hopeless," declared Don in frustration. He turned on his heel and ran over to the low door where he ducked his head to exit without slowing down.

Margeaux stood there not knowing what to do until she saw Don awkwardly steering a long weather-beaten ladder through the low door. As he took it off his shoulder and placed it against the wall under the roof beam, Margeaux wondered if it was the ladder from the side of the church where Squeaky's body had been found.

"Give me your flashlight," he instructed.

He grabbed the side rails of the ladder firmly, placed one foot on the highest step he could reach, and then stood motionless.

"Are you okay?" Margeaux asked a moment later when Don, looking up into the darkness, still had not moved.

"I'm not sure I can do this," he said. "Perhaps we should wait for the scaffold."

"Don, we've got to see what's up there."

He stayed frozen to the floor.

"Is it the height?" she asked.

Don bit his lip and said nothing. Margeaux took the flashlight from his hand and moved him aside with a firm push.

Centered in front of the ladder, Margeaux put her foot on the first rung and gingerly tested it before she pulled herself up with her hands. The ladder creaked loudly as if it were protesting her weight. Standing still until nothing more happened, she stepped to the next rung, then the next, and continued climbing cautiously higher and higher. Don tried to steady the ladder at the bottom, listening apprehensively to its occasional groans.

As Margeaux approached the top, a rung cracked loudly under her foot. The ladder shuddered awkwardly as Margeaux quickly shifted her weight off the rung to regain her balance.

"Are you all right?" Don called up to her.

"Yes," she answered in a voice that sounded far away. "It didn't break."

He could feel the side rails of the ladder tremble as Margeaux climbed the last few rungs at the top. All he could see was the silhouette of Margeaux's head as she pointed the flashlight up at the roof beam.

Margeaux said nothing. A moment later, Don could stand it no longer.

"Margeaux, what's up there?"

She still remained silent.

Very slowly, Margeaux started to make her way down the ladder. The flashlight scanned about in random jerks as her hand went from rung to rung.

"What did you find?" he demanded when she reached the bottom.

"You had better look."

He looked unnerved.

"You want me to go up on the ladder?" His face paled.

"Don, I think you should see what's up there," Margeaux insisted once again.

He swallowed hard, took the flashlight from her, and stepped over to face the ladder. He tried to take a deep breath, but his breathing became faster and shallower. Feeling lightheaded, he heard only the distant din of the wind outside as he started to climb.

Haltingly at first, Don climbed up into the darkness rung by rung. Then, despite the occasional creaking complaint from the ladder, he started to feel a rhythm in his steps until he realized how high he had climbed. He could not help but glance down. Margeaux seemed miles below him. He closed his eyes to stop the dizziness that came over him. After a couple attempts to breathe deeply, he was relieved to feel the dizziness pass and opened his eyes to start climbing again.

There in the beam of his flashlight, on the rail of the ladder, was a dark crimson stain.

"Squeaky's blood," he thought.

"Don!" Margeaux shouted as she saw him sway from the center of the ladder. "Maybe you should come down."

At the sound of her voice, Don managed to steady himself. With a determined shake of his head, he carefully placed his hand above the blood stain and began climbing again. His heart skipped a beat every time he felt the length of the ladder flex and sag under his weight as he neared the top. The pungent odor of wood preservative mixed with the chalky smell of dust made his queasy stomach churn. He stopped when his eyes finally came level with the worn ends of the ladder's rails.

Gripping the top rung as hard as he could with one hand, he pointed the shaking flashlight in his other hand up at the roof beam.

"No," he groaned as he shut his eyes and turned his face to the side. When he could, he forced himself to look back up.

The wooden gargoyle's constant smile appeared jubilant as the long nailed fingers of one claw clasped the ankles of a delicately sculpted infant hanging upside down with its blood carved in furrowed streams flowing from its heart into the other cupped claw of the elated demon.

FIFTEEN

1532

To the Church Wardyns of St. Clement's in the Parish of Atwelle,

Upon the dethe of Peter, born of this parish to parents unknown, I gyft to the Church in his name the account of £10, mony saved from my own accounts as my needs are few and my requirements are humble, so that he may be beryd in the Churchyard of the parish he served and be remembered with the purchase of two sylver candlesticks to be placed on the altar of the Church remade to the Glory of God.

He is not but a corps with an arme mysteriously mangled. He is my frynde whose soul rests in heavyn.

Seculum seculi Amen.

Father Regis Hollowell

2017 "More bills to pay," grumbled Miss Daunting as she leaned over to pick up from the floor the small pile of envelopes that the postman had slipped through the mail slot of her front door. Standing up stiffly, she tossed some of her long gray tresses back over her shoulder before heading to the kitchen where she dropped the mail on the table.

"Bills, bills, and more bills as usual, I suppose," she mumbled as she carefully poured hot water from the tea kettle into the pot, delicately replaced the chipped lid and covered the pot with a tea cosy stained from decades of use. Setting the teapot on the table, the old woman sat down to start working her way through the pile by picking up each invoice, acknowledging it with a disapproving grunt, and placing it unopened on a new pile to the side.

"Here—what's this?"

She held up and studied an envelope with her name and address handwritten on the front. Instead of placing it with the other mail, she set the letter on the table in front of her before pouring herself a cup of tea. Stirring her tea absentmindedly, she picked up the envelope and examined it once more.

"Maryhouse Hall," Miss Daunting read out loud as if there were people sitting around the table waiting to hear her announcement of the return address. Ignoring her tea, she slid the blade of a letter opener into the envelope and after a few tugs upward had torn it open. She carefully removed and unfolded the fine heavy stationery. Holding it in both hands, Miss Daunting read the letter with her lips moving silently with each word:

Maryhouse Hall
Cambridge

Dear Miss Daunting,

I thought it might be nice for the two of us to take the opportunity to get to know each other better since we've both been working in the church these few months. So I'd like to invite you to be my guest next

Friday to dine at Maryhouse Hall. I thought you might enjoy the experience and privilege of dining at High Table with the fellows of a Cambridge College.

It also occurred to me that I might able to be of some help to you. You've mentioned several times that you sometimes have difficulty making ends meet on your pensioner's income. As it happens, there may be some funds related to my project at St. Clement's that could be used to compensate you for assisting me in my project. It would not be difficult work and it might be quite helpful to you financially. Perhaps we can chat about this when we get together.

I'll happily pick you up in Atwelle, and then we can drive to Cambridge, have sherry in my study, and dine in Hall. You'll be home by bedtime, I promise.

I do hope you can make it. Just ring me and let me know if you can join me.

Yours,
Margeaux Wood

Miss Daunting set the letter down with a surprised and pleased look.

"Thank you very much, dearie," she said, looking over at the pile of unopened bills. "Thank you very much indeed."

SIXTEEN

1532 The Greene Man Tavern had served ale to the residents of Atwelle for as long as anyone could remember. Through wars, plagues, storms, fires, and every lean time for the villagers, The Greene Man had survived. For centuries, year in and year out, men with tankards of ale had ducked their heads under the heavy beams in its low ceiling to make their way to the stones of the great hearth that were fired warm in winter and shaded cool in summer.

"Good sirs, as you ordered," said a slightly nervous publican as he set two tankards of ale on the table separating two men who had never before been seen there together. "This should do to refresh a parched throat."

Grabbing the flagons before them, Francis DuBois and Richard Lanham ignored the man as they cautiously eyed each other with a mixture of longstanding familiarity and current distrust. DuBois thought Lanham's plain cap without jewels or feathers matched his unimaginative personality. Lanham on the other hand looked disapprovingly at the colored fabric and furs worn by DuBois that were not permitted under the sumptuary laws for a mere gentleman who was not of a higher rank. After a long draft of ale, the men set down their tankards and resumed their scrutiny of each other.

"Lanham," DuBois finally spoke after drinking again and wiping the ale from his mouth, "you are as tight as a frog's arse underwater."

Lanham's eyes narrowed as he glared back at DuBois.

"And you couldn't hold onto a coin if it were sewed into your glove."

The exchange was like the first clash of blades by two wary swordsmen who were feeling each other out.

"All right," said Lanham, "the priest wanted us to talk. What do you want to talk about?"

"Look, Lanham," DuBois made the first thrust. "We have the chance for ships to drink from the water of an inland port in Atwelle that will make us both wealthier men. And you have managed to piss in the well with your bumbling politics and communications to the lord chancellor."

Lanham glowered in return. "I don't think you mind one whit that having no access to the sea prevents me from sending the salt from my mines to very profitable markets while the pope ponders what the Bible says about who can marry whom. And your pope has managed to mire the Royal Court in a swamp of theological claptrap that prevents anything from happening for the benefit of the realm."

Lanham emphasized his words by throwing back a quick swallow of ale and banging his mug firmly on the table.

DuBois scowled back at him. "Do you not think that I, too, would like to have ready access to those markets for my wool and grain?"

They were silent, both with jutting jaws. Retreating from their impasse, they sat back and took an aggressive swig of ale and then another. There was a lull in their thrust and parry while both men seemed to be reflecting into their tankards.

"More?" DuBois looked up and asked Lanham.

Lanham nodded. DuBois beckoned to the attentive publican who hurried over with two more flagons of ale. Both men took another deep draught and set down their tankards without speaking. The tension between them finally seemed to ease.

"He's not the same king now," remarked Lanham a moment later with sorrow in his voice. "Do you remember our last battle in France?"

When a wan smile appeared under DuBois' beard Lanham continued, "The king was right there with us. He was a man of action. He did not hesitate for a moment in deciding to do battle."

"And a good thing for us," replied DuBois. "Kings going to war have made our families a fortune for centuries."

Lanham's chest rose and fell with a small sigh. "Now the king will not even go to the royal privy without consulting the lord chancellor or seeking the pope's permission."

"Richard," DuBois responded as if they once again were colleagues in arms, "you must not discount the power of the Church. The land holdings of the churches and monasteries are significant. Its wealth continues to grow. And the people are as close to the Church as they are to the king. If anything, their loyalty is greater to the Church's power over the hereafter than to His Majesty's power over the here and now."

DuBois leaned forward and looked Lanham straight in the eye. "If the king and the pope are at odds, it is imperative that you and I not war with each other."

After a moment, Lanham nodded in agreement. "Only if we act together is there a chance of the king granting the rights to the port and its revenue."

DuBois made the next move.

"I need to act to show my allegiance to the king and alleviate his concerns about my relations with the Church. And you need to show the king that his grant of rights and revenues will not fall into the hands of the Church through your inheritance to your son.

"And yet we must do nothing to harm our relations with the church, for if the pope concedes to a new marriage, the Church and the king will continue to act in concert."

The men pretended to puzzle over the dilemma as they sipped at their ale until they simultaneously interrupted one other with the same solution.

"Our children must marry."

"We must marry our children."

At first, a smile came over their faces. Then, raising their tankards in an unspoken toast, they laughed out loud and drank like old comrades.

When their flagons fell back to the table, they hunched forward to plan the order of battle.

"We have two problems," began DuBois. "Your son intends to become a monk."

"Yes, that seems to be the case," said Lanham. "But I am taking steps to change those plans."

"I am aware of this already," replied DuBois.

"And the second problem?" Lanham asked.

"A marriage to my daughter will require a financial payment from you."

"What do you mean?"

"Just as I have said. If you want my leave to allow your son to marry my daughter, you will have to pay for the privilege."

"Now hang on. It is you, the bride's father, who should be paying a dowry to the groom."

"And I am happy to do so," replied DuBois, "out of your payment to me."

"That is preposterous!" Lanham angrily exclaimed. "What do you think you are doing, turning the dowry on its head?"

"I seek simply to settle the arrangements for our mutual desire to have our children marry," DuBois responded matter-of-factly.

Lanham studied DuBois for a moment as if he suspected something more, some cunning behind DuBois' demand perhaps. "How much do you seek?"

DuBois calmly stated his price. Lanham's mouth dropped open.

"Surely you jest, sir!"

"There is no jest in my terms, Richard. That is the price of my partnership."

"You would bargain with the flesh of your own daughter?" There was scorn in Lanham's voice.

"My *only* daughter," DuBois clarified. "So I won't bargain. You have heard my terms."

Lanham's face grew red with anger. DuBois looked at him calmly.

"And what about you? You seem perfectly willing to trade the desire of your son's heart for the money that will go into your pocket from shipping the salt of our earth. The price of my daughter's body—in exchange for your son's soul. That seems a fair bargain."

Lanham considered the offer for a moment. His agitation gradually eased.

"What assurances do I have on this arrangement?" he asked.

"Once you sort out the saving of your son from the Church and using him for your own ends, you have my daughter in a marriage to him without recourse. She is effectively a hostage."

"And what assurances do I have?" DuBois retorted.

"You'll have your money. And is my son in marriage to your daughter not your hostage?"

"And what of the grant of rights for the port and its revenues?" DuBois leveled the question at Lanham like a crossbow armed with an arrow.

"We shall combine our petitions to the king."

"And if one of us falls out of favor because of any action by the pope to support or oppose the king?"

"If the king will grant the petition to one of us only, then you and I agree between us to divide the revenues from the port through our united families," answered Lanham.

After a moment's silent deliberation, the two men looked each other in the eye. Lanham lifted up his tankard.

"DuBois, you are as tight as a frog's arse underwater."

"And you, Lanham, could not hold onto a coin if it were sewn into your glove."

The two men laughed, drank, and rose to give each other a hearty handshake.

2017 "More tea, Margeaux?"

"No thank you, Master Hodges," replied Margeaux.

The Master of Maryhouse Hall poured himself another cup of tea and walked back over to the large desk in his office. He sat down to face her.

"Tell me, how is your research going?" he asked in his deep voice.

"It's going well, thank you," she answered, trying to sound convincing.

"Tell me about your funding situation," he said as if finally reaching his agenda.

"Well, Master Hodges, I have some private funding in the works. But that's too preliminary at this point to comment upon," she hastened to add.

"Very well, then." The master did not look encouraged. He looked at his desk calendar for his next appointment.

"Master Hodges," she took back his attention, "there is one more thing that I thought I should bring to your attention as it may affect my project funding."

"Yes?"

"There have been some rather unfortunate incidents at St. Clement's of late. Rather horrible, actually. Two murders of staff and the disappearance of a baby in the town."

"Yes, I read about them in the papers," he frowned. "Mutilated bodies. Very bad business."

Margeaux looked slightly surprised.

"How is it that you know details about the bodies?" she asked. "There's been no description of the bodies in the press. The police have been keeping very quiet."

The master glanced away with an uncomfortable look and cleared his throat.

"I have some sources of information in that area." He paused and then looked at her with a serious expression. "Do you fear for your safety at all, Margeaux?"

"Well, I confess that dealing with this situation is disconcerting. I'm a little unnerved maybe, but at the moment not so frightened as to leave my project."

"Yes, well I'm glad to hear that." He glanced again at his calendar as he rose to end the meeting. "But you must let me know if you become afraid for your well-being at any point.

"By the way," the master said as he led her to the door, "that was a rather interesting-looking guest you had at High Table last week. Her hair was most . . ." he paused for the right word, "unique—for a woman of her age, that is," he tried to end diplomatically.

"Yes," Margeaux responded in agreement. "She's actually from Atwelle, a volunteer at St. Clement's."

"You two seem quite good friends," he commented as he opened the door.

"Yes, we are now. We've surprisingly managed to become quite supportive of one another," Margeaux answered with a pleasant smile.

"How nice," the master replied. "Good to see you again, Margeaux. Do keep me informed about your research."

After closing his study door and returning to his desk, he picked up the phone.

"Jane, has Father Adams arrived yet?

"Very good," he added after a pause. "Please bring him in at once."

SEVENTEEN

1532 The sergeant nodded casually to a man coming out of The Greene Man when he turned into the narrow lane behind the building and tried to appear that he had no particular purpose there. Once he drew nearer to Molly's house, he glanced around to check that he was not being watched. His insides grew tight as he felt the usual anxious anticipation of seeing her while still steeling himself to face the inevitable disappointment of rejection.

Upon reaching her house, the sergeant once again stopped and looked around carefully. He could see no one, and no one could see him. Nervously, he smoothed his mustache with a gloved hand before reaching out to knock on the door. His hand stopped in midair when he noticed the door was slightly ajar.

He slowly pushed the door open. "Molly?" he called out tentatively.

Hearing no answer, he stepped inside and called out her name once more. After a moment's silence, he closed the door quietly and took two measured, muted steps into the room. Then he saw a few drops of blood on the floor next to the thick wooden post that supported the stairs to her bedroom.

The sergeant slowly slid his sword from its scabbard. He stepped noiselessly over to the wooden post and studied the blood. Preparing to move guardedly up the stairs, he looked up at the door to Molly's bedroom.

With a jerk of his head, his eyes jolted shut as something splashed on his brow. Before his hand reached his brow, another drop hit his forehead. The sergeant stepped away and wiped at his face. When he saw the wet red smear on his fingertips, he looked up to see the drops of blood beginning to fall steadily from the top stair.

The sergeant bounded to the top of the stairs with astonishing speed and banged open the bedroom door with the hilt of his sword.

"My God—No!" he cried out.

He turned his head away, his fist gripping the handle of his sword pressed against the side of his head. Squeezing his eyes shut, he tried to force from his mind the sight of the pool of blood spreading from Molly's headless corpse.

The sergeant finally forced himself to look back on the room. His eyes searched for any sign of her beautiful blonde curls until he could stand the sight of the horror before him no longer. Stumbling back, he spun around and careened down the stairs where he blindly lurched back over to the wooden post.

"No!" he cried out again in a voice filled with pain.

Tears streamed from his eyes as he looked once more at the drops of her blood falling on the floor.

"No!" he shouted once more, this time in rage.

He raised his sword above his head with both hands and struck the thick wooden post below the stairs with a stunning blow. Chips of wood flew across the room as he raised the sword above his head a second time.

"No!" he yelled again as the sword hacked another deep wound into the wood of the post.

"No—no—no—no!"

With each successive strike of the sword to the wood, his cries became fainter. Breathing hard, he paused before slowly raising the sword even higher over his shoulder and striking the post with a final great blow that made the whole house shudder. The edge of the sword buried itself into the wood so deeply that when the sergeant tried to yank it out, the sword would not budge. He tried once more without result. With a frustrated sob, he gave the sword a third, much weaker pull, that again was unsuccessful.

Grabbing the handle of the sword with both hands, he balanced on both feet spread wide for a last effort to lurch the sword free when suddenly he stopped. His shoulders dropped. His hands fell from the sword and his arms hung limp. Slowly his legs buckled until his knees hit the floor with a thump.

The· sergeant's head hung between his hunched shoulders. He breathed hard as he remained kneeling. Without raising his head, he lifted an arm and rested his hand on the handle of the sword stuck solidly in the wooden post.

Surrendering to reality, his breathing turned into small sobs until his big shoulders started heaving uncontrollably with weeping.

2017 It was as if the low threatening clouds above St. Clement's had seeped inside its walls to brood over the people filling the church. Surrounded by Brandi's many friends, Margeaux and Don sat next to Miss Daunting and Father Lanham to pay their respects at her funeral. Though hearts were heavy at her mysterious death, there also was unspoken anxiety weighing on every villager from the unsolved disappearance of Nigel Green's son.

Father Adams stepped into the pulpit slowly and opened the large Bible lying in front of him.

"From the Book of Job," was all he announced without raising his eyes. His deep sonorous voice made the words sound as if they were directed individually to each person sitting before him.

And the Lord said unto Satan, From whence comest thou? And Satan answered the Lord, and said, From going to and fro in the earth, and from walking up and down in it.

And the Lord said unto Satan, Hast thou considered my servant Job, that there is none like him in the earth, a perfect and an upright man, one that feareth God, and escheweth evil? And still he holdeth fast his integrity, although thou movedst me against him, to destroy him without cause.

And Satan answered the Lord, and said, Skin for skin, yea, all that a man hath will he give for his life. But put forth thine hand now, and touch his bone and his flesh, and he will curse thee to thy face.

And the Lord said unto Satan, Behold, he is in thine hand; but save his life. So went Satan forth from the presence of the Lord, and smote Job with sore boils from the sole of his foot unto his crown.

And he took him a potsherd to scrape himself withal; and he sat down among the ashes. Then said his wife unto him, Dost thou still retain thine integrity? Curse God, and die.

But he said unto her, Thou speakest as one of the foolish women speaketh. What? Shall we receive good at the hand of God, and shall we not receive evil?

Father Adams slowly looked up at everyone and asked them, "And shall we not receive evil? We come here to present ourselves before the Lord, as the people of Atwelle have for centuries. Would not Satan, going to and fro in the earth and walking up and down in it, also come among us?

"We receive good at the hand of God, but does that mean we should expect to receive only good at all times? Shall we not also receive evil?" he asked again.

"Would not Satan and his agents commit his evil rites that touch our bone and our flesh? And just how could Satan come among us? Is it the vicious act of one deranged person who would do the Devil's bidding? Or would he test us all on a grand scale to see whether all of us will eschew evil and hold fast our integrity?

"Has Satan not tested us by using the foundations of our society to smite all of mankind with sore boils from the soles of our feet to the crown of our heads? For the society of mankind is a history of satanic rites.

"In a 'civilized society,' slaves were tortured with the rending of their flesh and the denial of their freedom while they lived. In our 'civilized society,' the entire lives of serfs were given by force to feudal lords. Our 'civilized society' was revolutionized by the greed of industry, sickening men and women as if the Devil himself invidiously commanded that the very labor of their hands should smite them with sore boils.

"Satan claimed to God that 'Skin for skin, yea, all that a man hath will he give for his life.' Does not mankind use the skin of one race to suppress another 'for his life' as if committing a rite directed by Satan himself?

"And how better to curse God to His face than to destroy the great gift that He gave to sustain us by cannibalizing the planet on which we live to satisfy our human appetites for pleasure instead of meeting the needs of human suffering.

"The rites of Satan in our lives every day, whether through the acts of men and women or through our so-called civilized society, touch our bone and flesh with the sore boils of war, violence, crime, hunger, and suffering, from the soles of our feet unto the crowns of our heads."

Father Adams fell silent as his eyes met those looking up at him.

"And shall we not receive evil?"

He paused.

"We know from Brandi's death that we shall. The question is whether we will remain upright, fear God, and retain integrity in the face of such evil."

His voice turned ominous.

"Or curse God and die."

With a concluding gesture, he bowed his white head and closed the Bible. Several minutes later, the service ended. Margeaux and Don stood in line to exit the church.

"Not much solace there," Margeaux commented.

"Well, he did leave out the fire and brimstone," offered Don.

When they stepped outside, the fresh air, even under the gray sky, raised their spirits until they heard their names called out by a familiar voice. Detective Steele approached them, accompanied by an official-looking person.

"Miss Wood, Mr. Whitby, this is Chief Inspector Russell. He is assisting in the investigation, in light of its increased complexity."

The chief inspector gave each of them a brief businesslike handshake as if the contact had successfully secured their fingerprints and DNA. With a neatly trimmed gray mustache and thinning hair combed over his bald pate, he looked old enough to be Steele's father. Like Steele, he wore a raincoat, but his was a khaki color to Steele's dark blue.

"Nice of you to come to the service to pay your respects, Detective," said Don. "Or is it part of official duty in the investigation?"

He could tell from the look in response that Detective Steele did not appreciate the question.

"Both," the detective gave a clipped reply, "if that's what you'd like to think."

Margeaux shifted uncomfortably as Detective Steele went on. "I mentioned to Inspector Russell your theory about there being a connection between the incidents here in Atwelle and the gargoyles you have been discovering."

"Yes," Inspector Russell joined in. "It's an original theory, I'll give you that. But I'm afraid it's a bit of a reach, if you know what I mean."

"But Inspector," Margeaux replied, "you have to admit that the coincidence, if that's what it in fact is, is rather extraordinary."

"Coincidence, extraordinary or not, doesn't really tell us who committed the crimes and certainly will not convict the criminal," Inspector Russell responded. "More likely a psycho serial killer who's associated with or hangs around the church."

"Or maybe more than one killer," said Detective Steele.

Spotting Father Adams, Inspector Russell excused himself to head over to talk to the vicar.

"What about Nigel's missing baby?" Don asked Detective Steele.

"Still no information on the infant's whereabouts," he answered. He looked around and lowered his voice.

"But I do have a surprising lead and may be coming close to making an arrest soon."

"Who do you think—," said Margeaux, but her question was interrupted by Detective Steele's upraised palm.

"Sorry. Police business," he said, watching their reaction with a grim, polite smile until he turned to go join Inspector Russell.

EIGHTEEN

1532 "You sent for me, Father?"

Christopher Lanham looked around the door into his father's study. Richard Lanham stopped pacing in front of the dark wood paneling. With his arms folded, he looked up and smiled.

"Come in, son."

When Christopher entered the room, he saw Francis DuBois sitting at his father's desk.

"Good morning, Christopher. Good to see you," DuBois offered a pleasant greeting.

"And you, sir," Christopher replied with a respectful bow.

DuBois noticed the young man was not wearing a monk's cowl. Instead he was dressed in casual clothes and appeared to have been outside already, despite the early hour. "Have you been hunting, Christopher?" asked Lanham.

Christopher hesitated.

"In fact, I have Father."

DuBois looked pleased. "If I may say so, Christopher, I am happy that you and my daughter—"

"I am indeed sorry to interrupt you, good sir," Christopher addressed DuBois before turning to his father. "But I must be off to see some servants."

His father frowned. "Christopher, I had hoped you would join us to meet with the sergeant. We are conferring with him in a moment to address the unfortunate criminal acts that have occurred in Atwelle of late."

"I am afraid, Father, that I am obliged to meet with Geoffrey and his wife."

He looked at Lanham and then at DuBois with an apologetic explanation.

"Geoffrey and his wife have been faithful servants at Lanham Manor as long as I have been alive. They are doing me a particular service and are expecting me just now to do my bidding. And I fear I am in need of their aid at the moment."

"Very well then. Go tend to your matter," said Lanham who did not look happy at his son's decision to go visit their servants instead of joining the conversation.

"Gentlemen," Christopher bid them adieu with a small bow as he backed out the door. Hurrying off in the direction of the small cluster of servants' huts near the animal barns, Christopher did not notice the sergeant, who slipped behind a tree and watched him closely until he entered the house of the servants.

A few moments later, the sergeant was standing before Lanham and DuBois in the study. Without his usual good humor, he stood silently before them, looking tired and drawn. Lanham, his arms still crossed, avoided looking at the sergeant by turning to stare out the window as DuBois spoke.

"Sergeant, we have asked you here to address the regrettable incidents that have occurred recently in Atwelle. Now I know the unfortunate souls may not have been of a station that would bring concern to many, but such incidents nevertheless can have harmful consequences."

The sergeant's eyes narrowed at DuBois as his expression became even grimmer. DuBois continued without noticing.

"We are trying to promote Atwelle as a potential center for commerce, perhaps the biggest market town in Norfolk outside of Norwich if the king gives us a grant of rights for the port in Atwelle. We want nothing to raise fear in those who would otherwise be inclined to come here to buy and sell their wares."

DuBois looked at the sergeant for some sign of assent, but was confronted only with an unsmiling stony face. Lanham continued to avert his eyes from the conversation.

"Moreover, if these crimes, given their horrific nature, are not solved and the perpetrator is not brought to justice, the chancellor might even use the situation as an impediment to the king's granting our petition for the rights to the port. Even a delay of the king's action on the petition from your failure to bring the criminal to task with dispatch could be an economic disaster for us."

DuBois paused, disappointed at the sergeant's silence.

"Sergeant, it is imperative," DuBois said with concluding emphasis, "that you bring the criminal to speedy justice with utmost expediency and without any mercy."

The sergeant thought of Father Regis's identical request. But more for Peter, it seemed, for Father Regis had barely mentioned Molly, and then had referred to her only as "that woman." He also recalled with indignation the reaction of Molly's father to the news of her death as if the man had merely lost a casual acquaintance.

Uncertain of how to deal with the sergeant's reticence, DuBois looked over at Lanham. Lanham's arms were now crossed more in self-defense than as a gesture of authority. His gaze did not turn from the window. With no response from Lanham, DuBois struggled for something to secure the sergeant's acknowledgement and assumption of the task.

"It is reported, Sergeant, that the workmen at the church are saying that the murders are a sign of evil spirits about and that they may readily desert the construction and flee the town."

The sergeant still said nothing. Now DuBois began to grow angry at the man's refusal to reply. Though Dubois started to turn red at the sergeant's apparent insolence, his anger was nothing like the seething rage behind the sergeant's emotionless mask. The sergeant thought nothing of their commercial risk, of the priest's concern, of the church, or of justice. His whole being was focused solely on a single undistracted, undiluted desire.

Revenge for Molly's murder.

"Have you taken any action at all to find the person responsible for these murders?" DuBois demanded.

"I have," the sergeant answered in a threatening tone. His fist tightened on the handle of his sword. "And I will apprehend who it is that did murder—though you gentlemen may not like it when I do."

Lanham's head turned away from the window. He and DuBois looked at each other and then at the sergeant. A moment of tense silence was broken by the study door suddenly swinging open. Father Regis rushed into the room.

"The wood-carver's baby—has been abducted!" the winded priest managed to gasp between breaths. "He was taken during the night."

Father Regis looked from Lanham to DuBois and then up at the sergeant. There was a panicked plea in his eyes.

"You must do something! The workers will leave if Bittergreen goes."

2017 There was a definite look of uncertainty on Miss Weatherby's face. Her pursed lips and furrowed brow set several of her piercings pointing off at odd angles.

"Do you really think this essay assignment would be within my expertise, Miss Wood?"

"My dear, you're an undergraduate studying something vaguely resembling medieval and Tudor history. You don't have any expertise," patronized Margeaux. "Besides, if you can sort out black clerical collars as well as you did, you should be able to sort out this subject."

Miss Weatherby was drawn magnetically over to the window of Margeaux's study to ponder this new challenge.

"It sounds a bit more—well, you know—legal rather than historical."

"The two fields are not mutually exclusive, Miss Weatherby," Margeaux responded. "The postulate is that certain legal documents such as trusts and bequests from which wealth was conveyed are an accurate, and indeed even quantifiable, measure of ecclesiastical versus secular authority in the pre-Reformation period of the Church in England."

Miss Weatherby looked as if she still had her doubts. Margeaux went on.

"This could be a whole new theoretical approach to assessing the timing and degree of power shifts underlying the division of the Church of England from the Church of Rome."

"But I don't have any background at all on trusts and bequests."

The legal terms came out of Miss Weatherby's mouth as if they had a bitter taste.

"Nor, I suspect, do you have any knowledge of how trusts and wills could be undone," confirmed Margeaux. "That's why I checked these books out of the law library for you."

Margeaux picked up several large tomes from her desk and plunked them one at a time next to Miss Weatherby, who looked at the pile with trepidation.

"Did Gutenberg print those?" she asked.

"I have every confidence in your abilities, Miss Weatherby. Start by explaining for me how trusts and wills were written and how they worked. Then describe how they could be dissolved or nullified. Now I'm afraid I have to run."

Margeaux started putting on her coat as Miss Weatherby lifted the heavy pile of books with a grunt.

"Any news from your brother?" Margeaux asked, watching her struggle to balance the stack of volumes.

"No," she answered. "I'm getting quite concerned."

"Don't be," Margeaux responded. "I'm sure he's trying to get his life back together after prison. He'll likely be in touch when he's ready.

"Just pull the door closed behind you, won't you," Margeaux called over her shoulder as she hurried down the stairs.

Miss Weatherby lurched off balance to lean the books against the door jamb to keep them from falling from her grasp. As she struggled to close the door, the books began falling and hitting the floor with accelerating thumps.

"Careful with those," Margeaux warned from the flight of stairs below. "They're checked out in my name."

Miss Weatherby looked down in frustration. The jumble of books hid her feet.

"If you want me to learn how trusts and bequests were done, why do you want me to figure out how they were undone?" she asked with no one around to hear or answer.

Margeaux drove to Atwelle in record time. By now she had driven the route to the village so many times that she knew precisely where road conditions or lurking police cars required vigilance, and where she could drive fast and with less caution. Her arrival outside St. Clement's was punctuated by a short screech as her car skidded to a quick stop. Miss Daunting stood waiting for her at the church's front door.

"My work on your project is going better than expected. No one knows a thing," the older woman reported to Margeaux. "I'm actually enjoying it more than I expected."

After their hasty huddle, they went inside. Don, standing some distance down the nave below the repositioned scaffolding on the left, noticed them and waved to Margeaux. The two women walked briskly down the main aisle to the front pew where they turned with military precision to join him.

"Any more news from the police?" asked Margeaux.

"None that I've heard," Don answered. "I spoke briefly with Nigel. He stopped by before heading back home to his wife. He's pretty distracted, poor man."

Margeaux nodded and asked, "Have you been up there yet?"

"No. I waited for you," he replied as he stepped back from the ladder to let her go first.

The metallic sounds of Margeaux's steady steps were followed by the irregular syncopation of Don's hesitant tread below. Don's halting footfalls ceased as they both stepped over to the illuminated roof beam and clicked on their flashlights.

Their eyes studied momentarily the gargoyle before them once again. It had a grim appearance as the carved lips covered its crooked teeth without a grin. Still the sharp-looking fangs in the corners of its mouth threatened danger to what sat before it. Don and Margeaux shifted their flashlights quickly down to the second smaller carving.

"*Chevalier?*" Margeaux murmured her guess in French.

"Do you think so?" Don asked. "A knight?"

"Well, the prominent sword in front seems to suggest that."

"Hmm," mumbled Don in reply as he studied the male figure standing upright with his hands resting before his chest on the hilt of a tall sword whose blade extended down his body to where its point rested at his feet.

"But he doesn't have any sort of armour or shield," noted Don. "So I'm not sure he's a knight in arms."

They puzzled over the carvings a few minutes, unable to reach any definitive conclusions. Margeaux looked across the church at the opposite roof beam. Don turned and squinted in the same direction.

"Still too dark to see anything," she observed. "When can they move the platform over there, do you think?"

"That's odd," Margeaux heard him comment. Turning to look at him, she saw his gaze had redirected to the corner at the end of the church next to the large stained glass window.

"What?" she asked, unable to see anything particularly surprising.

"There's no gargoyle on the last roof beam in the corner. At least, there doesn't appear to be one."

Margeaux could see that the corner was enclosed by two dark wooden planks that formed a long rectangular box covering the base of the roof beam above the stonewall.

"What do you suppose that is, covering the bottom of the roof beam?" she asked.

"I'm not at all sure. It's not structural, but there's one in the other corner as well."

The beams of their flashlights barely illuminated the opposite corner on the other side of the stained glass window.

"It doesn't make sense—ten carved figures. There are always twelve," insisted Don.

"Well, the number twelve comes from the number of Disciples, doesn't it?" Margeaux replied. "And these carvings are definitely not Disciples."

"But why have carvings on all the other roof beams but not the ones in the corner?" mused Don.

They puzzled in silence for a few minutes as their heads turned back and forth from the carving before them, to the invisible carving across the church, to the corner roof beams that had no carvings.

For a brief moment, some rare sunlight in the early winter gloom broke through the clouds and gloriously lit up the stained glass window. Then as quickly as the light came, it began to fade away. But from their vantage point on top of the scaffold, Don and Margeaux were able to make out some of the colored panes at the peak of the large window.

"I thought I saw a couple coats of arms," said Margeaux. "Did you see them?"

"Yes. Some sort of heraldic figures, perhaps."

"Well hopefully I'll get a look at them someday—if that day will ever come," Margeaux said with a note of frustration. "When will the scaffolding be moved across the way?" she inquired again.

"At least a couple days. Probably longer. I'll talk to Nigel when I can. Our work here is the least of his concerns at the moment."

NINETEEN

1532 Father Regis looked around the crowded marketplace for the sergeant. Seeing no sign of the large man's red hair and moustache, Father Regis turned his attention to a cart of apples. The farmer selling the apples was busily rearranging them so the best were on top.

"Martin Dankwood, a good day to you."

"A good day to you, Father Regis," the farmer replied.

"How is your father doing, Martin?"

"Not well, Father. I fear it is near the end of his time."

Father Regis placed his hand on the farmer's shoulder. "The end of our time on this earth should be nothing to fear, my son. I will pray for him."

"Thank you, Father,"

"I will take a couple extra apples today, Martin."

"A good thing, Father," said Martin Dankwood as he waved away the coins offered by Father Regis. "With All Hallows' Eve upon us, winter is comin' and the apples are soon gone."

Father Regis nodded his thanks and looked for the sergeant once more without success before strolling on to the baker's stall.

"Lizzie, you are looking well today. I will be needing my usual soul cakes for All Hallows."

"Good day to you, Father. I have them, indeed," the baker's plump wife answered as she turned around and bent over to fetch a basket for his selection. "My husband has baked a good many with All Hallows on the morrow."

Father Regis discreetly looked away from the large woman's behind.

"Will you be havin' many soulers stoppin' by to earn some cakes by prayin' for souls?" she asked as she lifted up a large basket full of the small round cakes. "After all," she said as she turned back to show the cakes to Father Regis, "there's enough souls newly dead in need of the prayin'."

Lizzie's smile disappeared and her face went white as she realized from the priest's stern look that she had made her casual market chatter to the wrong person.

"I am sorry, Father. I did not mean to—."

"No matter, Lizzie," he said as he abruptly took some cakes and handed her a coin. Stepping away, Father Regis looked sadly at the cakes sitting in his basket, thinking of how he would have set some of them aside for Peter who gamely made his best effort every All Hallows' Eve to fashion a prayer for the year's departed souls of St. Clement. Peter, who had no family name, would remember each of theirs, Father Regis recalled while wiping away a small tear.

He continued wandering about the market, but the joy that he usually felt at being among the townspeople of Atwelle was gone. While the market buzzed with its typical activity, the priest's thoughts ran to all the difficulties masked by the usual business of the day.

The work on the church was slowly grinding to a halt. Faced with the possibility of not being paid, more workmen were leaving every day, concerned about supporting their families through the winter. And those who remained and waited faithfully for All Hallows' Day would find that Father Regis's promise to pay them in full for their work on the church was not to be fulfilled. His mouth went dry as he imagined the men's reaction.

Even worse, he saw no prospect of any funding that would cover the completion of the church's construction. Reports of the heightened tension between the king and the pope were more frequent. The conflict of unspoken loyalties had a paralyzing effect on his attempts to raise funds. Father Regis knew the test would come soon from a king's tax on the church and the clergy followed by a Peter's pence that would represent a direct challenge between the authority of the king and the Church.

It would be the end of St. Clement's. He pictured the walls of the church forever standing stillborn like ruins without a roof. He would have to answer to the Bishop of Norwich and face the black cowl of an unforgiving Father Cuthbert.

His heart grew even heavier as Father Regis thought about the murders and the missing baby. The threat of their mystery hung over the town like the low gray clouds coming in on All Hallows' Eve. He had gone to the sergeant many times in the last week to check on the progress of the investigation, but had learned almost nothing. First of all, the sergeant always seemed to be sleeping during the day. And when he did speak with him, he could not get the large man to talk of anything but the murder of the prostitute. Was the sergeant doing nothing on Peter's death and the disappearance of Bittergreen's baby, Father Regis wondered.

"Father? Father Regis?"

The sound of his name brought him out of his thoughts. He realized he was staring absent-mindedly at some pheasants hanging from a wooden rack. A man in rough clothes who was known for poaching was looking at him uncomfortably.

"They were fairly caught," the man said defensively. With a worried look at the priest who remained silent, he held out a bird whose head hung limply over the man's fist. "Here, this one is for you, for free."

Father Regis at first took the pheasant with a natural momentary happy thought of how much Peter would enjoy it for dinner. But then the reality of Peter's brutal death returned to blacken his mood even more. With a distracted gesture, he handed the bird back to the man and moved on, his mind returning to the murders of Peter and the prostitute.

"Does the sergeant have the same suspicions I have?" he wondered. Peter had seen both Richard Lanham and Francis DuBois visit the prostitute, and they had seen Peter. Either man was capable of killing

Peter to prevent damage to his reputation and the campaign to control the inland port and its revenue. Either man had a motive to kill the prostitute for the same reason.

A sudden sobering thought brought Father Regis to a stop. He remembered the sergeant's demand to Peter that he stop hanging about the lane where the prostitute lived. Could the sergeant have killed Peter and the prostitute at the command of either Lanham or DuBois?

"Or on the command of both?" he asked out loud. Feeling the villagers' curious looks from his question still hanging in the air, he moved on to the next market stall.

"But what of the missing baby?" he puzzled in his mind. "Why would they bother with a workman's child?" There was no apparent connection. It must have been the act of another criminal, he concluded. "Is it one, or two, or three criminals?" Whatever the solution, it did not bode well for finishing the construction of the church, he concluded.

"Father Regis!"

The booming voice above him brought him up short. He realized the sergeant was surveying him from atop the man's tall horse. There were dark circles under the sergeant's fatigued eyes. The entire length of the sergeant's sword passed through the priest's vision as the large man dismounted from the horse and lowered himself to the ground.

"Let me walk you back to the church—or what there is of it," he suggested in a grim voice.

They walked without talking until they left behind the commotion of the market. Just as Father Regis started to ask the sergeant about his investigation, the sergeant stopped and looked down over his moustache at the priest. Father Regis watched the horse shake its head and mane. He could not bring himself to look the sergeant in the eye.

"I know who is responsible for the murders of Molly and poor Peter," the sergeant announced in a quiet but firm voice.

Father Regis looked anxiously at the sergeant.

"For a big man, I can move quickly and quietly, Father." He wiped the length of his moustache with a gloved hand and gave a heavy sigh. "And I have followed unlikely people to unlikely places."

"Who is it?" the priest immediately asked.

"I shall not say, Father, but you would not believe it."

"Can you not tell me?" Father Regis urged.

"I must speak to DuBois and Lanham first. Then you will know."

Father Regis felt his stomach sink. The sergeant remounted his horse.

"Justice will be done," he assured the priest below him. "Whether it be the king's—or my own," he added, laying his hand on his sword.

Father Regis hurried in the direction of the church after watching the sergeant ride away. He felt as if he would be ill. A major patron of his church would be accused of a capital crime. With that loss and the controversy of the levy of Peter's pence, there would be no hope for rebuilding the church.

Even worse, he realized he was about to meet again with Christopher Lanham and Margaret DuBois. In a few minutes, he would be trying to encourage them to marry, while he knew one of their fathers would be arrested shortly for murder. He did not know how he could carry out such deception.

Father Regis soon met the two young people outside the walls of the unfinished church. Christopher and a family servant rode up on their horses as Margaret arrived in a driven carriage. He was pleased to see the two of them greet each other pleasantly before he welcomed them. The three of them, followed by Lanham's servant, wandered along the church walls underneath the gray sky toward the shells of the families' chapels. Christopher commented favorably on how much progress had been made despite the rumors of workmen deserting their labors.

"I assure you both, the workmen have not been a problem," Father Regis responded.

Christopher gave him a skeptical look.

"But I have heard talk that the murders in the town and the disappearance of the carver's infant son are thought by the workmen to be evil signs of a curse on the place?" he asked.

Father Regis tried to look as if the very idea was an affront. "This is consecrated ground, my son. There is no evil here."

He was surprised when the two young people walked past the family chapels to the area of the chancel where the altar would stand next to the entrance to the crypt. There they turned and looked back down the length of the church under the open sky. Father Regis sensed a feeling of doubt about the place from them both.

"Besides," he tried to assure them, "the sergeant has told me that he knows with certainty who has committed all the assaults upon the civil peace of our town and that he will make an arrest of the guilty in short order."

Christopher looked at Father Regis with surprise.

"Well that is certainly good to know, Father. Do you feel better for having heard that news, Margaret?"

The young maiden nodded demurely and lifted her skirts to step around the entrance to the crypt as she walked back toward the Du-Bois family chapel.

2017 As Margeaux drove into Atwelle, it seemed as if the village was deserted. The recent funerals and the missing baby cast a lingering pall over the place like the gray clouds that seemed these days to be permanently painted on the sky above. When she eventually stepped into St. Clement's, the church, like the town, was empty and silent.

Walking toward the altar, Margeaux saw that the scaffolding had been moved down the right wall of the church below the next unexamined roof beam. She was relieved after driving the distance from Cambridge that Don had managed to see to the reassembly of the structure in Nigel Green's absence. As if out of nowhere, Father Lanham appeared from behind the altar and approached her.

"Have you seen Don?" asked Margeaux. "I'm supposed to meet him to look at the final gargoyle."

"I don't believe he's here yet," the young man answered.

"And Father Adams?" she inquired.

"He's gone to Cambridge again."

"Has he been going there a lot?" she asked warily.

"A fair amount."

Margeaux looked around the church.

"Where's Miss Daunting?"

"Tending to her duties, I assume," replied Father Lanham. "Oh, there's Don now."

They watched Don march down the center aisle of the nave, cut through a random row of pews to the right wall, and turn again to approach them.

"Hello," Don greeted them both without much zest. Grabbing the corner pipe of the scaffold, he tested it to see that the assembly was solid.

"I see you were able to have Nigel's workers move the scaffolding," Margeaux noted.

Don nodded.

"Any news about the baby?" she asked.

Don sadly shook his head and looked at Father Lanham.

"None, I'm afraid." Father Lanham looked up at the entire height of the scaffold. "Well, I'll leave you two to it. Let me know what you find," he said as he headed off.

Though they appeared to be at the last of their discoveries, there was not much enthusiasm shared between Margeaux and Don before beginning the slow climb up the ladder to see the final gargoyle.

"Margeaux, you must be concerned about all the terrible things going on around here. We didn't sign up for all of this, after all."

She looked unhappy at the reminder of all that was going on. "What I want to know is where are Father Adams and the police." Her voice was agitated. "They should be doing something to get to the bottom of all this."

"Father Adams?" Don asked, a bit surprised at her statement.

"Well somebody should be doing something to stop what's been happening," she snapped back at him. "They haven't said much publicly about the murders or even asked people to report suspects."

"Detective Steele did say he had leads and might be making an arrest," suggested Don.

Margeaux had already turned her back to him and taken an angry first heave up the ladder, her small rucksack bouncing violently on her back. Don followed slowly. At the top, they started their usual routine with their flashlights.

The gargoyle was noticeably happy once again. Its somber countenance had been replaced by the grin filled with crooked teeth between its two fangs. But it crouched there among the spider webs without company. The second carved figure was gone. Instead of the carved figure resting its hands on the hilt of the sword, the gargoyle alone firmly gripped the sword's handle in both its claws.

Neither Don nor Margeaux said anything for some time, until Margeaux pulled a pad of paper from her rucksack and started making notes.

"What do you make of it?" Don finally asked.

"Not sure," was her curt reply. "The knight, or whatever the armed authority figure was, is gone and his sword is still there in the grasp of the demonic figure."

Don decided to leave her obvious observation alone to avoid irritating her further, but then changed his mind.

"We have to come up with its explanation—to find what it's saying. It's too important," he insisted. "The other gargoyles have been predictors of two murders and the baby's disappearance. We've got to figure out what this one means and what could happen next."

For some time, they stared at the gargoyle in frustration. Its nasty grin seemed to grow with their increasing vexation. It was as if the creature enjoyed warning them without revealing the threat.

Don grew more fearful as he silently named all the people he could think of who could be at risk. "But how? And why?" he kept asking himself. He looked over at Margeaux, who had turned the beam of her flashlight on the upper right-hand corner of the large stained glass window.

"See anything?" he asked as his flashlight joined her search.

"No," she shook her head. "Too grimy."

Margeaux and Don stared at the gargoyle for a few more minutes until they could no longer tolerate the irritation of his secretive smile. They began climbing down the ladder. Suddenly, flashing lights started sweeping repeatedly through the windows and across the walls of the church.

When they reached the floor of the church, they saw the figure of Inspector Russell in his khaki raincoat striding toward them down the center aisle with a constable in tow. Two other policemen fanned out behind him to converge from the side aisles next to the walls. Another stood at the church door. They were surprised when Inspector Russell held up his police identification when he approached them.

"Mr. Whitby, Miss Wood, I need to ask you some questions. Would you please come with us?"

"I'd be happy to answer your questions, Inspector," answered Margeaux, "but I have to be off to Cambridge in a minute."

"I'm afraid you don't understand," Inspector Russell replied with a stern look.

"I'm taking you both into custody."

TWENTY

1532 The message was delivered to Father Regis just after sunset by the young son of Martin Dankwood who had sold him apples in the market earlier that day. The farmer's elderly father lay dying. Father Regis was asked to come to their farmhouse to administer extreme unction to the old man.

Grabbing a vial of holy oil, he hurriedly followed the boy down the spiral staircase from his room. At the bottom, the boy stopped suddenly. Father Regis almost stumbled into him. With a frightened look, the boy stepped back, squeezing next to the priest on the tight stairway. Father Regis looked past the boy into the back of the church where beams of wood and blocks of stone were scattered about.

A woman crouched in the shadows rose to her feet. There was a wild look on her face framed by her disheveled hair. She pointed menacingly at the priest.

"You!" she screamed. "You are evil!"

The accusation echoed back and forth between the tall walls of bare stone. Startled, Father Regis felt the farmer's son slip behind him to hide. He tensed as a man ran up behind her. The man put his arms around her shoulders to control and comfort the distraught woman. When the man finally looked up at the priest, Father Regis recognized Bittergreen, the wood-carver.

Bittergreen tried to calm his shaking wife for another moment until her anger melted into deep sobs. Holding her to keep her from collapsing, Bittergreen turned on Father Regis.

"I work for you here and my family goes hungry. And then I lose my son to the devil!"

At these words, Bittergreen's wife began to wail with grief. Father Regis could feel the hatred coming from the workman.

"There is evil in this place!" Bittergreen hissed.

The man's words stung Father Regis like the cut of a sword. Even in the growing darkness he could see the anger in the wood-carver's eyes. Behind him, Father Regis heard the farm boy start to whimper as Bittergreen half carried his wife out the door in the church wall. Father Regis tried to calm his own rattled nerves before moving toward the door. He was startled again as the boy sprinted past him in the direction of Martin Dankwood's home.

When Father Regis arrived at the farmer's house, Dankwood cautiously opened the door part way.

"I've come to help your father, Martin," Father Regis said, breathing heavily from his haste.

The farmer glanced over at the elderly man lying on a bed pulled up next to the fireplace, and then looked uncertainly back at the priest. When a groan came from the old man, Dankwood finally opened the door to the priest.

Father Regis hurried over to the bed. As he gave the sign of the cross over the man, he saw out of the corner of his eye the Dankwood's son hiding in the shadows of a corner. Although Father Regis anointed the old man with the holy oil and continued to pray over him, the priest knew from the gurgling sound of his labored breaths that only God could save the man now. Father Regis continued praying over the man long after he stopped breathing.

"I do not know when the soul enters the body," he reminded himself, "nor do I know when it leaves."

Yet he recognized there was another reason that he continued to pray for Martin Dankwood's father. It seemed as though death had surrounded him in Atwelle. He wanted it to stop. He wanted to do something to stop it. Father Regis kept praying until he conceded from the tears and grief of the family around him that no comfort was coming from his prayers. He rose from his knees.

"We can bury him on All Hallows' Eve when souls are moving freely between earth and heaven," he said trying to comfort the farmer and his wife. "And the soulers in the parish will be praying for his soul even as it rises to heaven."

Before he left, he looked about for Dankwood's son, but was saddened that the boy was nowhere to be seen. He felt a great weight on his shoulders as he walked through the darkness on the road back towards the town. He had failed.

He had failed Martin Dankwood whose father had died. He had failed the farmer's son who saw him as evil. He had failed Bittergreen and his wife. He had failed their baby. He had failed the workmen and the Bishop. He had failed the townspeople of Atwelle by not building their church. The unrelenting thoughts kept repeating in his head like an unending confession until he trudged through the door of the church and looked up into the sky where the roof should have arched above the stone walls.

"I have failed the Holy Church," he sighed as he turned toward where the altar was to have been constructed above the entrance to the crypt.

"I have failed God." His voice broke as he muttered out loud his final soul-crushing admission.

Through his tears, Father Regis saw a glint of metal where the altar was meant to stand. Not knowing what it was or from where the reflected light had come, he moved wearily down the length of the dark church under the clouds above. He squinted at something on the ground as he grew nearer to the entrance to the crypt.

The black clouds gathered above him enveloped the whole church in complete darkness. Father Regis kneeled down and reached out to feel for what lay there. He knew immediately the feel of the cold metal under his touch.

The sky lightened slightly. Father Regis could barely make out the sword resting on the chest of the large figure lying on the entrance to the crypt. He reached over to grab for a gloved hand but could not find it. With growing horror, he realized the lifeless body lying before him had no arms. Suppressing his fear, he reached over to feel the hair of a thick moustache along with something like smooth cloth.

As if to signal the midnight arrival of All Hallows' Eve, the clouds parted momentarily to let a shaft of moonlight fall on the figure lying before Father Regis. Next to his shaking hand he saw a rosette made of ribbon wrapped over the face of the sergeant.

2017 The cup of coffee sitting on the table in front of Inspector Russell had grown cold long ago. Tired from hours of questioning, Don sat opposite him at the table, looking around at the bare cement walls of the small interrogation room in the bowels of the Norfolk police headquarters in Norwich, waiting for the next question.

"If I had to design a room that would make me feel guilty of a crime so that I would confess, this would be the room," thought Don. "Then again," he reconsidered when another question did not immediately come at him, "if I thought I might be spending the rest of my life in a place like this, I'd never confess."

Inspector Russell studied the notes scribbled on a pad of paper on the table in front of him. The two of them had spent hours repeatedly tracing all of Don's activities and movements over the previous several days. Don summoned every ounce of patience to wait quietly for each question, no matter how often it was asked or the delays in asking it. He was on his best behavior. The police were deadly serious.

Between Inspector Russell's long absences from the room, he asked for exhaustive details of what Don knew about Margeaux. Don wondered how she would be answering the same questions and tried not to reveal how worried he was about her. They had been driven to Norwich in separate police cars and had not seen each other since leaving the church.

Next, Inspector Russell went through the list of victims.

Father Charleton. Don told the Inspector he had met the vicar briefly in a couple of interviews with the church committee before they decided to hire him. He had been looking forward to working with the older man, but then the vicar disappeared.

Squeaky. Don had only known him a few weeks, saw him working occasionally around the church, and used to joke about inviting him to climb up the scaffolding to see the roof beams.

"You mean to see the gargoyles?" asked Inspector Russell.

"Yes, I suppose so."

"Did he see the gargoyles?"

"I'd be surprised if he did. I don't think so."

Brandi. Don had met her only briefly on the day they found Squeaky. She was on vacation most of the time he was there, before her death, that is. He didn't really get to know her.

"Did you socialize with Miss Knowleton?"

"No."

"Do you know where she lived?"

"No."

"Do you remember having any conversations with Miss Knowleton?"

"Not really. If I did, they were very casual."

"What do you mean by 'casual'?"

"I guess I mean I don't even remember what we talked about."

Nigel Green. Don had known him for years in the building trade, a good man. He'd done Don a favor by making the scaffolding available at a low cost for the project at St. Clement's.

"Do you know where he lives?"

"I believe he has a place in the country about ten or fifteen miles from Atwelle."

"Have you ever been there?"

"No."

"Do you know his family?"

"Not really. I know he was a proud new father."

"Have you met his wife?"

"No."

"Would she recognize you?"

"As I said, I've never met her. Inspector?"

"Yes, Mr. Whitby?"

"I know you're supposed to be asking the questions. But if you don't mind my asking, is there any news on Nigel's baby boy?"

"You're right, Mr. Whitby. I'm supposed to ask the questions. How did you know Mr. Green's baby was a boy?"

"He told me the day after the baby was born—several times."

"What was the child's name?"

Maybe it was the stress of the day. Maybe the fatigue. Don's mind came up blank.

"I don't recall. I'm sorry."

"He told you about his new baby several times the day after it was born, and you don't recall his name?"

"Yes. It's silly I know. But I just can't recall the name."

Don was mentally kicking himself, trying to remember the name of the baby. Inspector Russell looked at Don a few moments without speaking.

"Mr. Whitby, tell me about your famous gargoyles."

"Well, first off, they're not mine and they're not famous," Don snapped at him and regretted it immediately.

"I'm sorry, Inspector. Just getting a bit tired. What would you like to know?"

"Is it true that you 'discovered' them?"

"Sort of. Margeaux and I noticed them when we were looking at the ceiling through binoculars. I'm sure someone at some time must have known they were up there in the roof beams. But no one now seems to remember them, and because it's so dark, you can't see them unless you're right up there next to them."

Inspector Russell's questions led him through a description of the discovery of each of the ten gargoyles, which resulted in several pages of detailed notes.

"Besides you and Miss Wood, who else has seen the gargoyles, Mr. Whitby?"

"No one that I know of. Oh, I suppose Nigel or his workmen might have seen them when they finished assembling the scaffold next to each of them."

"Did anyone say anything to you about seeing them?"

"No."

"Did you tell anyone about the gargoyles, Mr. Whitby?"

Don paused.

"Well, the two vicars, Father Adams and Father Lanham, and I suppose Miss Daunting. She's a volunteer staff person at the church."

"Anyone else?"

"No."

Don watched Inspector Russell's pen touch down on the paper without writing for a moment.

"Detective Steele reported that you predicted from the gargoyles there would be more murders. Did you tell Detective Steele about the gargoyles?"

"Oh, right. Yes, we did. Or Margeaux did, actually."

"When was that?"

After all that had happened, Don struggled for a moment to remember his conversations with Margeaux.

"I believe Margeaux first had suspicions about the gargoyles after Brandi's death."

"What did you do about her suspicions?"

"Nothing at first. I didn't put much stock in them."

"When did you change your mind?"

"After Nigel's baby went missing and we saw the gargoyles on each side of the church holding a baby."

"Did you tell Detective Steele about your suspicions then?"

"Yes, when he questioned me in connection with the baby's disappearance. He questioned all of us at the church," Don added hastily.

"Tell me exactly what you told Detective Steele."

"I don't remember exactly. Just the general similarities between the figures in the carvings and the murders. I still couldn't figure out how the gargoyles could be connected to anything or who could be doing anything suggested by the carvings."

"Did you talk to him after looking at any other gargoyles?"

"Just when he introduced us to you after Brandi's funeral."

"Why didn't you talk with him after seeing the final gargoyle, the one with the sword?"

"Don't have a particular reason. Didn't see him and didn't really have any further particular suspicions, I guess."

Inspector Russell paused again with pen to paper.

"Do you own any guns, Mr. Whitby?"

"Good heavens, no."

"Do any shooting of any sort?"

Don gave him an odd look.

"No, Inspector."

Inspector Russell picked up his cup of coffee and then set it back down when he realized it was cold. He leaned back in his chair.

"Have you ever had a previous run in with the law, Mr. Whitby?"

"No, sir."

"That's not true, is it Mr. Whitby?"

Don gave him a blank look.

"Isn't it true that you've had six speeding offences in the last fifteen years driving a"—he flipped to another page of his pad—"a 1956 MG?"

Don looked down at the table and took a deep breath.

"If that makes me a suspect, Inspector, you've got a lot of suspects who own MGs to interview. Perhaps you'd better get on with that."

The Inspector stood up.

"Thank you, Mr. Whitby. You can wait upstairs while I finish with Miss Wood. Someone will be driving you and Miss Wood back to Atwelle when I've finished with her. It shouldn't be long."

A policewoman escorted Don upstairs and invited him to sit in the car in which she would be driving them to Atwelle. He climbed into the back seat while she went back to get Margeaux.

"Bloody hell!" Don exhaled in exhaustion.

He leaned back, rubbed his tired eyes and then opened them to look about. There was Father Adams walking up to the entrance of the police station, where the vicar stopped to take a long drag from a cigarette. Don watched him flick the glowing butt onto the sidewalk before pulling open the door and entering with a purposeful stride. A moment later, Margeaux walked out through the same door with the policewoman.

"What the hell was that all about?" he asked Margeaux before she had even finished climbing into the back seat with him.

She did not look any happier about the experience than he was.

"And why ask me all those questions about guns?" he asked in exasperation.

Margeaux gave him a shocked look.

"They didn't tell you?"

Don shrugged and shook his head.

"No. What?"

"Detective Steele was found murdered—with his own gun."

TWENTY-ONE

1532 Father Regis felt every nerve was on edge as he threw a handful of dirt into the grave of Martin Dankwood's father. He gave a final prayer and benediction along with the sign of the cross as the sun started to set on All Hallows' Eve. Then after a consoling word with the farmer, he hurried toward the spiral staircase and climbed to his room.

The priest sat on the side of his cot and simply stared at the floor. The shock of finding the sergeant's mutilated body right there in the church had kept him awake all night and had not left him all day. When not thinking of the sergeant, he was equally unsettled at the prospect of facing all the workmen with no wages to pay them. That mental picture kept coming to different endings, none of them good and all of them tensing his insides. It appeared to be the end of St. Clement's. There would be inevitable embarrassment before the Bishop of Norwich. He was too despondent even to pray.

"It matters not for there is no apparent solution for which I can pray," he concluded without hope.

In the distance he heard the singing of the soulers as they made their way to the church. "They will be here soon," he thought as he looked over at the basket holding the soul cakes he had purchased in the market for their arrival. He waited numbly for the group of soulers to arrive in the All Hallows' Eve tradition at the church after having gone around the parish asking the more affluent residents for soul cakes in exchange for praying for their souls and the souls of their families.

Father Regis tried to prepare himself to give them cakes for their prayers on behalf of the souls of all the parishioners who had died in that year. But his mind kept returning to the final question that kept tormenting him.

"With the sergeant gone, who will bring the murderers to justice, including his own killer? Who can stop the evil?"

The priest felt a presence and looked up with a start. His heart was pounding as a tall dark figure stepped into the candlelight. With a wave of relief, he recognized the black cowl.

"Father Cuthbert, welcome."

"Father Regis."

Father Cuthbert pulled back the hood covering his face to reveal a grim look. At the sound of the approaching soulers, his somber face took on a frown.

"Praying for souls for a bite of cake. Pitiful really. If it worked, there would be no need for us."

Father Cuthbert walked over to the basket where he picked up a soul cake and took a bite.

"Were it not such a tradition, I believe I would find it to be heresy. Only God has the power to enter a soul into heaven. It is heresy for people to claim they have the power to make that happen, for cakes or otherwise. Do you know who promises people that he can take care of their souls?"

"Priests," thought Father Regis.

"The devil himself," Father Cuthbert answered his own question. "That is why the prayers of the soulers are nothing but heresy. I know the devil's ways."

Father Regis looked uncomfortable. He wondered what he should do with Father Cuthbert there when the soulers arrived with prayers to earn the cakes.

"Father Regis." He heard the soulers call out his name from the bottom of the spiral staircase. "We are here to pray for the souls of the departed from St. Clement's."

Thunder rumbled in the distance. Father Regis gave a hesitant look in the direction of the black cowl.

"Go on. Give the fools their cakes and send them on their way before the storm drenches them," said Father Cuthbert as he stuck the rest of the cake into his mouth.

After dispensing the cakes, Father Regis hurried up the stairs to his room. Father Cuthbert had rolled out a blanket on the stone floor.

"May I share your roof, Father Regis?" he asked.

"Of course, brother. But please take my bed."

"Thank you no. I sleep on stone every night to remind me of the suffering of our Savior for the forgiveness of our sins."

"Then at least let me prepare some food for you," Father Regis offered.

"It is not necessary. I will start my fast for All Hallows' Day in a few hours in any event. There is no need for your trouble."

Father Cuthbert sat down on his blanket with his back against the wall.

"As I am here, I should tell you about the decision to levy a tax for the church."

"Peter's pence?"

"Yes. A signal of the church's resolve and strength is going to be sent to His Majesty in response to his pressure on the pope."

Father Regis felt hollow. He had now heard the final death sentence for St. Clement's.

"There will be other signs of the church's power shown to the king throughout the realm. Even here in Atwelle when the new church is finished and consecrated. The Bishop of Norwich is eager for its completion and will consecrate the church himself. Are you feeling unwell, Father?"

Father Regis sat down on his bed. His face was pale. He swallowed and sat quietly for a moment.

"The bishop honors us. But is it wise to risk the wrath of the king in such sensitive times?"

Father Cuthbert gave him a cross look.

"These are matters above your station, Father Regis. Do not presume to understand them or question the Church's decision."

His face softened as he pulled his black hood around his head and stretched out on his blanket.

"But that is not why I am here. You will be told of these things when the decision is announced among the clergy for administration of the tax in the dioceses."

Father Regis gave him a questioning look.

"Then why are you in Atwelle?"

Father Regis stared at Father Cuthbert's face long after he had finished the answer.

"Father Cuthbert, come with me immediately."

It was more of an order than a request. Father Regis stood and headed for the door.

"Now see here, Father," protested Father Cuthbert. "I take my orders from the bishop—"

Father Regis whirled around to face him.

"Now, Father Cuthbert!"

Stunned by the unexpected fierce look and harsh command from the humble parish priest, Father Cuthbert scrambled to his feet.

2017 Don scowled at his phone after leaving another message for Margeaux. He had heard nothing back from her for two days.

"That's the best we can do I'm afraid, Mr. Whitby," one of Nigel Green's workmen said after climbing off the scaffolding. "I can't keep the men any longer, and there's a big storm comin'. Plus you know what's on the telly in an hour," he added with a knowing look.

Don didn't have a clue what was on television that evening, but knew he wouldn't win any argument for more time from the workers. He looked up at the narrow scaffold that Nigel's men had hastily constructed at Don's request.

"Is it safe to climb up?" Don asked.

"Safe enough," the workman responded. A long low rumble of thunder sounded outside.

"Well, we're off." He turned to leave with a wave. "Good luck, Mr. Whitby."

"Thanks, Joe. And give my best to Nigel when you see him, will you?"

Without turning back, the man waved in agreement as he headed past the altar down the length of the church.

Don gave another uncertain look up the slender scaffold that snaked its way up the corner of the church next to the stained glass window.

"Looks a bit undernourished, Joe," he mumbled to the workman, who was no longer within earshot.

A flash of lightning came through the window as if someone outside had quickly flipped a light switch on and off. Don pulled his phone out of his jacket pocket and tried to call Margeaux again. After a few rings, irritation filled his face once more.

"Hello, Margeaux. This is Don again. I've been trying to reach you for a couple days. So if you get this message soon, give me a call. I'm at the church in Atwelle. I've decided to take a further look at the roof beams."

Following another doubtful look at the scaffold, Don dashed over to the low side door. After pushing it open, he dodged through the gravestones in the churchyard to wave down Joe in his car.

Joe rolled down his window. "Yes, Mr. Whitby?"

"Joe, do you have anything I can use to cut away some wood?"

"I think I have an old hand axe in the back. That's it."

"Can I borrow it?"

"Sure." Joe climbed out of the car, opened the boot and dug out a small axe, which he handed to Don.

"Many thanks, Joe. I'll get it back to you."

Another duet of lightning and thunder came out of the distance as random raindrops started to fall. Don hurried back to the church where he ducked through the low door.

The church had grown dark. Don saw a light switch near the scaffold and turned it on. A small spotlight above focused its beam on the altar. The rest of the church was swallowed by one vast shadow.

Don's jaw was clenched as he walked up to the ladder. A clap of thunder sounded nearer. He didn't like any of this one bit. But he hefted the hand axe in one fist and grabbed the metal ladder with the other.

He looked up again at the ceiling before starting to climb. He could barely see the wood that enclosed the bottom of the roof beam where it met the stone wall.

"There has to be another carving there," he thought. "There are always twelve."

Pulling himself up the ladder with one hand, he forced himself to take a breath with each step. The head of the axe in his other hand often clashed clumsily against the metal pipes of the scaffold, sending an echo into the shadow that lurked beyond the altar below. His worries about Margeaux and what he might find at the top of the scaffold started to meld in his mind. When he finally reached the top, Don stayed on his knees after climbing onto the small platform.

"Don't look down," he gave himself the order and closed his eyes. With the vain hope that Margeaux might call, and fearful of what he might find in the shadows, he allowed himself to remain still on the platform for a few moments. Finally, the silence, interrupted only by the thunder outside, compelled him to look at the dark wood before him.

Carefully, Don reached out to touch the two wide planks of wood that joined to form a casing around the base of the roof beam. He felt the dry rot under the surface of the wood give slightly against the pressure of his fingers. The planks were not made of the same hard oak as the roof beam. Swallowing hard, he lifted the hand axe, took aim at the center of a plank, and struck.

The blade of the axe sank into the soft wood with ease. Don twisted the axe to widen the cut and then yanked it out to strike again. After a few more blows, there was a split in the plank big enough for Don to reach in and start pulling at the rotting wood. He forgot where he was as he alternately hammered the axe and tore at the decaying wood with his hands. Finally, when he could grab hold of each plank with both hands, Don managed with two great pulls to wrench them away from the roof beam.

"Margeaux!" he called out as if she were there to hear his warning in the darkness of the church.

Don took a moment to scan one more time the carving before him. The face of the demon was like the other gargoyles except that a circle of tonsured hair wrapped around its head like a monk. Below the fangs of its open mouth, sitting in the claws of its hands, was the head and torso of a woman.

Scrambling over to the ladder, Don descended as quickly as he could. The fragile scaffold shuddered with each hurried step. At the bottom, Don dropped the axe to the stone floor with a clatter and fumbled to pull his phone out of his jacket. Fear for Margeaux gripped him firmly when there was still no answer from her.

Don hurried over to the low stone doorway and ran out into the rain. Another flash of lightning lit up the graveyard around him as he dashed toward his MG.

"It's like All Hallows' Eve," he shuddered as he slammed shut the door of his car. "My god, it *is* All Hallows' Eve," he realized as he started the engine and peeled out onto the slick wet road.

With the storm raging around him, Don pushed Sally around the slippery turns and through the large puddles stretching across the low points of the wavy roads to Cambridge. The tiny beating wipers did little for his visibility through the small windscreen. He dialed Margeaux's phone number repeatedly without success while he drove on. Fortunately the heavy rain had kept much of the rush hour traffic off the streets of Cambridge where he ran as many red lights as he could.

Sally screeched to a stop as close as possible to the main gate of Maryhouse Hall. Don leaped from the car to run down a cobblestone passage, then through the college gate and into the Porters' Lodge. When Don burst through the door, Gerald looked up calmly at the intruder without surprise or alarm.

"May I help you?" His unperturbed inquiry conveyed his authority in the territorial domain over which a head porter had exerted unquestioned control for centuries.

"I'm looking for Margeaux Wood," Don blurted out.

"I'm sorry, sir. The college is closed to visitors after business hours."

Seeing the extreme agitation in Don's face, Gerald's hand dropped invisibly behind the counter to the phone where the press of a button would summon the police.

"I'm—" Don was almost frantic. "I'm working on a project with Margeaux and haven't been able to reach her for two days. I'm very worried about her. Can we see if she's in her study?"

Gerald looked over at the mail slots for the fellows and saw that Margeaux's box was full of unretrieved mail and messages. Without hesitation, Gerald threw on his bowler and led Don out into the main court of the college where they leaned into the blowing rain. A group of students mustered around the entrance to the college bar parted for Gerald like the Red Sea before Moses. Entering the next college court, Gerald disregarded the rules by stepping off the cobblestones to cut across the grass of the court toward the stairwell to Margeaux's study, where they bounded up the three flights of narrow stairs. At her door, Gerald knocked firmly.

While they waited for a response, Don read the notes taped to the door. The first was dated the day before.

"Miss Wood, I was here for our appointment and apparently missed you. I'll check back tomorrow—Joan Weatherby."

"Miss Wood?" Gerald knocked again more firmly with his ear cocked for an answer. Don quickly read the next note on the door. It was dated that day at 2 p.m.

"Miss Wood, I checked back for you. I have the answers to your final questions on the mechanics of Tudor trusts and wills. Please call me when you want to meet to discuss. Here's my mobile number. . . ." It was again signed "Joan Weatherby."

Don turned to Gerald.

"Do you know where Margeaux lives?"

"I have her address."

"Can you go see if she's there?"

Gerald nodded and turned to head down the stairs. Returning to the main gate, the two were drenched from the heavy rain. Don handed the porter his card.

"Here's my mobile phone number. Call me when you know anything. Can I reach you here if necessary?"

Gerald gave Don his personal number as well as the college number. Don dashed back to Sally and with a squeal of tires headed to Atwelle. His mind raced as he flew up the road toward Norfolk. He turned on the radio to listen to news reports, but the static from the electrical storm surrounding him rendered the old radio nearly useless.

Don turned off the radio and pressed harder on the accelerator. He knew where he needed to go to find out what might have happened to Margeaux. One last unseen gargoyle remained in the church.

TWENTY-TWO

1532 The two clergymen leaned into the hard wind. Muttering a prayer in Latin, Father Cuthbert pulled the hood of his cowl forward with both hands as the cold rain started to pelt his face. Atwelle disappeared behind them as they pressed on down the road leading into the fields surrounding the town. When he finished his prayer, Father Cuthbert looked over, as he squinted from the rainfall.

"Why do you bring me out on such a night? How can you disregard what this night is? The souls of the dead and the spirits of evil are about on All Hallows' Eve."

Father Regis knew before his companion had finished speaking that it was not the weather or the late hour that was the problem. He too said a silent prayer for protection as he looked away from the skeletal tree branches that seemed to grasp wildly at them from the dark of the growing tempest.

"I fear it is those very spirits that we may have to confront this night," he warned.

Father Regis could feel the damp of the rain starting to seep through the cloth of his cassock as he turned off the road under the violently swaying oak trees leading up to the entrance to Lanham Manor. When he reached the main door of the darkened building, he pounded on it steadily until he finally heard the wooden bar sliding away on the inside. A servant opened the large door a few inches and peered over a flickering candle to see who would knock at such an hour.

"It is Father Regis," the priest announced impatiently as he pushed open the door and led Father Cuthbert into the entrance hall. "We are come to see Christopher. Go and wake him now."

"What is the meaning of this?" Richard Lanham's stern voice came out of the darkness as he came around the corner, closing a cloak around his nightshirt.

"I am sorry to disturb you, Richard. But we must speak with Christopher immediately."

Lanham looked at the ominous dark figure of Father Cuthbert standing behind Father Regis.

"And who is this?"

"This is Father Cuthbert. He serves at the pleasure of the Bishop of Norwich."

"Father Cuthbert, this is Richard Lanham, lord of this manor and Christopher Lanham's father."

After a brief look of surprise at Father Regis, Father Cuthbert bowed his head slightly at Lanham.

"Now we must see Christopher at once," Father Regis persisted.

Taken aback at Father Regis's uncharacteristic insistence, Lanham gave him an unhappy look but nodded to his servant. "Would you please fetch Master Christopher."

The servant made his way with his candle up the oaken staircase, leaving the men standing uncomfortably in the darkness. A few moments later, the servant returned alone.

"I could not rouse him," the servant informed them.

Lanham frowned, took the candle from the servant, and led them all up the stairs to a door at the end of a long hallway.

"Christopher?" Lanham called out quietly.

When there was no response, he tapped lightly on the door.

"Christopher?" Lanham repeated in a slightly louder voice.

After another moment's silence, he gently opened the door. Peering into the darkness, he lifted the candle and stepped softly into the room. Father Regis and Father Cuthbert followed closely behind.

The curtains were not drawn around the four posts of the bed. It was empty, the bedclothes undisturbed. With a surprised look, Lanham turned to his servant.

"Where was Master Christopher this evening?"

"I believe he paid a visit to Geoffrey and his wife," the servant replied. "I did not hear him return before I went to bed."

Lanham spun around to face the two clergymen.

"What is this all about?"

Father Regis looked over at Father Cuthbert.

"Tell him why you have come to Atwelle."

Father Cuthbert pulled his black hood from his face and gave Lanham a look of forewarning.

"I am here at the instructions of the Bishop on behalf of the brothers of the friary at Walsingham to examine your son."

The monk paused.

"Yes?" said Lanham who knew there must be more.

"I am to determine whether your son is suitable to take his vows to become their brother, or—"

Father Cuthbert hesitated once again. He was unsure of the reaction on Lanham's face, which took on a surprising look of hopeful expectation.

"Or whether his acute interest in the study of satanic rights, as reported by the brothers in Walsingham as well as the brothers of the monastery at which he studied in Bavaria, is unhealthy or even—"

His voice grew even more serious.

"—heresy."

The hopeful look on Lanham's face changed to confusion and then anger. Before Lanham could speak, Father Regis turned to walk toward the door.

"We must go quickly, Father Cuthbert."

Father Regis looked back to Lanham.

"Richard, you will come with us," he ordered before moving speedily down the hall despite the dark.

2017 For a few minutes, the black sky turned less angry as the lightning abated. Don's grip on the steering wheel finally relaxed a little as he drove through the steady rain down a mercifully straight stretch of road. He tried to fidget away the clammy discomfort of his wet clothes against the leather of his seat.

Don's worry about Margeaux pounded at his thoughts. His mind bounced around all sorts of scenarios in which she alternately was perfectly safe or in mortal danger. Somehow he believed he could find the answer by looking at the final gargoyle hidden behind the wood casement in the corner. Yet he didn't even know for certain that there was another gargoyle. And if there were, would it reveal a possible threat to Margeaux, as the other gargoyles had conveyed their foreboding messages? Glancing down at the speedometer, Don saw that he had slowed down during the distraction of his worries. He focused on the road and sped up significantly. Another bright flash of lightning told him the storm was not yet over. His hands tightened hard on the steering wheel once again.

"Dammit!" he muttered a few minutes later after throwing a glimpse at his rear view mirror. The flashing lights of a police car trailed him about a quarter mile behind. "What are they doing out here?"

Don's mind jumped back two days to his interrogation at the police station, then ahead to what he might find at the church, and finally back to the mirror to judge the distance between Sally and the police car. He made his decision.

"Come on, Sally," he urged under his breath as he pressed down even harder on the accelerator.

Looking back repeatedly, Don saw the police car keeping pace in the distance. He felt the undulations of the car rising and falling over dips where the road had settled next to the flat fields of the fens. Great splashes kicked sideways out of the car's wheel wells from standing water in the road. He knew the stretch of straight road would soon end and he would have to slow down through the curves that followed ancient thoroughfares of past centuries.

Sally's headlights illuminated a deep water slick across the first curve. Don yanked the steering wheel against the car's sideways skid, but could not keep the car on the road. With two large bumps, Sally settled luckily into the mud at a break in the hedge where farm equipment accessed the field.

Don angrily pounded the steering wheel with his palms and sat waiting in the stalled car for the police. About twenty seconds later, the flashing lights filled his mirror. He was trying to come up with an explanation for the police when, to his amazed relief, the police car splashed through the standing water at a more reasonable speed and continued on past him.

Climbing out of the car, Don realized that in the dark, the car's position between the hedges had managed to hide the car from the road. He walked around to the back of the car to sort out the situation. The police car's flashing lights disappeared around the next curve. He looked down to see Sally's rear wheels partially buried in mud.

With no real choice, Don climbed back into the car, wiped the rain from his face, started the engine, and put the car in reverse. When the rear wheels started spinning in the mud, he immediately eased off the accelerator, not wanting to bury the wheels deeper.

While Sally's engine purred in the rain, Don opened the door and slopped through the mud to the rear of the car. There he reached around into the boot and grabbed his MG insignia car blankets. He wedged a blanket under each rear tire to give the car some chance of traction in the mud. After standing up to head back to the open car door, he suddenly crouched back down as the lights of the police car flashed by in the reverse direction after losing its quarry.

Thunder rumbled around him as he crawled back into the car, sat down, and slowly pressed on the gas pedal. He felt nothing for a second as the wheels spun in the mud, but then he sensed a slight lurch as the blankets worked their way under the tires. With perfect timing, he gently accelerated when he felt the blankets catching the tires. The tread of the tires moved back onto slightly drier ground, spun for another second, and then caught some traction, springing Sally free. Don carefully negotiated his way in reverse back to the road, then jammed the gearshift forward to speed off down the road away from his pursuers.

Sally's headlights soon caught the road sign to Atwelle. The town was twelve miles away. Don leaned forward as if that could make the car go faster. His soaked shirt clung to him like a second skin, and the wet muddy wool of his trousers itched his legs. When he finally pulled up to the church, the storm had reached its full fury with lightning and thunder alternating in the howling wind as if nature were singing out an unpredictable call and response.

Don sprinted down the outside of the church, the blowing rain stinging his face. Reaching the side door that remained open under its low arch, he hastily ducked through. The altar was still illuminated by the spotlight above. He paused when he thought he heard something, but after a moment of silence, ran over to the scaffolding in the corner.

As if to confirm that he had really seen the gargoyle above him a few hours earlier, Don stared for a long moment up into the blackness above. Then he looked down, picked up the hand axe lying in the shadows at his feet, and hurried over to the opposite corner. Once again, his eyes tried to pierce the darkness above to see the wood enclosing the roof beam at the corner.

Laying down the hand axe, Don ran back to the low doorway. The stone floor was slippery from the wet glaze and reflected the dim light. After a few paces along the outside wall of the church, he reached into the tall wet grass where his hands felt for the old ladder.

The buffeting wind kept Don off balance after he lifted the long ladder and tried to maneuver it through the door. Its ends bounced off the ground like a teeter totter as he slipped on the ground. By the time he had threaded it under the low archway and carried it over to the corner of the church, his arms and shoulders were aching.

When Don placed the ladder firmly against the wall, he felt the flex in its long rails that extended up the wall into the dark above. The cold rain on the back of his neck, along with the fear of what he was about to do, sent a shiver through his body. He tried to shut everything out of his mind as he grabbed the hand axe from the floor.

"Just climb!" He gave himself the command out loud over an ominous rumble of thunder when he placed his foot on the first rung.

Flashes of lightning followed one another in close irregular succession, illuminating Don's steady ascent. He could feel each rung sag under his weight, but he pressed on without stopping. Then, when nearly at the top, he heard a loud cracking sound an instant before a rung gave way under his foot.

Don clutched the rail with his free hand and his other hand fumbled to keep the axe from falling while his muddy shoe flailed against the rail until it found a solid rung. Steadying his body and his fear, he closed his eyes and leaned his forehead against a rung of the ladder. He could feel his heart pounding.

A sharp, vibrating clap of thunder right outside the stained glass made him flinch. Opening his eyes, he grimaced as he saw his hand clutching the rail at the spot stained brown with Squeaky's blood. The awful sight spurred him on to the remaining rungs at the top.

Don steadied himself only a second before he started smashing the blade of the axe against the planks covering the corner roof beam at its base. Oblivious to the swaying ladder, he rained repeated blows to the wood. Shards of wood stuck to his wet face and hair. His only thought was about what could be happening to Margeaux. With the frenzied hope that a twelfth gargoyle was there waiting to tell him, he forced his aching arm to keep hacking at the splintering casement.

Large chunks of wood started falling away. His free hand ripped away loose pieces of planking. Don leaned in to see what lay in the dark corner.

"Come on!" he tried to compel nature to give him a well-timed bolt of lightning. Squinting into the shadows, he waited until an obliging flash of light through the blood-red stained glass gave him a momentary glimpse of the ceiling's final secret.

Under long wavy hair sculpted around its face, the fangs and teeth of a female demon were bared over the head of a man held out in front of her between the claws of her hands. A second flash of lightning through the stained glass indelibly imprinted the horrifying picture in his mind.

Don's thoughts raced to figure out its meaning. What was the gargoyle telling him about Margeaux's disappearance and the danger she was in? Holding on to the ladder tightly, he felt confused, vulnerable, and powerless.

"No!"

The cry rang out through the church. Looking down, Don saw Father Lanham hurriedly approaching the base of the ladder. Then he saw more movement. The white hair of Father Adams became visible as he ran down the side aisle of the church toward the ladder. Both figures in black converged below, where they each grabbed the ladder before grappling to pull the other's hands from the rails.

Clinging to the ladder, Don watched the two men wrestle below. Each struggled to put the other off balance until they banged into the base of the ladder. Don lurched to one side and dropped the axe as he grabbed a firmer hold on the ladder to keep from falling. Spinning around, the two men jostled the ladder again.

Don reached out to catch hold of the wooden carving on the roof beam. He managed to hook his hand around one of the gargoyle's arms that was holding the head in front of the she-devil just as the scuffle underneath jarred the ladder once more. When the men both caromed hard off the ladder, Don reached over to grab the carved head with two hands while he tried to steady the ladder with his feet. The clash below went quiet, but Don could not look down from the precarious position of his twisted body.

Suddenly the ladder was wrenched away from under his feet. His arms were jolted straight down from the carved head, from which he now hung suspended. His fingers dug into the wood as his legs swung back and forth beneath him. All Don could see was the gargoyle leering at him with her fangs bared.

The wood between his hands cracked loudly. Dangling there desperately, he looked down at the stone floor far below and quickly back up. His panicked eyes searched for something else to grab until, with a splintering snap, the carving broke away from the roof beam.

Don's hands clawed at the air helplessly from the heights he hated as he felt himself fall and fall and fall . . .

TWENTY-THREE

1532 "I demand to know where you are taking me and what is going on."

Richard Lanham attempted to reassert his authority as he struggled to keep up with Father Regis and Father Cuthbert. They ignored him as they pressed on down the dark road. Though he received no answer, Lanham did his best to stay right on their heels.

"Your insinuations about my son are preposterous." Lanham tried a few minutes later to raise them in argument once again. "Satanic rites—ridiculous!"

As before, the clergymen kept striding forward without paying him notice. The wind at their back began to ease. Soon, Lanham realized where they were headed. The large silhouette of the DuBois manor house loomed ahead.

It took a while for a servant to respond to Father Regis's loud knocks on the entrance door.

"Father Regis?" the surprised woman asked sleepily as she cupped her hand around the fluttering flame of the candle to protect it from the breeze that blew through the open door.

"Lord Lanham!" she exclaimed, surprised once again as she peered at the men behind Father Regis.

"Go tell your master we are here," Father Regis told her. "And hurry," he added as they stepped inside out of the wind.

"See here, Father Regis. There is no reason for my being here," Lanham objected once more. "You will have to answer to the both of us for this impertinence to me and DuBois."

His threat was met with a stony silence from the priest and the monk.

"I fear no man, save the king," he warned them when he got no reply.

"Then do you fear God?" Father Regis responded. "And do you fear for your soul? For you should with what you could face tonight."

Lanham stood there without replying while they waited in grim silence for DuBois. A moment later DuBois was hurrying down the staircase with his wife close behind.

"Sirs, why are you here at this hour?" he asked. He surveyed the night visitors with a lingering glance at the unfamiliar monk in the black cowl.

"I am sorry to raise you from your slumber, Francis," Father Regis apologized. "But we are here out of concern for your daughter."

"Margaret?" DuBois looked surprised. "Who is this monk?" he asked, trying to understand the reason for their appearance and interest in his daughter.

"This is Father Cuthbert. He is here for the Bishop of Norwich," answered Father Regis.

A solemn nod tipped towards DuBois from the black hood. DuBois gave a questioning look at Lanham while his wife had an expression of deep concern.

"Is Margaret here?" Father Regis asked.

DuBois looked at his wife and back at Father Regis. "Of course. She is asleep in her bed."

"That is as it should be," said Father Regis. "I fear we may well have disturbed you unnecessarily. But may I still check to be sure she is safe from any harm?"

"That will not be necessary, Father," DuBois replied.

"No, it is right that I do so, especially on All Hallows' Eve," he insisted while approaching DuBois' wife on the stairs. "There may be evil about on this night. Please take me to her room. I will not wake her."

With a frightened look at him, the woman turned and led Father Regis up the stairs. The other men followed close behind. Quietly opening the door to Margaret's bedroom, her mother held out a candle to reveal a figure lying still under the blankets of her bed. The men gathered at the door.

"See," DuBois turned to them. "She is sleeping."

Father Regis spoke softly to Margaret's mother.

"I must make amends. May I bless her as she sleeps to allay your concern? I am sure I will not wake her."

"Of course, Father. Thank you," she replied.

Father Regis moved to the bed. He raised his hand with his fingers poised to make the sign of the cross. Suddenly he reached out with his other hand and threw back the covers with a swift forceful pull.

"Father!" DuBois called out in alarm. His wife threw her hands to her mouth.

Uncovered on the bed lay nothing but a mound of blankets and clothes.

2017 Don lay very still on the cold stone floor as he regained a foggy sense of consciousness. His throbbing head soon sensed the aches he knew would become bruises. Carefully moving each limb, he winced as a sharp pain shot through his ankle. At the sound of a groan next to him, Don opened his eyes.

There lay Father Adams alongside him with the vicar's arm trapped underneath Don's body. The man's glazed eyes were trying to fix on Don's face. Don sat up quickly and backed away on his hands and knees. His movement seemed to bring Father Adams's vision into focus.

"Are you all right?" Father Adams's voice was weak.

Don nodded. The vicar could see Don was wary of him. He took as deep a breath as he could to speak.

"I am not who you have to worry about," said Father Adams. "I called the police earlier. They should be here soon." His face grimaced as his hand went to his chest.

Don realized the old man could not move and posed no threat. "Where are you hurt?"

"It's my heart and my ribs," answered the vicar after some labored breaths. "You fell directly on me."

"Let me loosen your collar," said Don as he reached out for the tight black clerical collar surrounding the man's neck.

"No. There's no time," he wheezed. His hand moved from his chest and reached into his coat where he struggled to pull something from his breast pocket. With an effort, he held up a large, heavy key.

"Here, take this key. It's to the chest in—"

Father Adams ran out of breath and could not finish the sentence. Slowly drawing in as much air as he could, he gave Don an urgent look.

"Go open the chest in my study. Quickly!" He stopped to take another breath. "It will tell you what you need to know."

Don looked around. "Let me get you some help."

"The chest!" the vicar insisted, his shaking hand pointing in the direction of his study.

Don took the key and started to stand when the vicar grabbed his arm weakly.

"And Micah," he said in a struggling whisper.

"Who's Micah?" Don asked him.

"Three."

Don could hardly hear his fading voice.

"I don't understand, vicar."

"Go!" Father Adams ordered with the little breath he had left.

Rising from the hard floor, Don felt his body ache all over from the fall, and his right ankle hurt worse than he expected. He limped as quickly as he could down the length of the church to the small entry to the ancient spiral stone staircase leading up to the vicar's study. At the top of the stairs, he pushed open the door. A low light came from the lamp sitting on the vicar's desk. There in the corner sat the long low massive chest.

Don quickly called for an ambulance for Father Adams before hobbling over to the chest. He inserted the key into the lock. The lock initially resisted until the key finally turned with a heavy clicking sound. But when he tried to lift the long lid, it didn't budge. Don grabbed the lid at a different spot and tried to wrench it free. It still refused to open.

He ran his hand along the length of the lid and realized the problem. There were two more keyholes barely visible around each corner on the side of the lid. The two keyholes looked smaller, and he feared they needed a different key. Relieved when the large key fit at first, he frowned when it would not move after he tried to turn it. He tried again and again with no luck. Frustrated, he jiggled the key and moved it around. To his surprise, the entire key slid into the lock up to its handle at the end. When he tried to turn it again, he heard the lock give way. Don scrambled on his hands and knees to the lock on the other corner. He pushed the key up to its hilt into the lock and turned it until he felt the lid free up with a final click.

In the shadows of the room, Don at first could not see anything but darkness inside the chest. The darkness inside, he soon discovered, came from black vestments carefully folded and filling the chest. Don grabbed them and tossed them aside on the floor as he dug down, until he could peer deep into the chest. There was a shelf with a wooden handle on top. Grasping the handle, he carefully pulled. Up and out of the shelf slid a three-sided wooden box. The open side revealed a piece of thick aged parchment folded several times with two large wax seals next to each other on the top fold.

Don hobbled over to the vicar's desk. He swept to the side everything on the desk including the vicar's worn Bible. Then he carefully unfolded the ancient parchment document and positioned the desk lamp directly over it. Studying its script quickly, he paused often to reread carefully some of the words. When he reached the signatures at the end of the document, Don shook his head in wonder before refolding the document and placing it in his coat pocket.

His whole body hurt as he stood up. When he walked around the corner of the desk, the sharp pain in his ankle took away his breath. He leaned on the desk a moment to steady himself. His hand pressed down against the vicar's Bible. Pausing a moment to let the pain pass, he looked down at the worn book filled with bookmarks.

"Micah three," Don muttered as he flipped open the Bible.

"The Book of Micah," he confirmed as he found chapter three bookmarked in the Old Testament by a small envelope tucked between the pages. Don read the opening verses of chapter three that were carefully underlined in pencil:

> And I said, Hear, I pray you, O heads of Jacob, and ye princes of the house of Israel; Is it not for you to know judgment?
>
> Who hate the good, and love the evil; who pluck off their skin from off them, and their flesh from off their bones;
>
> Who also eat the flesh of my people, and flay their skin from off them; and they break their bones, and chop them in pieces, as for the pot, and as flesh within the caldron.
>
> Then shall they cry unto the Lord, but he will not hear them: he will even hide his face from them, at that time as they have behaved themselves ill in their doings.

He turned the envelope over to look at both sides. The front was covered with so many stamps there was only a small open space where the letter was addressed to Father Adams in Haiti. Don hastily slipped a single-page letter out of the envelope and read it quickly before standing up once again to head to the door.

Feeling his way down the stone stairs, he entered the nave and shuffled as fast as he could back to where he had left Father Adams. Don felt the beads of sweat on his forehead though the air in the church was cold on his face. Questions for the vicar swirled in his mind along with his concern for the man.

"Vicar?" Don called out as he limped hurriedly into the chancel to the corner of the church where he had left Father Adams. But the only thing in the shadows on the floor were the remnants of the broken gargoyle to which Don had clung for his life. The vicar was nowhere to be seen.

TWENTY-FOUR

1532 The storm passed over Atwelle, and the bright moon of All Hallows' Eve filled the sky as Lanham, DuBois, and the two clergymen hurried down the road toward the town. An eerie stillness fell over the land and silenced the laymen as Father Regis and Father Cuthbert spoke in hushed tones.

"They could be anywhere among the souls who have been denied entry to both heaven and hell," Father Cuthbert said to Father Regis. "Tonight is the first of the dark half of the year. It is the night when both hell and heaven can find their way to Earth."

"If these spirits are neither in heaven or hell, where do they go?" Father Regis asked. He was not thinking of spirits as much as he was thinking of Christopher and Margaret.

"That is difficult to say. This night they are active as they move through our world in search of an eternal home," Father Cuthbert replied.

Father Regis looked over at the black hood that hid Father Cuthbert's face.

"And because the spirits are active on this night, we bless our homes to protect the people inside. And we pray beside the graves of our loved ones for their souls."

"But it is not only the spirits who haunt this night," said Father Cuthbert, who worried about the children of Lanham and DuBois. "It is also the goblins and witches and agents of the devil that celebrate their black rites to claim the lost spirits and souls of the dead roaming the earth."

Where the men should go suddenly became clear to Father Regis.

"Father Cuthbert, where do we pray for our dead?"

"In the graveyard and in the church where they lie."

"And if we pray to protect our homes, where is our home, Father Cuthbert?"

"The church," he answered.

"And where in Atwelle would one celebrate rites for souls roaming the earth lost between heaven and hell?" Father Regis asked.

Father Cuthbert stopped short and looked at him. "A place that is part of the earth and yet part of heaven."

"An unfinished church that is partly consecrated," Father Regis finished the answer.

"Should they come with us?" Father Cuthbert asked the question as though Lanham and DuBois could not hear him.

"Oh yes," answered Father Regis without hesitation. "They shall come with us," he said firmly as he walked even more briskly toward the town.

Winding their way quickly through the streets and along the waterway of Atwelle, the four men finally arrived at the church. They entered through the door standing open to the roofless shell of the church. The moon shone brightly, and deep shadows were cast on the grounds surrounded by the uncompleted walls.

Once inside, they moved cautiously down the length of the church, not knowing what to expect. They saw and heard nothing until a small light appeared on the ground toward the end of the church. Then a second light lit up next to it like a small flame.

"Evil spirits rising," whispered Father Cuthbert until fear froze the words in his throat.

All four men knelt low to the ground behind a stack of timbers that were waiting to be carved into roof beams. The lights continued to rise until they illuminated the hands and arms holding them.

"The sergeant's missing limbs," said Father Regis in a horrified whisper. "Coming out of the ground."

Lanham and DuBois were white with terror as they too recognized the man's gloves. Father Cuthbert was transfixed by what appeared before them.

"On this night, the souls of the dead revisit their homes," he said in a low murmur.

"Wait—look!" Father Regis interrupted in a hushed voice.

As the candles continued to rise, the full figure of a man appeared to be holding them. The man's figure was accompanied by the silhouette of a woman who stood behind him with her arms raised up. Both DuBois and Lanham were seized with fear at the sight of the apparitions floating out of the ground.

"The sergeant and Molly," the two of them whispered almost simultaneously without hearing one another.

"They are not coming out of the ground." Father Regis leaned forward. "They are coming out of the crypt," he realized.

The ghost of the sergeant turned to face the woman he loved. The light of the candles fell on her face and stiff arms raised high.

DuBois reached over and grabbed Lanham's arm. It was Lanham's son holding the candles in the sergeant's gloves. Margaret DuBois stood before him. Above her extended arms, she held the still body of a naked baby.

While murmuring a short unintelligible chant, Margaret laid the infant's body on the ground. Christopher responded with a similar rhythmic incantation in Latin. When he finished, he handed one of the candles to Margaret before picking up a goblet sitting next to the entrance to the crypt. Raising up the cup, he made the sign of the cross with the candle in his hand above the goblet and then made a slow measured gesture with the candle below the goblet.

"The sign of the devil!" hissed Father Cuthbert.

Margaret began waving her head about wildly, her hair flying back and forth around the candle in her hand. She seemed to be chanting once again as if speaking in tongues. Christopher raised the goblet high in the air and called out another phrase in Latin.

Lanham and DuBois saw the two clergymen tense with a start at Christopher's words before he turned to hand the goblet to Margaret. She passed her candle to Christopher and placed both hands around the cup. Drawing it to her lips, she tipped her head back as she drank.

Even in the moonlight, the four men could see the dark lines of blood running from the corners of her mouth. Her head came forward, and she passed the cup to Christopher. He handed her the candles as he took the goblet in his hands.

Watching Christopher raise the cup to drink, Richard Lanham stood suddenly.

"No!" he yelled at his son.

Christopher gave a startled look in the direction of the four men. Margaret, blood dripping from her chin, let out a scream of fright and then a shriek of fury. Christopher threw the goblet to the ground to grab the candles from Margaret. Their flames went out. The four men heard Margaret scream in the dark once more before everything went silent.

The four men moved forward carefully in the moonlight to the entrance to the crypt. Margaret and Christopher were nowhere to be seen. Father Cuthbert found the cold body of the baby and started praying over the small corpse. Hearing the prayers in Latin, DuBois and Lanham fell despondently to their knees, not knowing what else to do.

Father Regis turned on the two shocked men with an accusing look.

"These are the most horrific and ghastly acts that humans can commit anywhere and under any circumstances. But such vile deeds done in the shadows of this unfinished church—this holy ground—can be matched in God's eyes by no other sin."

The men kneeled on the ground in silence, unable to raise protest or defense.

"There can be no doubt," the priest continued, "that such abomination and heinous crimes shall be punished by excommunication through the pope's edict and by execution on the king's command. These are certain."

At this announcement, the shaken men looked up at the priest and monk. Father Cuthbert slowly nodded his head in somber agreement. DuBois spoke with a plea in his voice.

"Father, there must be some way mercy can be shown."

"Yes, Father," agreed Lanham. "What can we do?"

"You will do what any Christian who has responsibility for sin must do," the priest answered. "You will give confession and do penance for these evil works."

Both men nodded humbly. Yet the priest gave them another stern look.

"And it will be public confession and penance."

"That will not happen, Father," Lanham declared immediately as if the loathsome sight they had just experienced could be denied.

"It cannot be," confirmed DuBois. "That would be our doom, the end of our families."

"Hear me and make no mistake," Father Regis glowered at them. "You will confess all in front of God and the world, and pay a dear price for God's forgiveness if you are even to dare ask for His mercy."

As the two men started to object once again, Father Regis silenced them with a raised hand. Father Cuthbert stepped behind them as if to prevent their escape.

"Hear me out, for you have no choice in the matter," decreed Father Regis. "Your wealth and power will proffer no immunity. But your families and fortunes will not be destroyed if you listen well and follow my instructions.

"These words, written under your signature and seal, will state the manner by which you shall do your public confession and penance . . ."

TWENTY-FIVE

2017 Don stood there not knowing what to do. The hand axe and battered old ladder lay on the church floor among the scattered wood chunks and splinters from the gargoyle and its casing above. There were no signs of Father Adams or what had become of him.

The rush of gusting wind outside sounded like large waves hitting the shore. Another low flash of lightning came through the stained glass bathing the altar in a splash of unnatural reddish orange light. A low rumble of thunder followed seconds later.

When the sounds of the thunder and the wind ebbed simultaneously for just an instant, Don's ears perked up at an unfamiliar sound. He paused, trying to hear over the renewed gusts of wind. Then he heard it again. It sounded almost like a distant small cry. Puzzling over what it could be, he heard it again a second later. This time, the sound seemed to come from the altar.

Don limped on his throbbing ankle as quickly as he could over to the altar and circled it cautiously. He saw that one of the large ornate candlesticks was missing. A deafening crack of thunder and a bright flash of lightning spun his head toward the large stained glass window. His eyes fell on the grate over the entrance to the crypt. It was slightly ajar. He shuffled painfully to the grate and kneeled next to it.

"I hate churches at night," he mumbled under his breath as he pried the grate up with his fingers and slid it away to the side. He heard the sound again. There was no mistaking it. It was the distinct cry of an unhappy infant.

With a careful, halting hobble, Don made his way noiselessly down the winding staircase. Nearing the bottom, he saw the glow of candlelight at the entrance to the crypt and stopped. He could see a limp hand at the end of a black sleeve lying on the floor at the base of the stairs. After another step, Don saw the sleeve and shoulder attached to a black clerical collar. He hunched down and peered into the crypt.

There sat Miss Daunting on the small coffin, trying to quiet the baby in her arms as she brushed back a long strand of gray hair from her face. Next to them, Margeaux stood beside Father Regis's sarcophagus. In the steady glow from the large silver candlestick sitting on the sarcophagus, Don saw the surprised looks on their faces. He looked down at Father Adams' lifeless body on the floor.

"Margeaux, are you all right?" asked Don as he took the final step into the crypt. Before she could answer, he heard another voice.

"She's just fine, Mr. Whitby."

Don felt the sharp point of a knife blade on the side of his neck. The firm grasp of a hand on his arm and the pressure of the knife blade steered him over to the third coffin and pushed him to the floor. When Don looked up, he saw the long blade of a knife in the hand of Father Lanham.

"What's going on here, Lanham?" Don demanded.

"It's quite clear, Don," Father Lanham answered with sarcastic friendliness in his voice. "I discovered you here in the crypt after you killed Father Adams and then found that you were keeping Nigel's baby here after you abducted him. And now you've abducted these two ladies on All Hallows' Eve."

"*You* found *me*? You're saying I killed Father Adams and abducted the women?"

"Yes, with this knife."

The curate held up the knife with a look up and down its long sharp blade. Don saw numerous needle marks on the inside of his arm.

"Look, Lanham. I know what you're up to. Don't harm the women or the baby. The police are on their way."

"I know," answered Lanham. "I called them. They should be here just after I—or should I say *you* finished your dirty work here before I discovered you, wrestled you for control of your knife, and stabbed you in self-defense."

He smiled down at Don on the floor.

"I had planned to just tell the police I discovered you here doing your work of the devil before you fled. But now with a little improvisation, this new situation with you showing up should turn out quite splendidly. All very neatly tied up for the police."

"You don't have to hurt the women or the child, Lanham," urged Don. "There's no point in doing this. You can escape now before the police come."

"There most certainly is a point to all this, Mr. Whitby. But don't worry. I won't hurt them."

They all looked over at the stairway suddenly as they heard footsteps thumping their way down. With a surprised look, Lanham dropped the knife in Don's lap and stepped hastily over next to Miss Daunting, taking the baby in his arms. Don stood up with the knife in his hand just as Inspector Russell lowered his head to enter the crypt.

"Nobody move!" he ordered as he saw the body of Father Adams and drew a gun out of his shoulder holster. Inspector Russell's eyes scanned the crypt as he clicked off his flashlight. There was a brief look of relief in his face when he saw the baby in Father Lanham's arms.

"Mr. Whitby, drop the knife on the ground. Now!"

His gun was pointed at Don's chest. The knife clattered on the stone floor as Don immediately let go of it.

"Now slowly turn around and place your hands behind your back," the inspector ordered as he reached into his coat to grab his handcuffs.

"Thank you for coming so quickly, Inspector," said Father Lanham.

Inspector Russell locked the handcuffs around Don's wrists, turned him around, and firmly pushed him to the floor where he sat once again leaning against the sergeant's coffin. The Inspector walked over to Father Adams' body and kneeled down next to it. After feeling for a pulse briefly, the inspector stood up.

"Now explain what's going on here. First I receive a call from Father Adams and then I get a call from you, Father Lanham, to come to the church because of a murder threat."

"Inspector, I've had suspicions about Mr. Whitby and Father Adams for some time," Lanham explained. "After the awful deaths in the parish, I suspected that they related to satanic rites similar to those in Haiti where Father Adams lived for thirty years. I did some research into satanic rites which suggested that tonight, on All Hallows' Eve, something terrible might happen.

"I followed the vicar and Mr. Whitby to the entrance to the crypt and called you. Then I heard the vicar and Mr. Whitby arguing, followed by a scuffle. When I came down, I saw Father Adams lying there and then found the women being held against their will and the baby as well.

"It was horrible, Inspector. I was frightened to death to think of what those two men were going to do in this church to this poor baby and these women. I was doing what I could to prevent Mr. Whitby from harming them until you arrived, thank heavens."

"Is the baby all right?" Inspector Russell asked.

"Yes, thank God," answered Lanham.

"Ladies, you okay?"

Miss Daunting and Margeaux nodded at Inspector Russell. Margeaux started to speak, but the Inspector interrupted her with a raised hand before pulling out his phone and, with his gun still trained on Don, calling for more back up police and an ambulance.

"Inspector," Don addressed him, "everything you've just heard is a lie. I can prove it to you."

"Mr. Whitby, it would be best for you if you say nothing and wait to speak with a lawyer."

"Please Inspector, let me speak. I'll tell you everything," declared Don. "But first tell Father Lanham to give the baby to Miss Daunting. Please. The baby's sleeping. It will do no harm."

The Inspector looked uncertain.

"Please!" Don insisted.

Inspector Russell heard the urgency in his voice and hesitated. "All right, Mr. Whitby. But I don't want any trouble from you," he warned with a gesture of his gun. He nodded at Father Lanham who handed the baby to Miss Daunting.

"Thank you, Inspector," Don said and then carried on.

"Inspector, in my inside right coat pocket is a rather unusual document you need to see."

When the Inspector hesitated, Don twisted his body so the policeman could see there was a paper document inside his coat. The Inspector approached him guardedly.

"No funny business, Whitby," Inspector Russell warned with a wave of his gun as he cautiously reached into Don's coat pocket.

Stepping back, the Inspector held up the piece of folded aged parchment. His gun in one hand, he managed clumsily to open its several folds with the other hand. First he examined the elaborate seals on the back and then turned the document over to the first page. He looked up after a few moments.

"I can't read much of this," he announced. "The language is convoluted. The spellings are a bit odd."

"That's because it was written on this day, All Hallows' Eve, in 1532, Inspector," said Don. "The date is on the signature page at the end. It is a truly extraordinary legal document," he continued as the Inspector, holding his gun, looked at the parchment, "drafted by the priest of this church at that time, while the church was being rebuilt.

"I just had a chance to read it before I came down here and you arrived. Let me tell you what it says."

The Inspector lowered the paper and turned to listen to Don.

"The document was signed by two men who were the heads of the two most powerful families in Atwelle at the time, the head of the

DuBois family and the ancestor of the curate here, the head of the Lanham family. They signed it after the two men and the priest interrupted a cannibalistic satanic rite being conducted right here in this crypt by Lanham's son and DuBois' daughter."

A look of distaste came over Inspector Russell as he glanced uneasily around the crypt and continued to listen.

"In this document," said Don, "the two men agree to give public confession and pay penance for the crimes of their children and families.

"As penance, their entire estates were combined and their ownership placed under two trusts. The first trust was to fund the rebuilding of this church, St. Clement's, with a percentage of income from the trust to go to the families to support their living expenses.

"As for their public confession, Inspector, it was placed in the church for the public's viewing every time anyone stepped inside. Their crimes and confession are told by the gargoyles carved in the roof beams of the church for all to see. The gargoyles were to be carved specifically by a wood-carver named Bittergreen, for what looked to be a pretty handsome sum at that time, I'm guessing."

"What about the second trust?" asked Inspector Russell.

"The second trust sets aside some money from both family estates and rights from income from the Port of Atwelle for the funding of a secret society formed under this trust agreement. The society is called the Order of Black Vestments and is comprised of priests who are tasked with vigilantly preventing the families or their children from ever committing evil acts again. The priests were to wear only black vestments to remind them and the families of their vows of vigilance."

"Inspector," Father Lanham interrupted, "this history is all very interesting, but I fail to see how it has anything to do with—"

"Just a moment, Father," Inspector Russell stopped him. He turned back to Don. "How does this document prove that what Father Lanham has said is untrue?"

"In my left coat pocket, Inspector, you'll find another document that's much more recent. It was written a few months ago by Father Charleton just before he disappeared."

Inspector Russell stepped over, reached into Don's coat, and pulled out an envelope. Holding it up to the candlelight, the Inspector studied the address below a large number of stamps that filled most of the front of the envelope.

"The envelope is postmarked the day Father Charleton was last seen," noted Inspector Russell.

"It's a letter addressed to Father Adams in Haiti and signed by Father Charleton. Charleton's salutation to Adams and his signature refer to both of them as members of the Order of Black Vestments."

Inspector Russell listened to Don without bothering to open the envelope.

"The letter starts by telling Father Adams that Charleton has a solution to the problem of funding the current restoration of the church," Don said. "It turns out that the original trust for the rebuilding of the church in 1532 has never had much money in it because it was mostly spent to complete the church back then. However, the money in the other trust for the Order of Black Vestments has been compounding for almost five centuries with very little having been spent from it.

"According to the letter, Father Charleton's plan as the trustee of the Black Vestment trust was to dissolve that trust and move its money into the church's funds controlled by the church wardens for restoration of the church. Once that was done, several million pounds would become available for the restoration and operation of the church.

"But then he also warns Father Adams, the only other member of the Order of Black Vestments, that he believes there is someone among the people he has told about his plans who is not only a threat to his plan for the trusts, but now also a threat to his safety. He asks Father Adams to return as soon as possible."

Don paused. "Someone killed Father Charleton to stop him from moving the money in the trust for the Order of Black Vestments to the church's funds where the head of the Order cannot access and control it.

"But when Father Adams unexpectedly came back as vicar of the church to head up the Order and identify the threat to Father Charleton, he could not be killed as well on the heels of Father Charleton's disappearance without raising suspicion. So someone arranged the murders in this church to mimic the murders in the gargoyle carvings to prevent the trust for the Order of Black Vestments from being dissolved."

Don looked over at the others. Lanham fidgeted nervously while Daunting rocked the baby. Margueax looked at Inspector Russell to gauge his reaction.

"How would that stop the trust from being dissolved?" asked Inspector Russell.

"I'm no lawyer, but I know from working with church budgets that only a court can dissolve a trust, and it cannot be done if the express purposes of the trust still exist. If the trust was established to stop murders in the church and there are still murders in the church, anyone could object to the dissolution of the trust."

Inspector Russell concentrated closely on Don's words.

"And if the trust is not dissolved, then the next head of the Order of Black Vestments after Father Adams, say a young curate already in place at St. Clement's, could have access to the millions in the trust and could disappear with the money."

All eyes turned to Father Lanham.

"Inspector, this whole story has gotten out of hand," the assistant vicar objected as he calmly took Nigel's baby from Miss Daunting and started bouncing him playfully in his arms.

He suddenly pulled a knife and put it to the baby's throat. Margeaux gasped. Don scrambled to his feet.

"Nobody move!" the man ordered.

"Inspector, I want you to point the barrel of your gun into the palm of your free hand, and then take the gun by the barrel with your fingers and lay it slowly on the floor. And lay your phone next to it, if you don't want the baby to get hurt."

Inspector Russell carefully followed the instructions. Father Lanham turned to Miss Daunting.

"Go pick up the gun," he told her.

Miss Daunting walked over and gingerly lifted up the gun from the floor, her long gray hair cascading around her as she leaned over.

"Now kick the phone away from the Inspector," he directed.

The phone clattered across the floor against the wall of the crypt after she did what she was told. When she walked back to Father Lanham, she promptly handed the gun to him. Don and the inspector stared at her in surprise.

The curate laid the baby down on the sarcophagus in front of him and walked over to Margeaux with the gun pointed in her direction.

"Now we're all going be very calm about this," Lanham said. But instead of calm, he was jittery. "Miss Daunting is going to leave shortly with the baby, and I am going to leave with Miss Wood," he announced.

He waived the gun about nervously. Margeaux looked at him uncertainly.

"I want no interference of any kind. Do you understand?" he ordered with even more agitation. "Once we get out of the church, we'll leave little Junior for you to come and change his diaper, but we'll still have Miss Wood. Is that clear?"

"No," said Margeaux. "Just take me. Leave the baby. I'm the only hostage you need."

"Inspector," Don interrupted, "I've just now realized something else. The mastermind for this venture isn't Lanham."

Don looked over at Father Adams's body and then at Miss Daunting.

"There's only one person who knew everything about this situation—one person who first knew from Father Charleton about the huge amount of money in the trust for the Order of Black Vestments. A person who was not suspected and who was clever enough to put a plan in place to have complete control of the Order and its trust money once Father Charleton had mysteriously disappeared.

"Someone who then learned of Father Charleton's intention to dissolve the trust for the Order of Black Vestments to combine the trusts to fund the rebuilding project at St. Clement's—a glitch in the plan which would ruin control over access to the trust money. That person figured out the trust for the Order of Black Vestments could not be dissolved if its stated legal purpose, the prevention of evil and murders in the church, was still unfulfilled."

Miss Daunting looked nervously at the curate holding the gun.

"The person," Don concluded, "who also knew from reading the trust agreements in the chest in Father Charleton's study about the gargoyles on the roof beams that told of the confession for murders— murders that would prevent the dissolution of the trust for the Order of Black Vestments if they were repeated today."

With a questioning look, Inspector Russell waited for Don to reveal the person's name.

"If you want to know who that mastermind is, Inspector, I suggest you ask Miss Wood. Or perhaps you should address her by her real name, her family name in its original French— Miss DuBois."

Don turned to Margeaux. "My French is a little rusty, Margeaux. But I believe *du bois* is French for 'wood,' is it not?"

"Whitby's right," the young vicar unexpectedly exclaimed. Everyone turned to look at him in surprise. There was panic in his face. His whole demeanor changed in a heartbeat as his loyalty to the conspiracy crumbled with drug-addled fear. He let go of Margeaux's arm and stepped away from her.

"Her name is DuBois, but I'm not a Lanham," he said. "My name's Weatherby."

"Shut up!" Margeaux ordered.

"It was all her idea," Weatherby accused. "She was going to make me head of the Order of Black Vestments and take the trust money when we got control of it. I just got out of prison and needed money and a break. Margeaux came to me with the whole plan."

"Shut up, I told you!"

"The murders were all her idea!" the man protested as he threw the gun on the floor.

Lunging suddenly for the gun, Margeaux knocked over the candlestick. The crypt went completely black as the candle hit the floor. A loud gunshot and a ricocheting bullet reverberated throughout the chamber. Don heard the sound of shuffling feet stumbling about as he lurched awkwardly with his hands cuffed behind him to where he thought the baby lay on the sarcophagus. An instant later, it was deadly quiet in the crypt.

"Inspector, are you there?" Don finally called out into the darkness.

"Yes." The inspector's voice sounded like it came from the floor in the corner near the entrance to the stairs.

"There's a ventilation tunnel that exits off behind the sarcophagus," Don said to him. "They're probably trying to escape through that."

Inspector Russell's flashlight clicked on. In the light, Don was crouched over the baby. The three of them were alone. Don stood up and looked down in relief as the infant began to cry angrily.

With his phone at his ear, Inspector Russell reported that backup police were outside the church. "Let me take off those handcuffs," he said to Don.

"First, tell them the ventilation tunnel comes out inside the church-yard wall in the northeast corner," Don told him. "They can quickly find the grate over the opening to the tunnel by going to the only grave in that part of the churchyard. There's a large low slab of stone covering the entire grave. It has just the name 'Peter' carved on it."

A noise came from the floor by the stairs. The beam from the inspector's flashlight swung quickly over to the shadows where the sound of a low moan came from Father Adams as gunshots rang out in the distance.

EPILOGUE

The Master's Lodge. Maryhouse Hall, Cambridge England

2017 "Mr. Whitby, if you would please sign these documents."

Master Hodges gestured for Don to sit at the master's large oak desk in his study. Don felt quite important as he installed himself in the tall leather chair behind the desk, looked around at all the books covering the walls of the master's study, and picked up the pen lying next to the small stack of legal documents.

"Now if you'll just sign here, here, and here," the master's long manicured index finger pointed to the bottom of three pages carefully laid out for Don's attention.

"Thank you," the master said as Don finished. "And now you, Father Adams, if you would please sign just below Mr. Whitby's signatures; plus I need your signature on this additional document as well."

Don rose from the chair and handed Father Adams the pen as they exchanged places.

"Thank you, Father Adams," the master said when the vicar laid down the pen after his final signature. Father Adams looked relieved.

"Gentlemen," said the master as he picked up the documents and meticulously placed them in a file that he then tucked under his arm, "these will be filed tomorrow with the court, which will issue an order officially transferring the funds from the Order of Black Vestments to the new trust for the restoration of the Parish Church of St. Clement in Atwelle.

"You, Mr. Whitby, will then officially be one of the trustees of the restoration trust. I believe the trust will be well guided by your expertise," concluded the master.

Father Adams nodded in agreement.

"Thank you," replied Don. "But I have to ask, Master Hodges, how is it that you came to have responsibility for the trusts for the Order of Black Vestments and the monies from the DuBois and Lanham families?"

"It is a longstanding part of my responsibilities and emoluments of office as Master of Maryhouse Hall," the master responded. "When the trusts were founded in 1532, Father Regis, the priest at St. Clement's, was quite serious about preventing those powerful families from ever perpetrating any similar evils or abuses of power. Father Regis was thinking in terms of centuries. After all, the church and the families had been around for hundreds of years when the trusts were created.

"So who could be appointed to oversee the trusts to preserve their funds and see that their terms would be carried out for centuries? No bank or firm of solicitors could be counted on to last that long. Even the Royal house was not likely to last as needed. So Father Regis picked a person in a position with the ability to administer the trusts for such an extended period."

He smiled confidently at the two men.

"The master of an ancient Cambridge college. Maryhouse Hall had already been in existence around two hundred years when the trusts were formed. Father Regis, who had studied at Maryhouse, provided for the master of Maryhouse Hall to oversee the trusts, which each master has done faithfully for almost half a millennium."

Father Adams shook his head in disbelief.

"Ironically, I was visiting Maryhouse Hall regularly to meet with Master Hodges to plan for the transfer of funds in the trusts for the restoration of St. Clement's, while Miss Wood was plotting at the same time in the very same college to get control of the money in the trust of the Order of Black Vestments."

"It's still hard for me to believe that Margeaux would create such a plot, let alone do what she did to carry it out," said Don. He shuffled through the emotional memories of first meeting this beautiful woman when she swung her binoculars at him, when they shared the excitement of discovering of the gargoyles, and when he and Sally dangerously raced down wet country roads, fearing for her safety.

"She was a very bright, resourceful, and purposeful woman," Master Hodges responded. "She clearly was capable of conceiving the plot to gain control of the trust funds. But I too am surprised that her greed was so ruthless as to persuade, with the promise of great fortune, that fellow Weatherby to commit murders and Miss Daunting to abduct a baby."

"I suspect," offered Father Adams, "that she learned about the Atwelle confession trusts from her family history and her research into the trust documents in the vicar's chest, as well as from discussions with Father Charleton. After that, she recruited Weatherby, who had been in seminary before going to prison, to succeed Father Charleton to gain control over the funds in the Order of Black Vestments. But then, hearing of Father Charleton's plan to dissolve the trust, she quickly had to take Father Charleton out of the picture.

"But instead of her handpicked 'Father Lanham' taking over the trust funds for the Order, I returned to carry on Father Charleton's plan to transfer the Order's funds to the restoration of the church. Then she was clever and ruthless enough to come up with the idea of repeating the murders of the Atwelle confession to have cause to object to the dissolution of the trust."

"She definitely made certain that I knew there were murders that unquestionably perpetuated the purpose of the Order," added the master. "Her accomplice, posing as 'Father Lanham,' would have had ample legal grounds to prevent the transfer of the Order's funds."

"But for Margeaux to commit those horrible crimes . . ." said Don, still struggling to accept it all. "Did you have any suspicion of her, Father Adams?"

"After I received Father Charleton's letter filled with fearful warnings, I knew the motive for evil, but had no idea who was carrying out the crimes. So I was suspicious of everybody," answered the vicar. "Including you, Don, I'm afraid.

"I thought Miss Daunting was the least likely. She seemed harmless. I didn't suspect that Margeaux had brought her into the plan to hide the baby after he was abducted.

"I tested Margeaux by trying to scare her off her project at the church. I was generally unfriendly and even did silly things like banging on the door of the church behind her to frighten her. If she stuck around, then she was still a suspect, I figured. When she stayed with the project even after the murders, I remained suspicious of her, even though it seemed unlikely that she was involved.

"Your involvement, Don, was unclear. You really didn't know Father Charleton or have any connection with the trust funds that I could see. But you were friendly with everybody, making you a potential accomplice with anyone. Because there was nothing concrete to associate you with Father Charleton's concerns, I simply asked the police to check you out closely.

"Then, sadly, there was Father Lanham—I mean Weatherby. I had no inclination initially to suspect him of wrongdoing because he was a man of the cloth who seemed a sincere young man, and I simply didn't think anything of the name 'Lanham' since all the evils of the Lanham family occurred centuries ago. In that, I failed my obligations to the Order of Black Vestments.

"So I did nothing for quite a while until I started to check out his history and credentials in the middle of all of the horrible murders. When the results came back the afternoon of All Hallows' Eve, I found out that our Father Lanham was as phony as a three pound note.

"Then I knew anything involving him was seriously amiss. So when I happened to come out of my office and saw him heading for you at the top of the ladder, I knew I had to do something."

"Thank God you did," said Don.

"It's remarkable, Mr. Whitby," commented the Master, "how you put everything together for the Inspector in those dangerous circumstances in the crypt."

Don shrugged. "After reading the Atwelle confession document and Father Charleton's letter, it just came to me all at once that there had to be someone behind this who knew everything about the situation. I thought it was Father Lanham. But when Miss Daunting revealed that she was an accomplice, it occurred to me that there were more people involved. And then, I recalled the notes on the door of Margeaux's office here in college."

"What were those?" asked Master Hodges.

"When Gerald, the college porter, and I were frantically looking for Margeaux after she disappeared, we went to her office. On the door were notes from a student who missed a meeting with Margeaux. Her one note said that she had the answers to Margeaux's 'final questions on the mechanics of Tudor trusts and wills.' The phrase just stuck in my head. Then when I read Father Charleton's letter that mentioned dissolving the trusts, I thought it was an odd coincidence that I'd just seen the note about Margeaux's questions about the same thing.

"That eventually put it all together in my mind. Margeaux knew about the huge amount of money in the trust and the plan to blend the trusts together, which would ruin their access to the trust money. She also knew about the existence of the gargoyles, and she had research done on the mechanics of Tudor trusts. She was the one who would know that the trust could not be dissolved if the Order of Black Vestments was still required to prevent the same murders being committed in this church. I didn't want to believe it. But the plan was all there, and it was all hers."

The three men were silent for a moment, reflecting on the remarkable situation.

"What will happen to them?" Don finally asked.

"They will go to prison for a very long time, probably the rest of their lives," answered the Master. "Once in custody, Weatherby gave a full confession in a blink of an eye."

"He finally blinked," Don said softly to himself with a satisfied smile.

Wearing a mournful look, Father Adams stared at the floor. "A great price was paid in terms of human life and tragedy." Then his face brightened a bit as he looked up. "But at least the funds for the church's restoration are in place once again five centuries later because of the Atwelle confession. Our congregation is reenergized and many newcomers are visiting now to see our famous gargoyles."

"Yes, Father, but even with the funding secure, I have to tell you that I don't have the same enthusiasm for the project after all the losses we have suffered," Don said.

Father Adams looked directly at Don. "My friend, I urge you to take to this project the words of Paul in his epistle to the Romans:

But we glory in tribulations also:
Knowing that tribulation worketh patience;
And patience, experience;
And experience, hope."

"Hope? From all that's happened?" Don asked. "The greed? The murders?" There was still sadness in his voice.

"Hope," repeated Father Adams as his fingertips rose to touch the stiff black collar circling his neck. "*Seculum seculi, Amen.*"

ABOUT THE AUTHOR

Photo by Daniel Knighton/Pixel Perfect Images

JOEL GORDONSON, in addition to being a fiction author, is an international lawyer with degrees received in the United States and from Cambridge University. His first novel, *That Boy from Nazareth*, received critical acclaim. *Midwest Book Review* called this historical fiction adventure story set in biblical times "Profound, vivid, and highly recommended."

For more information, visit www.joelgordonson.com